Eg

The Dead Men's Wife

Serial Seniors

Tide of Death

Raven's Wing Murder Mystery Series

Strange Winds

Cursed Ground

Watching Woods

Magpie Cottage Murder Mystery Series

Mistletoe and Murder

WATCHING WOODS

A Raven's Wing Irish Murder Mystery

T.E. HARKINS

This is a work of fiction. Names, characters, places, and incidents either are the product of the author's imagination or are used fictitiously. Any resemblance to actual persons, living or dead, events, or locales is entirely coincidental.

teharkins.author@gmail.com

First paperback edition June 2025

Digital ISBN: 979-8-9894205-6-8
Paperback ISBN: 979-8-9894205-7-5

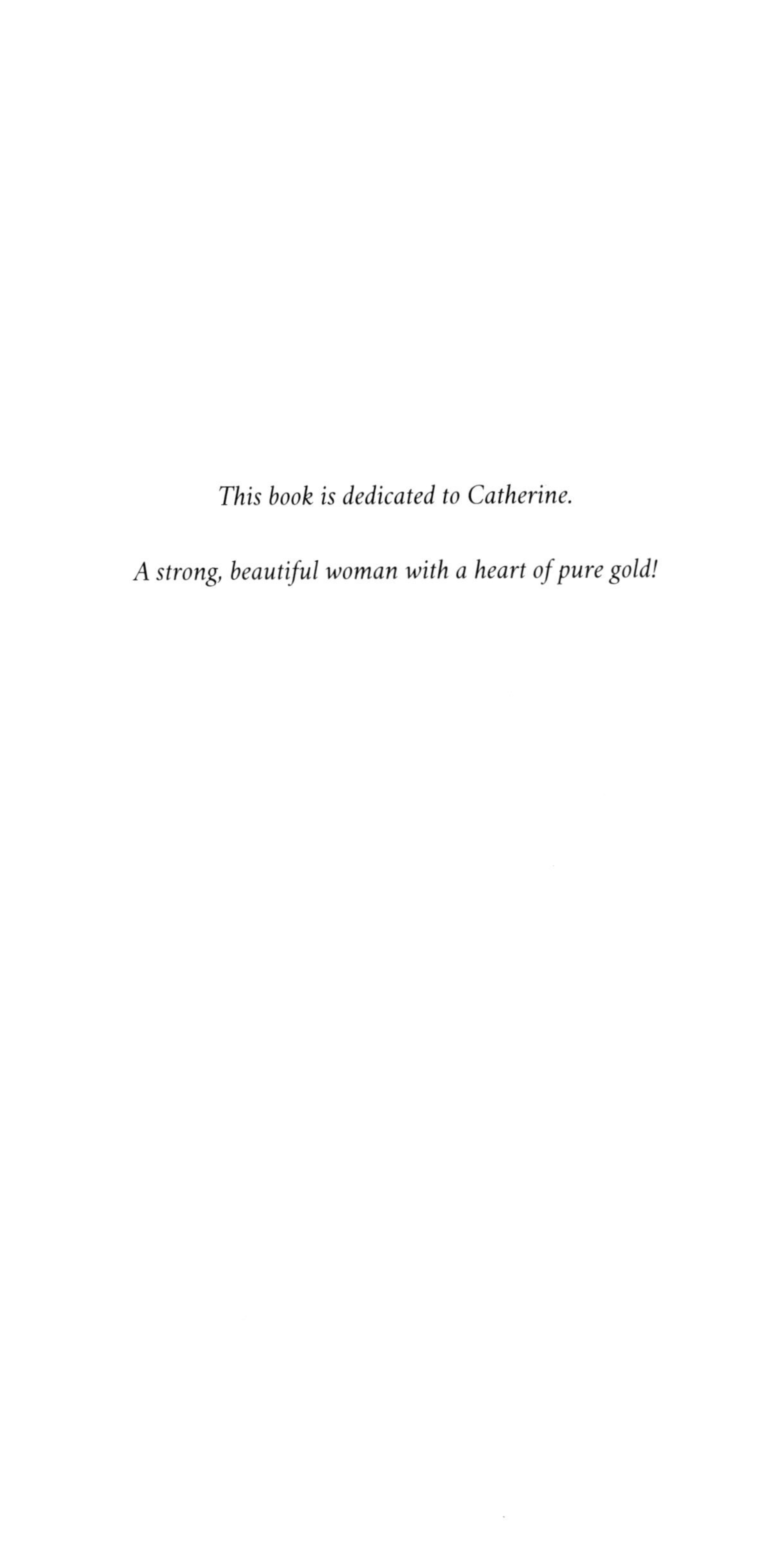

This book is dedicated to Catherine.

A strong, beautiful woman with a heart of pure gold!

PROLOGUE

The crunch of leaves beneath Jack O'Hara's boots shattered the silence as he stepped onto the wooded trail, the fading light of dusk casting long shadows through the trees.

He winced as some startled jackdaws launched from their perches high above, scattering into the encroaching dark. Jack placed his next step more carefully to avoid disturbing whatever wildlife remained. He'd come to the forest to find peace, not disturb it.

All day, he'd been surrounded by the merry chaos unfolding in the tiny village of Carrigaveen as locals prepared for the annual matchmaking festival. The constant buzz of hedge trimmers, the rumble of delivery trucks, and the hammering of nails echoed through his skull, hurting his head.

He'd taken medicine to soothe his anxiety, but it didn't even dull the edges.

Jack had seen it all before—the banners welcoming the lonely-hearted, the fairy lights strung across the streets, the tents and stages being erected to host events that would be attended by thousands of hopeful singles, all dreaming that they would get their shot at love.

He, at once, pitied them for their loneliness and envied them for the courage it took to open their hearts. Jack had never been one to let others in. His only meaningful relationship was with his work, and though he found his occupation fulfilling in its own right, it didn't keep him warm at night.

Jack sighed deeply, his loud exhale camouflaged by the gentle wind that whispered through the trees. In all the years he'd been coming to the matchmaking festival, he'd never before considered the possibility of finding a partner for himself. It simply hadn't occurred to him. In fact, he'd only recently become aware of his desire for companionship. But as soon as the notion of amiable domesticity formulated in his mind, it began to haunt his waking thoughts.

He made a nice living. He owned his own semi-detached home in Bantry. He was possessed of a patient and kind disposition. And, when motivated, he was even a decent enough cook. Surely, a good woman could do worse than to stand at his side.

Perhaps, he thought, he should put in his own application to have the legendary local matchmaker find him a mate. All he had to do was submit some lengthy forms and raid his bank account for the—what he considered extortionate—funds to cover the service.

Yet something held him back.

Deep down, he knew the whole idea had taken root in his brain because he'd already met the woman he considered his ideal mate. She just wasn't aware of it yet. And how could she be when he would never have the stomach to bring up the subject with her?

In frustration, Jack kicked at a clump of earth, panicking insects that had considered the soil a safe place to hide from the rest of the world.

Jack wandered deeper into the forest, following the trail as it weaved through the towering trees, a winding ribbon of dirt and shadow. His head began to feel lighter, calmer.

Then, not far ahead, a sliver of movement caught his eye —a flutter of golden hair and the glimmer of pale skin against the darkening palette of greens and browns. The sight of the beautiful woman, kneeling to pluck a wild blue-bell from the forest floor, stilled his feet and stole the breath from his lungs. He dared not move or call out for fear of spoiling the perfect moment.

He thought he recognized the woman, even in silhouette. Her name was Molly Jenkins. She was an American from Boston who had crossed an ocean to find her one true love, whoever he might be.

But Jack couldn't be sure. He'd only been face-to-face with her once, following a mix-up involving pints at the Knot & Lantern Pub the night before.

He watched as the woman stood up, a bouquet of delicate violet flowers clutched in her hand. Nervously, he ran a hand through his wild, black curls and steeled himself to announce his presence.

But before he could work up the nerve to call out, he heard the sharp whistling of something moving fast through the trees. The next sound that reached his ears was the distant yelp of pain that escaped the woman's lips.

In shock, his eyes traveled from her face down her body, where he saw an arrow protruding from her chest. A stream of crimson blood flowed from her punctured flesh, staining the fabric of her pale-yellow sundress.

"Jesus, Mary, and Joseph," Jack muttered under his breath, too stunned to move.

As if sensing his presence, the woman turned to face him, the orbs of her eyes wide with shock and pain. He watched her lips move, and though he was too far away to hear her or read her lips, he instinctively knew what she was saying.

Help me.

Torn between empathy and survival, Jack took a few tentative steps toward the prone woman. He'd barely begun to narrow the gap between them when the sound of another arrow whistling through the air dropped him to his knees. The deadly projectile buried itself in the tree above his head.

There was no glory in being killed by the same hand that felled the woman, he reasoned. Not when he had no weapon to defend himself against the unseen assailant. Silently vowing to return with reinforcements, Jack turned and ran.

He barreled through the woods, nearly crashing into trees as he sprinted along the path that led back to the village. His vision blurred, his lungs burned from exertion, and the tail of his unzipped leather jacket flapped wildly, slapping painfully against his hips.

His strides ate up the ground as he raced toward the Garda station, panting, desperate, and ready to set off the alarms that would rattle the cozy little village of Carrigaveen to its core.

CHAPTER ONE

The Wild Atlantic Way stretches before me like a coiled serpent. Hairpins of asphalt hug the coastline as I navigate my Honda CR-V around another impossible bend in the road. White knuckles grip the steering wheel tighter as the sole of my Vans sneaker connects with the brakes.

To my left, craggy cliffs plunge into the sea, and I know I'm only one mistake away from steering a path into oblivion. To my relief, the GPS in my car shows that I'm approaching my destination. As romantic as taking the scenic route might seem—and indeed, it has made my heart beat faster—I find myself longing for the comfortable boredom of a straight, paved road.

After spotting a sign for the village of Carrigaveen, I take the exit off the coastal road and begin heading inland.

"In two miles, your destination will be on the left," the mechanical voice of my navigation system informs me.

At long last, my shoulders relax, and I allow the flood of excitement I've been holding at bay during the long drive to finally flood over me. For the first time since arriving in

Ireland a few months ago, I've been commissioned to write a story about something other than murder. The thought of writing a heartwarming feature story is just what my imaginary doctor would order.

As I drink in the stunning landscape, amber-hued in the late morning sunlight, it's hard to imagine that weeks earlier, I'd nearly been killed while solving the twisted tale of an Irish construction magnate who died under suspicious circumstances.

What happened next was even more astounding. The articles I wrote for the local newspaper had been picked up by the international wire services. Suddenly, this Alabama transplant was being offered more money than any recent college graduate could dare hope for to write stories about events in Ireland.

My latest assignment—a three-page spread on the country's longest-running matchmaking festival—has brought me here to the remote village of Carrigaveen.

Population during the year: 263

Population during the annual festival: 6,000+

Because there are so few rooms for rent, most festival attendees are forced to seek accommodations as far off as Bantry, a good thirty miles away on treacherous back roads. Luckily, the magazine has secured me a room at the only hotel in the village. I am, officially, a member of the press corps.

If my mama were still alive, I know she would be so proud.

The car shudders as my car's front tire dips into a pothole the size of a serving bowl. My jaw clenches in reflex, then drops open in awe as Carrigaveen—resting like a patchwork quilt stitched into the emerald valley—comes into view.

Brightly painted cottages in shades of butter yellow, seafoam green, and coral pink line the narrow, winding lanes. Flower boxes bursting with cheerful blooms adorn nearly every windowsill, their sweet scent carrying on the salty breeze. The village looks almost *too* quaint and charming, as if it's been generated by artificial intelligence in response to a request for a picture of an ideal Irish town.

Yet, as I ease my car down the main street, I can't help feeling that something is off. I'd expected the village square to be bursting with activity as final preparations are made for the matchmaking festival's official opening tomorrow. Instead, the main street is eerily quiet. The few locals I pass hurry along the clean, tidy streets with hunched shoulders and furtive glances. Even the vividly painted festival signs that dot the roadside—complete with hearts and cavorting cupids—seem subdued.

"What in tarnation is goin' on here?" I mutter to myself as the GPS guides me out of the village toward vast fields littered with party tents and stages.

Finally, I spot a sign for the Abbey Wood Manor. Turning my car off the main road, I wind my way through a dense collection of oak and ash trees, their branches forming a natural archway overhead. Dappled sunlight dances on my windscreen like fairy lights.

Suddenly, Abbey Wood Manor rises up ahead of me like a castle fit for a cartoon princess. The massive structure stands tall and timeless, its golden stone walls accessorized with climbing ivy and leaded windows. The steep slate roof is crowned by large chimneys and turrets that, on a cloudier day, would seem to touch the heavens. Just ahead of me, at the center of a large roundabout, there's a statue of a cowled monk, his stone robe sweeping the ground as he cradles an open book.

Overwhelmed by the majestic beauty of the place, I don't notice that my car has veered off the pavement until gravel starts bouncing loudly off the undercarriage. I quickly right the car, my eyes still glued to the stunning building.

I could almost believe the imposing stone structure—a refurbished monastery originally built in the fourteenth-century—had been plucked straight out of a medieval tapestry. That is, if it weren't for the solar panels winking on the roof and the satellite dish hiding not quite out of sight behind a soaring turret.

A low whistle escapes my lips as self-consciousness bubbles in my belly.

I wish I'd done an internet search of the hotel before leaving Raven's Wing—my little cottage in Ballygoseir. The blue jeans and light sweater that had seemed like a good idea this morning now feel horribly out of place, almost like I'm about to walk into Sunday service wearing slippers and an old pair of pajamas. The worst part is, I didn't even pack any dresses for the trip. Then again, I only own one—a wrap-around thingamajig I bought for a funeral. My aunt Audrey had been horrified when I wore it with sneakers.

Well, there's nothin' I can do about it now, I think to myself. *Carrigaveen is just gonna have to take me as I am.*

As I near the roundabout in front of the hotel, I see a filigreed sign with arrows guiding visitors to the spa, the falconry center, and the parking lot. While the first two options spark my curiosity, I figure I should probably park and check in before I start exploring.

Emerging from the shadow of the statuary monk, I finally catch a glimpse of the hotel's ornate entrance. But it's not the large, carved wooden door flanked by medieval sconces that captures my attention. It's the sight of a Garda vehicle parked out front like an uninvited guest at high tea.

I pound my open palm against the leather-lined steering wheel.

"I knew there was somethin' goin' on," I say aloud to no one.

My interest piqued, I consider sidling my car up next to the Garda vehicle and asking, straight out, what the Irish police are doing here. But before I get the opportunity, the passenger door swings open, and out steps the last person I expect to see in Carrigaveen.

Detective Brian Mulhaney.

I watch my hopes for a light-hearted feature story go up in smoke.

Because if Detective Mulhaney is here, that can only mean one thing.

There's been a murder.

CHAPTER TWO

Moving with lightning speed, I navigate my car through the roundabout and stash it in the nearest available spot in the parking lot. Without missing a beat, I grab my suitcase and race back toward the hotel entrance, cursing the gravel for making it harder to wheel my rolling bag.

Despite the racket of my suitcase clattering behind me, Detective Mulhaney doesn't notice me approaching. He's too engrossed in his conversation with another Garda officer. Every so often, he pauses to jot something down in a small notebook.

I first met the detective not long after I moved to Ireland. He was exhuming a body, and I was trying to find out why. We've had a somewhat complicated relationship ever since. I like to think I've helped him solve some of his trickier cases, though I doubt he'd ever admit to needing my assistance.

Against my better judgment, I find myself appreciating the sight of the frustratingly handsome Irish lawman. His broad shoulders fill out a sleek navy suit in a way that ought to be illegal. I even allow myself to consider the possibility that he's not as obnoxious as I have made him out to be.

Then, when I'm less than ten feet away, he turns and spots me. As our eyes meet, he sighs deeply, breaking our gaze to stare at the sky.

"Heaven save me," he mumbles to himself before deigning to address me. "Savannah Jeffers. When I got the call to come here this morning, I should have known you wouldn't be far behind."

The young Garda officer beside Detective Mulhaney, a blond-haired man built like a linebacker, squares his shoulders. "Sir, would you like me to have the young lady removed from the property?"

Flashing the officer a sugary smile, I say, "I dare you to try."

The officer seems taken aback at first but then, probably not wanting to lose face in front of the detective, starts moving toward me.

Detective Mulhaney rests a hand on the junior officer's arm, stopping him. "Leave it with me, O'Dwyer. She might be the nosiest woman I've ever had the misfortune to lay eyes on, but she's not a threat."

And just like that, I no longer find Detective Mulhaney so attractive. "Since I already stand accused of bein' a busybody, I reckon I should live up to the reputation. So? Who's been killed?"

The young officer, O'Dwyer, snorts in disbelief at my forwardness.

Detective Mulhaney, on the other hand, seems to be fighting an internal battle between annoyance and amusement. "Why would you assume there's been a murder?"

I tilt my head and exhale loudly. "Are you tryin' to say they sent a homicide detective from Cork all the way out here for somethin' else? Like findin' a missin' cat?"

"Just as likely as you being here for a weekend spa retreat," he fires back.

I laugh. "Hardly. But since you *didn't* ask, I'll tell you. I'm here to write an article for an American magazine on the matchmakin' festival. See how easy that was? Now, go ahead. It's your turn."

His sparkling eyes narrow. "What makes you think this is a tit-for-tat situation?"

"I explained why I was here. It only seems polite to return the gesture."

"No, what would be polite is if you stopped interrogating me so I could get on with my job," he retorts.

I widen my eyes in exaggerated earnestness. "And I will. As soon as you tell me what's goin' on. You see, I'm a guest at this hotel, and as a concerned member of the public, I wanna know if I'm in any immediate danger."

"Only from me if you don't quit wrecking my head," he says, but a slight twinkle in his eye tells me his bluster is mostly for show. "Look, if it will bring an end to your incessant questioning, I'll tell you. I'm here investigating a reported murder."

My eyebrows draw together in a frown. "*Reported* murder? What does that mean?"

He sighs, his broad shoulders sagging slightly. "It means we don't have a body yet, Jeffers. Only the report of one. Filed last night."

I scratch my head, ruffling my long, red hair. "How can you have a report of a body but not the actual body?"

"Because the body wasn't where we were told it would be. So, I'm here to check the victim's room to see if I can find anything that corroborates the report," he explains tersely. "Now, if you'll excuse me, I have work to do."

"Just one more question," I implore him before he can walk away. "If the victim is stayin' at the hotel, that means they're not a local. And if they're passing through for the festival, it's a fair bet they came alone."

"Good Lord, woman. Is there a question anywhere in my future?"

"How'd you ID the supposed victim so quickly?" I blurt out.

"If I answer your question, do you promise to leave me alone?"

"I don't make promises I can't keep," I tell him. "But I promise to try."

Detective Mulhaney sighs. "Fine. The man who claims to have seen the murder says he recognized the woman after seeing her at the local pub the night before last."

Today is Friday. Which means the reported victim must have arrived in town on Wednesday, if not before. "Is the man who reported the murder from 'round these parts?"

O'Dwyer, who's been silently observing the whole exchange, seems incensed by the notion. "Jack O'Hara is hardly a local. As much as he likes to think he owns the place."

Only when Detective Mulhaney glares at O'Dwyer does he realize he's just given me the name of the man who reported the murder. O'Dwyer seems to shrink under his senior officer's disapproving stare.

"I think we've given you just about enough information for one day," Detective Mulhaney tells me, his eyes still on O'Dwyer. "If you have any further questions, I advise you to contact the Garda press office."

With a shake of his head, Detective Mulhaney turns away from me and mounts the steps that lead into the Abbey Wood Manor. Officer O'Dwyer follows on his heels like a scolded puppy.

I pause, my hand resting on the telescopic arm of my suitcase, wondering what I should do next. While I enjoyed pressing Detective Mulhaney's buttons—and I *had* been interested in the reason for his presence—I'm not sure how to feel about what he told me.

I'd accepted this feature writing job partly as an escape, a chance to write about something other than death and depravity. Yet, before I've even checked into my hotel, the specter of murder looms over my head.

But, the angel on my right shoulder argues, *it's only a reported murder. It's probably nothin'.*

The angel on my left shoulder disagrees. *It's not worth the risk. You nearly died the last time.*

Ignoring them both, I grab my suitcase by the handle and begin climbing the steps into the hotel. Detective Mulhaney has a job to do, and so do I. Whatever else may happen, I agreed to write a story about the matchmaking festival, and that's precisely what I intend to do.

CHAPTER THREE

Stepping into Abbey Wood Manor feels like walking straight into a fairy tale—only this once upon a time comes with central heating and free Wi-Fi.

The grand lobby has so many old-world curiosities I don't know where to focus my attention first. My eyes dart between the wall covered with thousands of tiny Claddagh medallions, the elaborate stone fireplace blackened by centuries of peat smoke, and the large, mullioned windows that cast a soft light on the antique furniture scattered around the room.

For an Alabama girl with a single mom who grew up moving from one tiny apartment to another, this hotel might as well be the Taj Mahal. I'm tempted to pinch myself just to be sure that I'm not dreaming.

My sneakers squeak against flagstones worn smooth by centuries of sandaled feet as I cross the fancy foyer to join the small check-in line. Through lowered lashes, I glance at Detective Mulhaney, standing twenty feet away, surrounded by a trio of local guards who seem eager to prove their usefulness.

Feigning interest in a pile of local newspapers stacked on a nearby antique console table, I strain to hear what tidbits of intelligence the officers seem eager to share with Detective Mulhaney. From where I'm standing, I can only hear snippets of their conversation.

"...maid flat out refuses to go into the room until..."

"...compromising situation a few years back..."

"...flew in from America..."

"...wouldn't put it past O'Hara to go stirring up trouble..."

I give my head a quick shake, trying to jolt the fragments of information into some kind of order. Did the maid catch the dead woman in a compromising position a year ago? Has the victim—if she truly has been murdered—spent time in Carrigaveen before? Is she an American? And who is this Jack O'Hara guy that all the guards around here seem to dislike?

As I'm trying to pull theories out of thin air, I catch Detective Mulhaney glaring at me. His eyes tell me he knows exactly what I'm doing and that I need to mind my own business.

Irritated that he's seen through my pretend disinterest, I pick up a newspaper and hold it up, blocking him from sight. On the front page of the *Carrigaveen Cryer* is a large article focused on the upcoming festival. Below the fold is a picture of an old farmer next to the headline, "Cattle Farmer Reports Theft of Grain Chemicals Overnight."

I find myself secretly hoping that the reported murder Detective Mulhaney is here to investigate turns out to be some kind of harmless—if tasteless—prank. And it seems there's a good chance it might be just that. I mean, the local guards sure don't seem to be taking it very seriously. And it would probably do me good to spend some time in a sleepy village where matchmaking and late-night barn raids are the biggest news.

Just as I'm starting to refocus my attention on the article about the festival, hoping to learn something that might be useful for my own story, I feel someone tapping my shoulder. Whipping my head up quickly, I see a forty-something man standing in line behind me, gesturing toward the front desk.

"It's your turn," he says with an American accent.

"Oh, thanks," I mumble, setting the newspaper on the console table. "I appreciate you not cuttin' in line while I was distracted."

"What can I say? My mother raised me to be a gentleman," the tall, gangly man replies, attempting a suave demeanor that's betrayed by the deep blush coloring his cheeks. "Can I help you with your bags?"

"No need," I tell him, already walking backward toward the counter. "My mama gave me two good arms and a suitcase with wheels. But I appreciate the offer, all the same."

I turn away from his crestfallen expression to face the middle-aged woman behind the front desk. She has rosy cheeks, curly auburn hair tucked into a messy bun, and a nametag that reads Dervla. Her expression is wary as if she's waiting for me to give her bad news.

"Please tell me you have a reservation." Dervla's voice is soft and lilting. "Sure, I don't think my poor nerves can handle turning anyone else away today."

I frown. "Have you had a lot of people showin' up without bookin' a room? Didn't they know there's a festival goin' on?"

She rolls her hazel eyes and throws her hands in the air in mock surrender. "That's just the thing. They're here *for* the festival. Flew in from the good Lord knows where. Come to think of it, I wonder if they bothered to book a flight or just showed up at the airport hoping to hitch a ride."

A smile forms on my lips. I just met Dervla, but I like her already. I rest my elbows on the counter and lean in conspiratorially. "Well, I hope for their sakes they packed tents.

'Cause they sure ain't gonna find any place in the village with a spare bed."

Dervla's gaze shifts to focus on something behind me. I turn to see what caught her attention and notice the gangly man who was in line behind me walking sheepishly toward the door with his large duffle bag slung over his shoulder.

I face Dervla, cocking my thumb in the direction of the retreating man. "Lucky for your nerves, we weeded out that one before he got to the front desk."

Dervla chuckles. "And for that, you have my undying gratitude. What's your name, love? I'll give you the best pick of the available rooms."

"The name's Savannah Jeffers," I tell her, reaching in my purse for my passport. "The company I'm working for should have already paid for the room."

Dervla's fingers fly across the keyboard, then she stops typing and looks at the monitor. "Yes, your room has been paid for in advance by—" she stops, doing a double take of the screen. "Wow! Do you really work for them? I love that magazine."

I can feel my face getting warm with embarrassment and, if I'm honest, a little pride. "They've only hired me to write one article for now. On the festival. So, if you hear of any good love stories, let me know. I need to make a good impression."

"I will, of course," she replies with a wink. "Not that there'll be any shortage of happily-ever-afters this week. It's what we're known for. But this year, you might even have a little intrigue to write about as well."

"How's that?"

Dervla tilts her head toward where Detective Mulhaney and the other guards are standing. "You didn't hear this from me, but there's been report of a murder in Carrigaveen. Now, mind you, no one thinks for a second that anyone has actually *been* murdered. Just some troublemaker setting the cat among the pigeons, more like. But it could make for a nice bit of drama for your article."

Wondering what else Dervla might know, I decide to play dumb. "Is that why the guards are at the hotel? Was the woman murdered here?"

Dervla frowns. "I never said the supposed victim was a woman." I'm starting to think I've blown my chance to get intel from Dervla when she shrugs and smiles. "Or did I? Sure, I've been run off my feet all day. If I don't slow down, I'll meet myself coming back."

On the outside, I'm smiling. On the inside, I'm kicking myself for making such a rookie mistake. Luckily, my blunder doesn't stand in the way of Dervla's desire to gossip.

"To answer your question, no. No one's been murdered here…that we know of. But the woman *reported* to have been killed is a guest of the Abbey Wood. I checked her in myself only two days ago. From America, like yourself. Though no one's seen her about since yesterday."

"So, the guards are here to check her room or somethin'?"

"That they are," Dervla confirms as she turns her back to me and pulls a heavy brass keyring from a cupboard on the back wall. "But they won't be bothering you none. You're on the floor below in room 214. It's one of our bigger, nicer rooms facing the river."

Wishing I had the nerve to ask Dervla to move me to the allegedly dead woman's floor, I merely smile and say, "Thanks for the upgrade."

Dervla returns my grin. "It's been a pleasure. And if you need anything at all, sure, you know where to find me."

I nod and step away from the counter, almost running over the toes of the person behind me in line with my wheelie bag. Muttering a quick apology, I walk toward the elevators.

Detective Mulhaney and the other guards are speaking to a man in a suit, probably the hotel manager. Despite my best intentions, I can't help wondering what Detective Mulhaney will find in the woman's room. Will they find a body? Will the woman's room be ransacked?

Cursing my own curiosity, I sigh as the elevator doors slide open. I step inside and press the button for level two, which in Ireland is really the third floor because the first floor is known as the ground floor here.

Whatever floor you call it, Detective Mulhaney will be going to the one above me.

I'll just have to ask Dervla what happened after the fact. Because she's right, a little mystery could spice up my magazine article about the festival.

Just as the elevator doors start to close, a hand appears in the gap between the metal slabs. Sensors catch the movement and the doors slide open, revealing Detective Mulhaney and his merry band of junior officers.

Without stopping to worry about the implications, I quickly tuck my room key into my pocket and reach for the panel to hit the button for level three—the supposedly dead woman's floor.

Detective Mulhaney, noticing that the buttons for two floors are lit up even though I'm the only one in the elevator, eyes me warily.

I tap my palm to my forehead. "Silly me. I got confused about what floor my room is on."

To my surprise, he doesn't grace me with some acerbic comment. Instead, we make the short ride in utter silence.

When the elevator opens again on the third floor, the four men turn to me, waiting for me to exit first.

"Oh, no. Y'all go ahead," I insist. "I don't want to get in your way with my bags and all."

The local guards begin walking down the twisty hallway.

Mulhaney lingers a moment longer, standing just outside the elevator. "Don't even think about following us."

"I wouldn't dream of it," I lie with a saccharine smile.

I step into the hallway and make a show of studying the sign that indicates which way to turn to reach which rooms. The hotel, I discover, is like a figure eight, with two blocks of rooms on either side of the elevator banks, each with a central courtyard in the middle.

With a final, distrustful look, Mulhaney storms off after the local guards.

Once he rounds the corner and is out of sight, I pick up my bag by the handle and, on tiptoes, chase after him. I get to the corner just in time to catch sight of him making another left turn. I hurry down to the end of the hallway and sneak a look around. In this maze of a hotel, I'm half expecting him to make several more turns before reaching his destination, so I'm surprised to spot him standing outside one of the rooms.

I set my bag down softly and lean against the corner wall, afraid to look in case he catches me spying.

"Are you sure this is the right room?" I hear him ask the guards.

"That's what the manager said," one of them replies.

"Alright, so. Here goes nothing."

I risk a quick peek around the corner just as Detective Mulhaney raises a clenched fist and bangs on the door.

"Miss Jenkins? This is the Garda Síochána. Please open up."

His knock is met with silence.

One of the guards holds up a heavy brass key. "Shall we open it?"

Detective Mulhaney nods, holding out his hand for the key. But just as he steps toward the lock, the door slowly opens from the inside.

CHAPTER FOUR

The door cracks open just enough to reveal a stunning woman in her early forties with sparkling blue eyes and long, golden hair. She's wearing a white robe with the hotel's insignia, which she pulls together protectively when she sees the group of uniformed male officers.

"Can I help you?" the woman asks softly. She's American. I can tell by her accent.

"Good afternoon, Ma'am. I'm Detective Brian Mulhaney with the Garda Síochána." He flashes his badge and waits while she leans forward and examines it. "I am looking for Molly Jenkins."

From my hiding spot around the corner, I watch the woman's brows draw together in surprise.

"I'm Molly Jenkins. Is there some kind of problem, Detective?"

The three local guards exchange self-satisfied, knowing looks. Detective Mulhaney never takes his eyes off the woman named Molly.

"Ms. Jenkins, we have some rather…unusual questions for you," Detective Mulhaney says. "Do you mind if we come inside?"

Darn it! I won't be able to hear what she has to say if they take the conversation out of the hallway. Unless I eavesdrop through the keyhole. But there are some levels to which even I'm not willing to stoop. I try to console myself that if there's been no murder, which seems to be the case, I won't be missing much.

Molly steps into the hallway, pulling the door closed behind her. "If it's all the same to you, I'd rather not invite four men I don't know into my bedroom."

Detective Mulhaney nods, his face stoic if slightly flushed. "Of course, if that's what you would prefer. We're here because a murder's been reported."

Molly's hand flies to her chest, and she draws in a sharp breath. "Oh my gosh, who's been murdered?"

"You," Detective Mulhaney says, not beating around the bush.

"Me?" she laughs, a nervous edge to her voice. "Is this some kind of joke?"

"I'm afraid not, Ma'am."

"Well, as you can see—" she uses her hands to indicate the length of her body, "—I'm right here and very much alive."

One of the local officers, I assume the most senior of the group, pipes up. "I tried to tell you, Detective. You can't trust a word—"

Detective Mulhaney silences the guard with a raised hand. He keeps his eyes focused on Molly. "I assure you, it's just as perplexing for us as it is for you. May I ask you about your relationship with Jack O'Hara?"

"Jack who?" Her face is a mask of confusion.

"Jack O'Hara. From what I understand, you crossed paths

at the local pub, the Knot & Lantern, two nights ago. That would have been Wednesday night," Detective Mulhaney attempts to jog her memory.

Molly tilts her head, searching her memory. "I vaguely remember speaking with a man on Wednesday night—that was my first day in the village—but I didn't catch his name. And I have no memory of what we talked about."

"So, you can't think of a reason why he might have reported that you'd been killed last night?"

"Certainly not! I don't even know the man. Could he have confused me with someone else? As you said, I only met him once. And very briefly."

Detective Mulhaney shakes his head. "He seemed to think it was you. But, then again, nothing he said is making any sense. You see, we haven't found a body. So, at this point, we don't have any reason to believe a murder has even taken place."

"Well, that's a relief. A murder would really put a damper on the festival," Molly observes. "Did this Jack person say how I supposedly died? Or where?"

Detective Mulhaney clears his throat. "He said you were picking violets in the woods when someone shot you with an arrow."

Molly's eyebrows shoot up in disbelief. "An arrow? That seems a bit archaic. Where would anyone even find a bow and arrow around here?"

"Sure, the Manor offers archery lessons," the officer I'd seen outside, O'Dwyer, helpfully supplies.

Molly stares at O'Dwyer for a moment before shrugging. "Regardless, I haven't set foot in the woods. And, last night, I was so worn out from the trip over here I spent the whole afternoon and evening right here in my room. So, you see, he couldn't have seen me in the woods."

The third guard, the youngest of the three, takes a wide-eyed step away from Molly. "Fetch!"

"Fetch?" Molly's forehead crinkles. "Is that what you said? Who's that?"

I'm glad she asked the question. I have no idea who the guard is talking about, either.

"Don't pay the sergeant any mind. Sure, he's just talking nonsense." Detective Mulhaney shoots the young guard a look of warning before focusing his attention back on Molly. "Is this your first time in Ireland, so?"

Molly's smile reveals glowing white if slightly crooked, teeth. "It is. I'm part Irish, so I've always wanted to visit the homeland, you know? But this is the first chance I've had to make the trip."

Detective Mulhaney nods as if he's heard it all before. "And you're here for the matchmaking festival?"

Molly's cheeks redden, but she holds her head high. "I am. I fell in love with the idea of it, I guess you could say. Online dating isn't all it's cracked up to be. So, I thought I would give this a try. And who doesn't love an Irish accent?"

Detective Mulhaney shifts his weight and scratches his head. "Yes, well. I hope you find what you're looking for." He stares at his notebook as if it holds the secret to world peace. "When we locate Mr. O'Hara, would you like us to press charges?"

A crease forms between Molly's brows. "What for?"

"We could book him for filing a false report," Detective Mulhaney offers. "Normally, we wouldn't bother. But seeing as how you've been inconvenienced by this whole business, we'd be happy to make sure he knows not to mess with you again."

Molly bites into her full, red lips as she mulls it over. "If it's all the same to you, I think I'd prefer to just forget about the whole thing. This man, Jack, seems more misguided than malicious. And I really want to focus on enjoying my time here, not sitting in a police station filling out forms."

I can't help but admire the woman's grace. It's not every day four policemen come knocking on your door to tell you you've been murdered. Yet she's remained cool, calm, and collected throughout the whole bizarre ordeal.

Detective Mulhaney tucks his notebook in his coat pocket. "If that's what you'd prefer. We'll leave you to enjoy your holiday, so. Don't hesitate to contact us if anything else...strange happens. Or if Mr. O'Hara bothers you in any way."

"Thank you, Detective. I will," Molly assures him with a gentle smile. "Though it's hard to think of anything that could top this for strangeness."

"Yes, Ma'am," Detective Mulhaney agrees. "We're sorry to have disturbed you. Enjoy the rest of your day."

"You, too." With a slight nod to the officers, Molly opens the door to her room and disappears inside.

From down the hall, I can hear the three guards whispering to Mulhaney about what a nuisance Jack O'Hara is and how foolish he's made them look.

I don't have time to focus on what they're saying. They'll be heading back to the elevator any minute now, and they'll find me standing here in the hallway with my suitcase.

Desperate for cover, I scan the doors along the hallway until I see one with a sign reading "Staff Only" in gold filigree script. I race to the door and push, relieved to find it unlocked.

Inside, I see what appears to be the maid's restocking room. But, between the shelves, the hamper of dirty laundry, and the cleaning cart, there's isn't enough room for me and my bag.

Hearing voices down the hall, I quickly shove my wheeled

bag inside. Then, I spin around to face a door across the hall. I rest my shaking fingers on the handle, hoping it will look like I'm exiting my hotel room when, seconds later, Detective Mulhaney and his entourage of local guards round the corner.

CHAPTER FIVE

"Detective Mulhaney! What a nice surprise to be seein' you again so soon." The fib makes my eye twitch. "I'm guessin' you didn't find what you were lookin' for."

His eyes narrow. "And why would you be thinking that?"

I search my brain for an explanation that doesn't involve me eavesdropping on his conversation with Molly Jenkins. "Well, if you'd found a dead body, I kinda doubt your buddies there would be lookin' so smug."

Detective Mulhaney wheels around to look at the guards trailing behind just as the smirks run away from their faces.

"So. It was a false alarm?" I press, hoping he'll spill the beans so I can stop pretending not to know that Molly is alive and well.

"Unless we've just witnessed the miracle of resurrection, yes. I suppose you could call it that," Detective Mulhaney says as he storms past me toward a bend in the hallway.

I chase after him, leaving the other guards in the dust. "Molly's still alive? Does that mean you'll be goin' to talk to Jack O'Hara to find out why he said she was dead?"

A few feet ahead, the detective pauses and turns around to glare at me, his dark eyes hard as onyx. "I never said the alleged victim's name was Molly."

Darn it! I got ahead of myself again. Feigning ignorance is a lot harder than it sounds. "Um, no. Dervla at the front desk let it slip. She's a chatterbox, that one. But back to the point, are you goin' to talk to Jack now?"

He runs a hand through his short dark hair and resumes walking. "What we do now is no concern of yours. Sure, don't you have a story to be writing?"

"Well, that's just it. I'm thinkin' this whole fake murder business could be worth includin' in my article," I say, practically jogging to keep up with his long strides. "I'd like to come with you when you talk to him."

I am slightly worried about leaving my suitcase in the maid's closet. But it can't be helped. I'd love to hear what this Jack fellow has to say for himself.

"Absolutely not," Detective Mulhaney says, not bothering to look at me. "This is an active investigation. Not take your annoying journalist friend to work day."

His words catch me off guard. "Aww. I'm your friend?"

He shakes his head as he approaches the elevator and presses the down button. "Of course, that's the one thing I say that you actually pay attention to."

"Come on, Brian," I dare to use his first name, but it feels weird on my lips. "Let me come along."

The three guards who'd been trailing behind finally catch up with us.

"All I'm saying is that Jack's probably halfway to Dublin by now," O'Dwyer says to one of his fellow officers. "That's why we can't find him."

Detective Mulhaney's chiseled jaw clenches. "That's just about enough out of you, O'Dwyer."

The implication of the young guard's words hit me like

Cupid's arrow. "Hang on a second. Has Jack O'Hara gone missin'?"

O'Dwyer, his cheeks newly rosy, has the good sense to avoid meeting Detective Mulhaney's stare.

"Well, has he?" I push the issue.

Detective Mulhaney sighs deeply and jabs the elevator call button again with his thumb. "Look, if it'll keep you from haunting me for the rest of the day, I'll tell you. No one has seen or heard from Jack O'Hara since he filed his report last night."

My mouth falls open. "He just up and disappeared after reportin' a murder? That's mighty suspicious, don't you think?"

"It is unusual, I grant you," Detective Mulhaney concedes. "But it's too soon to jump to any conclusions. He wouldn't be the first man in Ireland to sleep off a bender in some pub's back room. And if he fancies the odd pint, that could also explain why he was confused about what he saw."

The oldest of the three guards—a thirty-something redhead still outgrowing his freckles—shakes his head. "Jack? Naw. He's not a big drinker. Three pints max, like. And that's at a push."

"Thank you for your input, Sergeant Sweeney," Detective Mulhaney growls.

"I could help you try and find him," I offer. "I'm good at talkin' to people. They open up to me. I've got an honest face."

Detective Mulhaney opens his mouth to say something, then grins wickedly and closes his mouth. I should probably be grateful he didn't say whatever it was that crossed his mind. It probably wasn't very nice. And just after he said we were friends, too.

To the detective's evident relief, the elevator chimes, and the doors slide open. Detective Mulhaney steps into the lift, and the three guards jostle to get around me so they can join him.

I take a step toward the elevator to follow them, but Detective Mulhaney holds up a hand. "Oh, no. You can catch it on the next run. After we're gone. Write your article and leave the policework to us, Jeffers."

"Or what? Are you gonna threaten to arrest me? Again?" I challenge. In our past encounters, he's made numerous idle threats about putting me behind bars. Needless to say, he's never actually followed through.

Detective Mulhaney cocks an eyebrow as if daring me to find out.

Before I can say anything else, the elevator doors close, leaving me alone in the hallway. I try to look on the bright side. At least now I don't have to worry about leaving my suitcase in the maid's closet.

Sighing, I trudge back down the hotel corridor in search of my abandoned bag. I'm half hoping Molly will pass me in the hallway. I tell myself it's only because I think her story—coming halfway around the world only to have someone report her dead—would make a compelling narrative for my article.

But the hallway remains frustratingly empty.

After retrieving my bag, I take the stairs down to my floor and hunt for room 214. Using the big brass key, I unlock the door and walk inside. The room is much bigger and grander than I expected. Thick stone walls bearing large tapestries yield to plush rugs underfoot. A massive canopy bed dominates one side of the room, while a sofa, loveseat, and minibar fill the opposite end of the room. The bathroom is near the bed—a cleanly tiled room with a rain shower and a clawfoot tub.

The cleaning staff has left fresh flowers in a vase and a chilled bottle of wine on the coffee table. There's also a box of chocolates on the pillow. After the long drive, I'm tempted to pop open the wine, devour the chocolates, and take a long midday nap.

But before I can even kick off my sneakers, I hear the faint ringing of my cell phone from inside my crossbody purse. I already know whose number will appear in the caller ID.

As soon as I answer the phone, I blurt, "I'm sorry I didn't call sooner, Miss Audrey. I just got to my hotel room this very minute."

"Sure, I thought you'd have been there ages ago. What took you so long? Did you get stuck behind a tractor?" my aunt asks.

It's not outside the realm of possibility that's what happened. With the size of the roads and the prevalence of tractors in the countryside, a twenty-minute journey can easily become a two-hour odyssey.

"No, nothin' like that. I just got a little sidetracked. You'll never believe who I ran into when I arrived."

"It wouldn't be Detective Mulhaney, by any chance? Would it?"

I almost ask how she could possibly know that, but then I think better of it. Audrey has a way of knowing things. I guess after spending her whole career in Ireland's Special Detective's Unit, intelligence gathering is in her blood.

I plop down on the sofa. The cushions are so fluffy I sink a good two inches. "Yeah. That's right. Some guy reported that a woman had been murdered. But it turns out she's not really dead."

"Isn't she now?" There's a note of surprise in her voice. I guess she doesn't know everything after all. "I hadn't heard that. A friend on the force called this morning, saying there'd been a murder in Carrigaveen. When I didn't hear from you, I started worrying."

"Thanks for your concern. But there's nothin' to worry about. It was just a false alarm," I assure her.

"I'm glad to hear it. The last thing you need is to get tangled up in another murder investigation," Audrey says, but I think she's secretly disappointed that the mystery was resolved so quickly. "Now that's sorted, I'll let you get on with your day. Have you had lunch? You must be starving after that drive."

Now that she mentions it, I realize I am a little peckish. "I could eat."

"Go get some food, so. I'll talk to you later."

The line goes dead. Audrey has hung up without saying goodbye. She has a habit of doing that.

I consider going downstairs to the lobby. I think I saw a sign for a restaurant. But then another thought occurs to me. When I'd been listening in on the conversation between Detective Mulhaney and Molly in the hallway, he'd mentioned that Molly met Jack at the Knot & Lantern.

Maybe someone there can remember that meeting or tell me more about Jack. The local guards clearly have something against him. I can't help but wonder if their dislike is warranted.

I unlock my phone, still in my hand, and do a quick Google search. The Knot & Lantern is a pub in the center of the village. And lucky for me, they're open.

CHAPTER SIX

Pushing open the Knot & Lantern's heavy oak door, the first thing I notice is the noise—everyone's laughing and having a good time. Unlike the grim atmosphere that greeted me when I arrived in the village earlier, the local pub buzzes with happiness and anticipation.

Word must have already gotten around that the murder report was a hoax. Now, everyone can relax and enjoy the last bit of calm before the festival orientation kicks off later this afternoon.

My eyes dart around, taking in the scene—exposed wooden beams, gleaming copper lanterns, and walls adorned with old black and white photos immortalizing Carrigaveen's long history.

As I weave through the crowd, the scent of oak and old leather mingles with the aroma of Irish stew. My stomach rumbles. Patrons occupy all the tables, but that doesn't bother me overly much. Not only can I probably order food at the bar, but I've learned that the people with the best gossip in town are always the ones behind it.

At the Knot & Lantern, that would be a stout man in his mid-forties with salt and pepper hair. His clear blue eyes sparkle as he chats with a group of white-haired men on wooden stools.

"...so I say to him, Paddy, if that's what you call a good swing, then we need to talk about what your real golf handicap is."

The older men's laughter rises above the chatter and clanking of silverware that fills the large room.

I'll have to play it cool if I want him to open up to me. Audrey once told me the only way to earn a barkeep's respect is to give out to them as good as they give out to everyone else. Which means, it's time to bring my A-game.

I slide onto an empty stool, pretending to focus on the line of taps with little blackboards advertising the different types of beers. Without shifting my gaze, I sense that the bartender has pegged me as a new customer.

"Excuse me, gentlemen," I hear him say. "There's no point looking at your ugly mugs when a pretty lady just joined us at the bar."

"You must be drinking your own merchandise if you think you have a shot with the likes of her," one of the older men says.

"Oh, I know I don't," the bartender says. "That doesn't mean I can't enjoy the view."

I hear chuckles from the group as the bartender moves into my peripheral vision.

I look up and smile. "Hi there. Do y'all serve food at the bar? I'm so hungry I could eat a possum."

The bartender's eyes twinkle mischievously, and he opens his mouth to speak.

I cut him off. "I'm guessin' the next words out of your mouth are gonna be something like, *you're not from around here*. And you'd be right. I'm a reporter here to cover the festival. So can we skip the small talk and jump right to the part where you're pourin' me a shandy?"

My cheeks suddenly feel warm. The only person I ever speak to like that is Detective Mulhaney because, quite frankly, he deserves it. But I don't know this bartender, and I start to worry I may have taken Audrey's advice too far.

Then, the bartender's grin widens, and he reaches for an empty glass. "Well, with that attitude, you might as well be Carrigaveen born and bred. I have a feeling you'll fit right in around here. I suppose you'll be wanting a menu as well?"

"Naw. Just order me whatever's best. And if I don't like it, I'll make you pay for my next pint." I smile just to let him know I'm joking.

"You've obviously never had Caroline's steak and ale pie. Let's just say I'm not too worried about you settling up." He sets the frothy shandy on the bar. "The name's Cian, by the way."

I hold out my hand for him to shake. "Savannah."

He frowns. "I've heard of Savannah. It's in Georgia, right? Is that where you're from?"

"No. It's my name."

He shakes his head. "You Americans—naming children after cities, using surnames as first names. What's next? Little tikes named after foods, like potato or mac and cheese?"

"McCheesy O'Potato does have a nice ring to it, don't ya think?" I joke back, not taking offense. I've been in Ireland long enough to know that when someone picks on you, it means they like you.

Cian scratches his jaw, feigning deep thought. "Sure, that sounds like something we should add to the menu. If you don't mind me naming a dish after your firstborn, that is."

"Naw. Go right ahead. The world needs more cheesy potatoes."

"Truer words have never been spoken. Now, if you'll

excuse me, I'll put in your order. If you need anything else, give me a shout."

I thank him and pick up my glass as he walks away. Normally, I'm not a big drinker. I don't even like the taste of beer or the way it settles in my stomach like a lead balloon. But when mixed with 7-Up, I find it's not too bad. And I don't plan on drinking much. I'll just nurse this glass while I try to find out what I can about Jack O'Hara.

From my perch on the stool, I watch as Cian chats with customers who come up to the bar. Not only does he seem to know everyone, he knows them well enough to ask about their spouses and children by name. I'm more convinced than ever that if I can get Cian talking, he'll be able to tell me a lot more about the missing man who seems to have made up a murder.

My chance comes when Cian approaches me ten minutes later, carrying a steaming savory pie and cutlery.

"Caroline's finest, right here," he says, depositing the plate in front of me. "Will you be needing anything else?"

I'm starving, and the meat pie smells delicious, but I force myself to wait. "Can I ask you somethin', Cian?"

"I knew this would happen," he says with an exaggerated roll of his eyes. "Ah, look, I know it will come as a disappointment, like, but I'm a happily married man. So, I can't be your date to the festival concert."

"Just my luck. The good ones are always spoken for," I joke back. "But I did have one other question."

"Well, don't keep me in suspense," he prods.

"Have you heard anythin' about a guy reportin' a woman murdered the other night?" I ask.

"There's not a soul in the village who hasn't," he replies. "But don't you go worrying yourself. It was all a misunderstanding. The only thing being murdered around here is

Seamus's patience when it takes me too long to refill his pint."

He says the last bit loudly, seemingly for the benefit of one of the older gentlemen sitting farther down the bar because the man chuckles and raises his glass.

As curious as I am, I try to keep my voice light, so he doesn't feel like he's being interrogated. "So, you don't think there was anythin' to it?"

"Sure, look, when Jack came in here rambling on about how he'd just witnessed a murder, I took it seriously enough. We all did," Cian assures me. "The guards got involved, and everyone in town was fierce worried about the poor woman we thought had met her maker. But we learned today that the woman in question—an American like yourself—is alive and well."

But something has been niggling at the back of my mind since the moment Molly Jenkins opened her hotel room door. "But isn't it possible this guy, Jack, just got confused about who he saw? I reckon it's more likely he identified the wrong person than he made the whole thing up."

Cian considers the question as he picks up a clean glass and polishes it with a nearby tea towel. "You've clearly never met Jack. A bit of an odd fellow. Strung tighter than a nun at a stag party. And then you've got the locals whispering about Fetch. But I wouldn't pay that any mind."

I seem to remember one of the guards at the Abbey Wood Manor also mentioning that name. "Who's Fetch?"

"Not someone you'd ever want to meet. Especially at night. But that's all I'll say on that front," Cian replies with a steely glint in his eyes. "No, it's far more likely Jack was just up to his usual tricks. I wouldn't put it past him to be looking for more ways to upset the festival."

I wonder why Jack would want to upset the festival, but first things first. "Who is Jack? Is he from around here?"

Cian rolls his eyes. "For one month a year, he likes to think he is. But no, he lives up in Bantry. The man's like a shadow. You only catch sight of him when the light hits just right."

I have no idea what he means by that, but I choose to let it go. "Does Jack always come for the festival?"

"He does. Though, as far as I can make out, he's never had any interest in finding a woman." Cian's eyes roam down the bar, checking to ensure no one else is trying to get his attention. "No, that one's far more interested in benefiting his bank account than his boudoir."

"His bank account? Does he do work for the festival or somethin'?"

"Or something would be a more appropriate description," Cian says cryptically.

"What does that mean?" I ask.

Cian doesn't give me the satisfaction of a direct response. Instead, he sets down the polished glass and throws the tea towel over his shoulder. "Ah, look, I'm but a humble barman. I listen to gossip. I don't spread it." Then, Cian lowers his voice and tilts his head subtly to the other end of the bar. "It'd be bad for business if you catch my meaning."

I shift my gaze down the bar and catch several patrons turning away quickly, trying to pretend they haven't been eavesdropping on our conversation. Disappointed as I am, I can't blame Cian for not wanting to say more. "I understand. I was just curious, is all. I thought I might include somethin' about it in my article."

"Well, if you're in town looking for a good story, might I recommend a visit to Prose and Cons?" he suggests with a wink. "Orla Gallagher, the proprietor of our local bookshop, can probably help you find what—or who—you're looking for."

I smile back at him. "I'm always in the mood for a good story. Thank you kindly."

"No bother. Enjoy your meal, so."

Cian wanders off to attend to a man brandishing an empty glass, leaving me alone with the mouth-watering, savory pastry in front of me.

I find myself torn between wanting to run off to chat with Orla straight away and staying to eat my meal. If I'm interpreting Cian's words correctly, Orla might lead me to Jack. I can almost picture the indignant look on Detective Mulhaney's face if I'm able to find the missing man the guards have been searching for all morning. The image makes me smile.

But in the end, the needs of my stomach trump my desire to show up Detective Mulhaney, and I bite into the most delicious meat pie I've ever tasted.

CHAPTER SEVEN

A cheerful bell jangles as I step into Prose and Cons early that afternoon. The walk from the Knot & Lantern was short, though I had to consult the GPS on my phone to find it. The bookshop isn't on the main road but tucked away down a quiet, leafy side street, a peaceful escape from the lively bustle of the village center.

Closing the door behind me, I'm greeted by the musty aroma of old books and freshly brewed coffee. Warm golden light filters through the shop's large bay windows, casting a cozy glow over dark wooden bookshelves that stretch from the floor to the ceiling.

Prose and Cons is a treasure trove of literary delights, with books from every genre crammed onto the shelves. Some titles are arranged in tidy rows, while others are stacked haphazardly as if they've been set down and forgotten. To my left, a rolling ladder leans against the highest shelf, its brass railings gleaming.

Wandering deeper into the store, I finally come upon a petite woman in her early forties arranging books on a display table. Her dark auburn hair is pulled back in a ponytail, with wisps escaping that frame her freckled face. She moves purposefully, her delicate hands deftly organizing books in several distinct piles.

When I spot the book titles, I can't help but grin. One side of the table is stacked with bodice rippers featuring shirtless Fabios on the cover. On the other? A collection of self-help books with titles like *Gaslighting for Dummies* and *Trust No One: A Guide to Protecting Your Heart*.

The woman, who I reckon must be Orla Gallagher, steps back to admire her work with a self-satisfied smile.

I clear my throat. "I love what you've done there, but I'd be lyin' if I said it didn't kinda send mixed messages."

Orla's hazel eyes flick over to meet mine, a wry smile tugging at her lips. "I like to think of it as a public service, especially around festival time. Hope for the best, plan for the inevitable, as they say."

I laugh. "I don't think that's the way the sayin' goes. You plan for the worst. Sayin' the worst is inevitable is kind of depressin', isn't it?"

"Not in my experience. It's just good sense to be prepared," she says with a mischievous wink. "You've never been in my shop before. I'd certainly remember you. I'm Orla. Is there anything specific you're looking for today? If you're in town for the festival, might I suggest this one?" She holds up a book called *Red Flags and Why You'll Ignore Them Anyway*.

My grin widens. "No, thank you. I'm not in town for the festival. Well, I'm not lookin' for love, in any case. I'm here because Cian over at the Knot & Lantern said you might be able to help me with some information."

Orla's expression shifts, her playful eyes becoming more guarded. "Is that so? And what kind of information are you after?"

The weight of her stare sits heavy on my chest. I take a

deep breath. "I'm lookin' for Jack O'Hara. You wouldn't happen to know where I can find him, would you?"

Orla stares at me momentarily, then begins fiddling with a book titled *How to Spot a Liar*. The silence in the quiet bookshop deepens. In the distance, I can just make out the echo of laughter from the main street.

"Jack O'Hara, you say?" Orla leans her hip against the display table, her arms crossing over her cozy white sweater. "And why would you be wanting to find him?"

"I'm a journalist here writin' an article about the festival. Jack's name came up, and I'd really like to chat with him," I tell her truthfully while leaving out the part about him falsely claiming he'd witnessed a murder.

She raises one eyebrow. "And what makes you think he'd want to chat with you?"

I consider my response carefully. "Maybe he won't. But I reckon I have to try if I want to find out the truth."

"The truth?" A flicker of interest sparks in Orla's eyes. "Ah, so someone's finally going to dish on the festival's dirt. Is that why you're looking for Jack?"

I have no idea what she's talking about, but it's clear she knows something I don't. I need to keep her talking. "Uh-huh. Somethin' like that."

"Well, it's about feckin' time," Orla says with sudden passion. "But I'll warn you, if you start digging into this, you'll become just about as unpopular as Jack. And some of the locals sure haven't made things easy on him."

I'm dying to ask her what made Jack so unpopular in the village, but she might clam up on me if I do. If I want her to tell me where I can find Jack, I need to play along. There'll be plenty of time later to dig into whatever shenanigans are going on at the festival.

"I'm just here to do my job," I tell her. "All I care about is the truth."

"The truth is a slippery fish if ever there was one," Orla muses, tapping her index finger lightly against her chin. "But that's not to say some truths aren't more accurate than others."

"Ain't that right," I humor her, even though I have no clue what she means.

For a brief moment, I think she's about to tell me where to find Jack. Then, the lines around her mouth harden, and she resumes her task of stacking books. "Sure, I wish I could help you. But, like I told the guards, I don't know where Jack is. I haven't seen him since last night."

Disappointment hits me like a screen door in a hurricane —hard and out of nowhere. "I understand. Thank you very much for your time. If you do hear from him, I'm stayin' at the Abbey Wood Manor."

I'm about to head for the exit when I feel Orla's hand on my elbow.

"I can't tell you where to find Jack, mind—" Orla pauses mid-sentence, her eyes darting around the shop as if checking to make sure we're alone. Finally, she leans in close, her voice barely above a whisper. "But if you were inclined to take a stroll by the river, you might stumble upon some... interesting sights. There's an old willow at the bend that's quite lovely this time of year."

My heart skips a beat. Is she saying what I think she's saying? "Why are you tellin' me and not the guards?"

Orla shrugs. "I don't think Jack's particularly keen on speaking with the guards just now, if you catch my meaning. Sure, they're always trying to find something or other to charge him with. I'd like to think there's someone out there who's open to listening to whatever it is he has to say. Maybe that's you."

"I got no trouble keepin' an open mind," I assure her.

"I'm glad to hear it. But, like I said, I have no clue where

Jack is." Orla winks dramatically. "I just think it would do you good to get some time away from the hustle and bustle. To clear your head, like."

I nod, smiling back at her. "I do think better when I'm surrounded by nature."

"Just be careful," Orla cautions. "The banks can be slippery and the currents treacherous. Wouldn't want our American guest to end up falling in and drowning, now, would we?"

After saying goodbye to Orla, I step out of Prose and Cons onto the quiet street. The cool Irish air, even in Spring, nips at my cheeks and makes me shiver. Or maybe it has nothing to do with the weather at all.

I can't shake the feeling that Orla's warning wasn't just about the river.

CHAPTER EIGHT

According to Google Maps, there's only one large bend in the river. It's just south of the village, behind the Abbey Wood Manor. That's got to be the place Orla was telling me about.

To get there, I'll need to walk back toward the hotel. I opted to leave my car behind when I went into the village for lunch. After spending the whole morning behind the wheel, my legs had practically begged for a stretch. Now, in my impatience to track down Jack, I wish I'd been a bit lazier.

Tucking my phone into the front pocket of my messenger bag, I walk away from Prose and Cons to join the cheerful mayhem on the main street. Shop doors stand open, inviting customers to browse selections of jewelry, candles, Aran sweaters, pottery, and everything else that might appeal to tourists. With the festival starting this weekend, plenty of willing shoppers stroll along the bunting-lined street, their arms laden with goodies.

Still, I can't help but wonder how much business the shops do after the festival ends. All the locals seem happy and friendly now, but what is life like for them the other eleven months of the year?

I get the sense that Carrigaveen is like a freshly painted house—from the outside, everything looks lovely. But if you look closer, there are enough cracks to eventually bring the whole thing tumbling down.

Quit it, I tell myself. *Your imagination's runnin' wilder than a dog with a stolen pork chop.*

As I approach the end of the high street, a large bus belches down the road, spewing out a cloud of diesel fumes that makes me cough. It can only be headed to one of two places—the hotel or one of the large tents that have been set up in the empty fields to welcome festival attendees.

That's where I *should* be heading. I arrived early in the day mainly so I could be here to report on the welcome ceremony. I consult my watch. The event is scheduled to start at four o'clock. It's nearly two o'clock now. That should leave me plenty of time to wander into the woods, ask Jack O'Hara a couple of questions, and then mosey back to the tent before the ceremony kicks off.

Even after rationalizing the plan in my head, my conscience pricks me. Ambling down the country lane—following a footpath tread into the weeds—I watch the bus pull to a stop a short distance from one of the tents. A horde of eager tourists spills out onto the grass, smiling and chatting happily.

I should be interviewing them right now. And I really ought to let the Gardaí locate Jack and make him explain why he filed a false report. But I also know I won't. Can't. Especially not after Orla hinted there's more going on in this sleepy little village than meets the eye. And whatever that may be, it could make my magazine article stand out from all the other stories written about the festival over the years.

With one last glance at the crowd of matchmaking hopefuls, I continue down the lane toward the woods. Before long, the GPS on my phone directs me to a trail just east of Abbey Wood Manor. Following a wire fence, I make my way along the edge of a field, careful to avoid brushing against the nettles. Tall oak trees loom in front of me like petrified gatekeepers.

As soon as I step into the woods, the trees seem to close in around me. The skeletal branches cast long, dappled shadows on the ground, and the air is cool, with the scent of moss and earth hovering in the stillness. A shiver runs the length of my spine as I imagine someone poised with a crossbow behind every tree.

Waiting. Watching.

Then, a bird chirps in the distance, snapping me out of my nightmarish fantasy.

Get a grip, I order myself and continue walking.

The soles of my sneakers crunch in the underbrush as I follow the twisting path deeper into the woods. I walk and walk. All the trees are starting to look the same, and I'm sure I've seen the same rock at least three times. Getting frustrated, I pull out my phone to see if I'm still headed in the right direction. But the little bars at the top that show me the strength of my cell signal have all gone dark.

Oh, great! I'm lost in the middle of the woods with no service, and I have no idea whether I'm closer to the river or the road. If I don't figure out where I am, I could be wandering around this creepy place all afternoon.

My mama taught me how to use a compass when I was younger, which would be helpful…if I actually had a compass. I try to remember what else she taught me. Oh yeah, it was something about following the moss. Above the equator, it almost always grows on the north side of the tree because that's the spot that gets the least sunlight.

I check out several trees around me, trying to get my

bearings. Turning around, I begin heading in the direction I think is south, toward the river.

At last, like a distant whisper, I hear it—the soft gurgle of flowing water. Relief washes over me, and I begin to wonder why I let myself get so spooked. Picking up my pace, I follow the sound, pushing through a cluster of ferns until—there it is.

The river glints like polished silver in the afternoon sunlight.

Downstream, I notice that the land seems to jut out into the water. That must be where the river bends! The stones beneath my shoes are smooth and slippery, slowing me down as I race toward a large tree whose graceful branches cascade like a green waterfall into the current below. I'm no arborist, but I'd bet dollars to donuts that's a willow tree.

I squint my eyes, searching for any signs of Jack O'Hara. But the closer I get, the more my heart sinks. There doesn't appear to be anyone here, but I spot some fresh shoe marks in the mud. I hope I haven't missed him.

"Jack?" I call out, praying that he's still within earshot.

Only the wind and the water lapping at the shore answer back.

"Come on, Jack," I mutter to myself. "Where in tarnation are you?"

Not here. That's for darn sure.

I sigh deeply—both disappointed by the failure of my mission and dreading the thought of traipsing through the woods to get back to civilization.

I'm just about to return to the path when something catches my eye—a flash of color in the water just beyond a thick knot of reeds.

It looks like a wool blanket. Maybe left behind from a picnic.

My curiosity pulls me forward like a magnet. I edge

closer to the water, the mud forming a suction-cup seal around my sneakers.

My fingers tremble as I reach out to push aside the reeds. The icy water sends a shock up my arm. I lean in, my breath catching in my throat.

That's when I see the shoes.

But it's what's attached to the shoes that makes my body want to evacuate the meat pie I'd eaten earlier.

The body of a man floats face down in the river, his dark hair swaying gently in the current.

CHAPTER NINE

Numbness floods my limbs as I stare at the lifeless body.

The man lies half-submerged in the shallows, one arm hooked around a mossy stone as if he'd tried to pull himself ashore mid-drowning. The river licks at his shoes like a stray cat lapping a bowl of cream.

My knuckles ache from clenching the strap of my canvas messenger bag.

I can't breathe. I can't think. This can't be happening.

What have you gotten yourself into this time? I ask myself.

This has to be Jack O'Hara. I've never laid eyes on the man before, but something—some gnawing certainty—tells me this has to be him. And, though I don't have any proof yet, I'd bet the farm he was murdered.

With trembling fingers, I fumble for my phone, nearly dropping it into the river. Once I have a firm grip on the device, I search for signs of a cell signal. I couldn't get reception in the forest, but here, by the river, I have a single bar.

I scroll through my contacts, searching for Detective Mulhaney's number. In my flustered state, I briefly forget that I saved him as *Arrogant Arsehole.* Accurate? Absolutely. But at this moment, he's exactly who I need. With a sigh, I hit the call button.

As it rings, doubt creeps over me. Should I have called the local guards first? They're in charge of keeping the peace in Carrigaveen, after all. But Mulhaney? He may be cocky as all get out, but he's sharp. And, for all his faults, I trust him.

"Come on, pick up," I mutter, pacing along a small patch of riverbank. My eyes dart between the water-logged corpse and the trees. It dawns on me that I have no idea how long the body's been in the river. If he was murdered, the killer might still be nearby. They could be hiding in the trees.

"Brian Mulhaney, you better answer your phone, or I swear I'll—"

"Jeffers?" Detective Mulhaney's rich brogue crackles through the speaker. "This better be important. I'm driving back to—"

"I think Jack O'Hara is dead," I blurt out, my voice quavering.

Jack's annoyed sigh rattles down the phone line. "Come here to me, no one cares about your theories. So, until you have a solid reason for thinking—"

"Is a body solid enough for you?"

He pauses. "What's that now? What do you mean *a body*?"

"Exactly what it sounds like," I say, my own annoyance shining through. "I just found a body in the river near Abbey Wood Manor. I don't know for sure. But I'm thinkin' it was must be Jack O'Hara."

Silence stretches between us, heavy with uncertainty.

Finally, he says dubiously, "Go away. You're not serious, are ya?"

"Do I sound like I'm jokin'?" I practically scream at him. "Do you want me to text you a picture of the body?"

I can almost hear the gears turning in Mulhaney's mind. "Have you touched the body?"

"Of course not! I'm not an idiot."

"Good. Now, listen carefully. I left Carrigaveen about twenty minutes ago, but I'm turning around. If you haven't already, you need to call the local guards right now. Make an official report, like."

I nod, even though he can't see me. "Got it. Call the cops. Anythin' else?"

"Don't touch anything. Don't even breathe on the scene if you can help it. Send me your exact location. I'm on my way."

"Are you sure there's nothin' you want me to do while I wait?"

"Just ring emergency services. That's all you need to do," Detective Mulhaney firmly insists. "Let me handle the rest, alright? For once in your life, stay out of trouble."

He hangs up. That man really will do anything to get the last word.

Although I disparage him under my breath, I still follow his instructions—first, by sending him a pin of my location, and second, by calling 112. After reporting the body and telling the dispatcher where the guards can find me, I end the call.

The sudden silence presses down on me.

I stare at the body in the river, my mind speeding faster than a NASCAR driver on the final lap of a race. Part of me knows I should do exactly as Detective Mulhaney says—sit tight until the local authorities turn up. The last thing I need is to get caught up in another homicide. I came to Carrigaveen to get away from all that.

But my curiosity is like a living thing clawing at my insides.

Will the guards even suspect the man was murdered? Or

will they assume he accidentally drowned? And, if they're not used to investigating murders, what clues might they miss?

I've already helped solve two murders since arriving in Ireland. Chances are, I have more experience with this kind of thing than they do, tucked away in this sleepy little village on the edge of the Atlantic. I doubt there's ever been a murder here. Before now, anyway.

Chewing my lip, I weigh my options. If I nose around and get caught, I'll be in more hot water than a crawfish at a boil. But if I don't and something gets overlooked...

Mulhaney's voice—overbearing and authoritative—plays in my head. *Don't touch anything*. But he didn't say anything about *looking*, did he?

I glance around, making sure I'm alone, then—careful to avoid the fresh footprints in the mud—I inch closer to the river's edge. I move cautiously, like a cat hunting a field mouse. The wild grass squelches underfoot and water seeps into my sneakers, soaking my socks.

My gaze roams around the area, searching for anything that seems out of place—specks of blood, signs of a struggle, a scrap of fabric snagged on a branch. My mama always said I had an eye for details. That I could see things other people overlooked. She said it's what made me such a good writer.

And my powers of observation don't fail me now. Lying in the turf a short distance from the river, I spot a thin, pale object partially obscured by long blades of grass. I crouch down beside it, my heart beating fast.

"Well, I'll be," I breathe, pushing the grass aside gently to get a better view of the item. It's a toothpick, or at least it used to be. This particular toothpick has been chewed to within an inch of its life. It looks about as mangled as a dog's favorite squeaky toy. Despite that, it looks relatively clean, so it can't have been here long.

Who did this belong to? Was it Jack's? Or could it be the killer's?

In the middle of a crisis of conscience, wondering whether to leave the toothpick or preserve it as evidence, I hear twigs snapping and the crackle of a police radio coming from the woods behind me.

Not wanting the guards to catch me in a compromising position, I stand up and step away from the river. Seconds later, two uniformed men step out of the forest, blinking to adjust their eyes to the sudden sunlight.

I recognize one of the men—the thirty-something redhead—from the hotel. He'd been one of the guards sent to check out Molly Jenkins's room. I think the detective had called him Sergeant Sweeney.

"Miss, are you the one who reported finding a body?" His accent is thick enough to spread on toast.

"That'd be me." My voice sounds as shaky as I feel. "I was walkin' by and, well, stumbled across…him." I tilt my head in the direction of the body without looking. I've seen enough for one day.

Sergeant Sweeney's eyes narrow. "Sure, you were at the Abbey Wood Manor earlier, weren't you? You were asking that Cork detective about the Molly Jenkins business."

Uh oh! If I'm not careful, he might mistake my interest for involvement. "I'm a journalist here to write a story on the festival. I thought what y'all were workin' on earlier would be of interest to my readers."

Sergeant Sweeney eyes me warily and steps toward the shoreline, looking down at the drowned man. "Every few years, we get a floater in the river. The slippery rocks make it fierce dangerous down here."

The other guard, a younger blond man with a notebook in hand, turns to me. "What were *you* doing all the way out here? Sure, if you're writing an article, shouldn't you be in the village at the festival, like?"

I can feel sweat beading on my forehead, but I keep my cool. "I was takin' a little break before the welcome ceremony. Thought a walk might clear my head. Though I reckon today's walk has done the opposite."

The guards exchange glances, and I see they're not entirely buying what I'm selling. My fingers twitch, itching to tell them about the toothpick, but I know I'm already on thin ice.

Sergeant Sweeney steps toward me to demonstrate his authority. In the process, he steps right into the muddy footprint, destroying its potential as evidence. I try not to wince.

"Garda Murray here will take down your details," Sergeant Sweeney says, oblivious to the damage he's done. "We'll be needing a proper statement from you later on. But for the time being, we're going to need you to vacate the area. For all we know, this could be a crime scene."

I'm tempted to smack my palm against my forehead. Of course, there's a chance this is a crime scene! I knew I should have picked up that toothpick. These local guards don't seem to have a clue what they're dealing with. Who knows what else they'll miss or, worse, destroy if I don't keep an eye on them?

"But I spoke to Detective Mulhaney. He told me I should wait here," I argue, trying to buy time.

Sergeant Sweeney narrows his pale green eyes. "Detective Mulhaney has his jurisdiction. We've got ours. Now, unless you fancy obstruction charges..."

What is it with Irish law enforcement always threatening to put me in jail?

"Alright, alright," I concede, holding up my hands in surrender. "I'll be on my way. But y'all don't hesitate to call if you need anythin'. My name's Savannah Jeffers. I'm staying at Abbey Wood Manor, just up the road."

Sergeant Sweeney nods to Garda Murray, who takes me by the elbow and walks me back toward the woods. I can't help feeling like an adult who just got banished to the kids' table at Thanksgiving.

As I'm being led away, Sergeant Sweeney calls out, "Don't stray too far, alright? We'll want to talk further once we have a better sense of what happened here."

There's a warning in his tone. Almost as if he's putting me on notice that if they do suspect foul play, I'll be right at the top of their suspect list.

CHAPTER TEN

My thoughts spin faster than a trailer home in a tornado as I cross the impossibly green field to the festival's main tent. Is Jack O'Hara dead? And, if so, did someone kill him?

With the image of the dead body floating in the river still fresh in my head, it's hard to shift my focus back to the living. But I'm in town to write an article, and, at the very least, being at the welcome ceremony will keep my brain occupied while I wait for Detective Mulhaney to arrive.

According to my watch, I've made it back just in time. The ceremony is due to begin any minute. I pick up the pace, not wanting to miss any more of the orientation than I already have.

The big cream-colored marquee is decked out with green, gold, and white bunting, fluttering in the breeze. Inside, the atmosphere looks warm and welcoming. Long wooden tables draped in white tablecloths are covered with brochures, maps, and little bouquets of wildflowers. String lights and paper lanterns hang from the ceiling, giving everything a soft, golden glow.

Ducking beneath a sagging banner that reads *Céad Míle Fáilte,* I'm greeted by a cacophony of conversations, the squeak of folding chairs, and the clatter of someone dropping what sounds like an entire cutlery drawer.

The air smells like hope with a hint of hairspray.

My eyes dart around, taking in the lively crowd and their eager faces. To my left is a group of giggling twenty-somethings—their accents a mix of Irish lilt and American twang. To my right, an older man in a tweed cap fusses with his hearing aid while, behind him, two middle-aged women lean in close, whispering like they're plotting something scandalous.

Vowing to push what I'd seen at the river to the back of my mind, I focus on the task at hand. My mission is simple—identify a few people willing to let me follow their journey on the rocky road to love. The only question is where to start. The tent is teeming with people.

I spot a group of women standing next to the beverage table and start moving toward them, not realizing I'm stepping right in the path of a forty-something man carrying two full pints of Guinness. He must not have noticed me either because we collide, and his fermented drink spills onto my arm, soaking through my light sweater.

"Oh my gosh, I'm so sorry," I quickly apologize.

"No, you're grand. I wasn't watching where I was going," the man says, his weathered face breaking into a practiced smile. "Ah, would you look at that? I've spilled my drink all over ya."

"Don't worry about it," I assure him. "Ain't nothin' a little water and a tissue won't fix."

He tucks one of the pints into the crook of his arm and pulls a handkerchief out of his back pocket. "I suppose this as good a way to meet as any. I'm Senan."

He reaches out as if he's planning to dry me off himself,

but I snatch the handkerchief away, and dab at the moisture on my arm. "Savannah."

He adjusts the flat cap perched on his thick, dark hair. "Is that where you're from?"

With a significant amount of effort, I refrain from rolling my eyes. "No. But I've been there, and it's real pretty."

"Not half as pretty as you, I'd imagine," he says with a lecherous glint in his blue eyes. "Did you come all the way from America for the festival, so?"

"Oh, I'm not here for the festival," I say, worried he might be getting the wrong impression. "I mean, I am. But not the way you're thinkin'. I'm writin' an article for—"

Before I can even finish the sentence, he cuts me off. "You're a journalist?"

"I am."

He steps back as if I'd just told him I had a touch of Ebola. The look in his eye turns distinctly hostile. "Sure, look, I'm sorry about the spilled beer. But I'd appreciate it if you left me out of whatever story you're writing. I've no interest in the world knowing my business."

His sudden shift in behavior makes me think he's hiding something. If I had to guess, I'd say he has a wife and kids at home. "No problem. And, again, sorry for bumpin' into you."

He glares at me before turning and hurriedly walking away.

Chuckling to myself, I head to the beverage table for a bottle of water to rinse off my arm. The group of women I'd noticed earlier is still there, huddled together in animated conversation. After paying for a liter of Ballygowan and cleaning up the spilled Guinness, I sidle up next to them.

"Mind if I join y'all?"

"Of course not! The more the merrier," a pretty blonde woman in her early thirties replies in an Australian accent, making room for me in their circle. She introduces herself as

Emily and gestures around the group, naming her new friends from Canada, France, and Japan.

"Y'all traveled a long way to be here," I comment. "How'd you even find out about the festival?"

"Would you believe my aunt, Adeline, met her husband here over thirty years ago?" Emily says. "So, when I got tired of awful online dates, she suggested I give this a try. Adeline swears by Maeve. Says she's the real deal."

Emily is referring to Maeve McKewon, the local matchmaker-in-chief. I'd done a little research on Maeve and found that she comes from a long line of women who've brokered marriages for centuries. But, if the legends are true, Maeve outdid them all—turning their small family festival into an international event and making thousands of love connections over the past fifty years.

"*C'est vrai*," the French woman named Simone confirms. "My brother. He, too, met his wife at the festival five years ago. They are very much in love."

The Canadian, Becka, nods her head. "Maeve found a husband for my cousin, who is just about the pickiest person I ever met. So, I figured, what the heck? If Maeve can spare me one more bad date, I'm all in."

"But how does she know what you're lookin' for?" I ask, genuinely perplexed. "What is she, like, psychic or somethin'?"

The woman from Japan, Reina, frowns. "She knows all about us from the forms and essays, of course. Did you not have to fill them out?"

"I'm actually a reporter, here to write about the festival," I admit, hoping that won't put them off talking to me. "You had to fill out a lot of paperwork?"

All of the women groan in unison.

"You have no idea!" Emily laughs. "It took me weeks to fill it all out."

"I almost gave up halfway through," Becka says, smiling. "At this point, Maeve probably knows more about me than I do."

As the group jokes about the amount of paperwork required to meet a potential husband, I find my attention drawn to the other side of the tent. Molly Jenkins, wearing a tailored purple dress that hugs her curves, is in a conversation with Senan, the man who spilled his drink on me.

Though Molly is smiling politely, everything else about her is screaming 'not interested'—from the slight tilt of her head to the way she keeps glancing around the room as if looking for an escape route.

If I didn't suspect Senan was a bit of a lech, I might feel bad for him.

Suddenly, a hush falls over the crowd. I crane my neck to see what's caused the sudden quiet.

"She's here!" someone nearby whispers reverently.

My heart starts racing, and I chide myself for getting so worked up. I'm here as a journalist, for goodness sake, not some starry-eyed romantic. But as I feel the anticipation building around me, I can't help but be impressed by the level of devotion Maeve inspires.

Hundreds of pairs of eyes focus on the tent entrance as a petite woman with silver-white hair walks in, her arm linked with a tall, handsome man in his late twenties who—judging by the family resemblance—must be her grandson.

The crowd parts, creating a path for Maeve. As she passes through the sea of people, her piercing blue eyes scan the room, seeming to make contact with every person present. Her gaze lands on me for a split second, and I swear I feel a jolt of electricity. Her humble presence is electrifying. It makes me think she's either a natural leader or a brilliant con artist.

When Maeve reaches the makeshift stage at the front of

the tent, she turns to face the crowd. The silence in the tent is so deep I'd swear I can hear the grass growing.

"Welcome, dear friends, to the Carrigaveen Matchmaking Festival," she says, her voice rich with warmth and wisdom. "We gather here today in search of love, companionship, and, with any luck, a bit of craic along the way."

I can't help but smile at her mention of 'craic'—that oh-so-Irish word for a good time.

"Though, for many of you, love might seem as unattainable as winning the lottery, it's really nothing more than a genuine connection with another person," Maeve continues. "I will help you find that, but you have to do your part. So, if any of you eejits came here thinking that swiping right counts as courtship..." She whips an old flip phone from her skirt pocket, brandishing it like Excalibur. "I'm here to tell you that this here's the only technology required to arrange a decent date!"

The tent erupts in cheers. Maeve holds up her hand to silence the crowd so she can continue.

The applause still ringing in my ears, I'm jolted by the sudden buzzing of my phone. The sound is jarring, and I glance around sheepishly, feeling like I've committed some sort of sacrilege.

"Excuse me," I whisper to Emily, sidestepping past her with a guilty glance.

Finally free of the huddled masses, I slip into the gathering dusk outside the tent and glance at the caller ID. *Arrogant Arsehole.* I answer the call.

"Detective Mulhaney?"

He skips the pleasantries. "Jeffers, I'm going to need you to come to the Garda station and make an official statement. We've identified the body. You were right. It's Jack O'Hara. And it appears he was murdered."

CHAPTER ELEVEN

The village police station, nestled at the heart of the village just behind The Knot & Lantern pub, looks like it was someone's home long before it became the official outpost of local law and order.

The building's whitewashed stone walls are softened by climbing ivy, and the slate roof has a slight sag as if it's seen one too many intense Atlantic storms. I imagine it's the kind of place where a constable is just as likely to settle a dispute over a wayward sheep as he is to solve an actual crime.

I step inside and find an impatient Detective Mulhaney leaning against a government-issue metal desk in what probably used to be the cottage's front parlor.

"Took your time," he says, pushing his weight off the desk and jerking his head toward a narrow hallway. "Follow me."

"If you were in that big a hurry, you coulda picked me up," I grumble under my breath, softly enough that we can both pretend he didn't hear me. "This looks more like a house than a Garda station. Do the guards live here?"

Detective Mulhaney walks down a short hallway, halting

at an open doorway. "Technically, no. Though I've been told there's a cot upstairs for Sergeant Sweeney when his wife kicks him out for snoring."

He ushers me into a room that's roughly the size of a postage stamp, with barely enough space for the rickety table and two chairs crammed inside. The walls are a faded shade of green, and a single overhead light casts harsh shadows on the few pieces of furniture in the room. I settle into a chair, wincing as it creaks. Beside me, a radiator hisses, pumping out heat that smells vaguely of boiled cabbage.

Detective Mulhaney takes a seat on the other side of the table and pulls out a small notebook. All our teasing banter from this morning is gone, buried under the weight of his professional responsibilities.

"Well, now, isn't this cozy?" I comment, trying to break the ice.

Detective Mulhaney prefers to keep things frosty. "Save the jokes, Jeffers. As I mentioned on the phone, Jack O'Hara has been murdered. Since you—"

"Was he drowned? Did someone hold his head underwater?" I cut him off.

He quirks an eyebrow at my interruption. "It appears he was strangled before going into the river. Now, if you don't mind, I'll be asking the questions from here on out."

I give him a sarcastic salute.

His jaw clenches. "As I was saying, since you were the one who found the body, I'm obliged to ask—did you have anything to do with Mr. O'Hara's murder?"

I figure he has to be joking. "Oh, yeah. I just love goin' around offin' strangers in my spare time."

His dark eyes bore into mine. "This is no laughing matter. If you'd said that to any other guard, they'd have you in handcuffs."

"Oh, come on. You can't honestly think I had anythin' to do with this," I protest. "And besides, women *get* strangled. They don't *do* the stranglin'."

Detective Mulhaney just stares at me. "Your sarcasm isn't helping your case."

"Neither is your insistence on always treatin' me like a suspect," I shoot back, trying to reign in my temper. I take a deep, steadying breath. "Look, I'm not gonna lie and tell you I didn't go out in the woods lookin' for Jack. Because I did. But I never expected to find him dead. And I sure as shootin' didn't kill him."

He runs his fingers through his short, dark hair and leans back, assessing me. "Look, I know you didn't kill him. But will you take a minute and think about how it might look to the local guards?"

My seat suddenly feels very uncomfortable. "You mean how I was followin' you around at the hotel earlier askin' if I could go with you to find Jack?"

He nods. "Something like that, yeah. Not to mention, I've had word you were traipsing around the village asking anybody and everybody if they knew where you could find him."

"That's not true. I only asked two people and—"

This time, he cuts me off. "It doesn't matter how many people you asked. In case you haven't noticed, village gossip moves faster than a racehorse at the Grand National. You have to keep your wits about you, or the next rumor on their lips will be about how a flame-haired American showed up just before bodies started dropping."

"Well, that'd just be dumb. Especially since, from what I've heard, people 'round here didn't even seem to like Jack," I say, thinking of the disparaging remarks the guards and Cian had made about the dead man. Even Orla had said he wasn't very popular among the locals. "What do you know about him anyway?"

Detective Mulhaney sighs. "Not much. All the guards here will say about him is that he was a troublemaker. What that means, I don't have a clue. His record is clean, he doesn't appear to be on social media, and, according to his taxes, he's self-employed. I know he was staying down here for the festival, but I can't find any hotel bookings under his name. The man is practically a ghost."

It seems to me people who place that much value on privacy generally have something to hide. "The local guards said Jack liked to stir the pot, right? Did they say if he'd made any enemies?"

"None that they were willing to tell me about. But I'm not surprised. Villagers are fierce protective of their neighbors' secrets."

It occurs to me that I've heard a few people mention one name in connection to Jack. "Do you know anythin' about a guy named Fetch?"

"Fetch?" Detective Mulhaney looks at me like I just asked if he still believes in Santa Claus.

"Yeah, Fetch. I've heard his name a couple of times now. I reckon he might be worth talkin' to."

Almost immediately, I sense a change in Detective Mulhaney's demeanor. I half expect him to launch into a stern lecture about minding my own business. Instead, he starts laughing so hard a tear runs down his cheek.

After a minute of this, I start feeling the butt of a joke I don't even understand. "What's so funny?"

"I'm sorry. I just can't believe you thought Fetch was a person," Detective Mulhaney says, wiping a finger under his eye to wipe away a tear. "Some detective you are."

Annoyance bubbles inside me. "Well, if it's not a person, what the heck is it?"

"Nothing but a fairy tale. A fetch is said to be like a spirit double, an exact copy of a living person. Like a doppelgänger. But the fetch is different in that it only shows up before someone dies, or so the aul' ones say."

My eyebrows knit together. "So, it's like a Celtic grim reaper wearin' a real person's face?"

"Something like that. Legend says fetch aren't malevolent or anything like that. They're just precognition that a person is about to meet their maker. Unless you see a fetch in the morning. Then, I think it's supposed to be a good thing. Who can say? It's all nonsense, of course."

I can't help but wonder if the bartender, Cian, was making fun of me when he brought up the fetch earlier or if he genuinely believes in the old legends. Either way, it seems unlikely that the fetch had anything to do with Jack O'Hara's murder.

"Alright, so it doesn't sound like you have any good suspects. Do you think you can pull any DNA off that toothpick out by the river?" I ask. "It could be a lead."

"Toothpick?" Detective Mulhaney frowns. "What are you on about now?"

"While I was waiting for the local guards, I saw a chewed-up toothpick in the grass. It didn't look like it'd been there long." Watching Detective Mulhaney tense up, I quickly add, "I didn't pick it up, I swear. You told me not to touch anythin', and I didn't."

"I didn't see any toothpick out at the crime scene. And Sergeant Sweeney didn't mention anything about one either," Detective Mulhaney seems skeptical.

I throw my hands up in frustration. "I knew Sweeney would miss it. I woulda pointed it out to him, only he was already treatin' me like I was a suspect. I figured it was better just to keep my mouth shut."

"That must have been a first for you." Detective Mulhaney

squeezes his eyes shut as he shakes his head. "I can't believe I'm about to encourage you, but did you happen to see anything else before Sergeant Sweeney arrived?"

"Now that you mention it, there were footprints in the mud right by the river," I tell him. "But don't get too excited. I watched Sweeney trample all through them when he was tryin' to get a closer look at the body."

"Please tell me you took photographs? Of the toothpick or the footprints? Ideally, both."

I grimace. "I didn't. You told me to stay out of it, remember?"

"That's just great," Detective Mulhaney mutters under his breath. "If it weren't for bad luck, I'd have no luck at all." He pushes his chair back forcefully and stands up. "That'll be all, Jeffers. I'll let you get back to writing your exposé on the matchmaking festival. If we have any more questions, someone will be in touch."

I rise from the chair, slightly miffed by the rough dismissal. "You know I'm gonna be askin' questions around the village...for my article, of course. Why don't you let me help you? I think there is—"

"No!" Detective Mulhaney says sharply. "It's best if you just leave this with me. You're not a detective, and I'd appreciate it if you stopped playing around at being one."

I'm tempted to point out that my murder sleuthing skills are clearly better honed than any of the guards in Carrigaveen. But I'm too proud to offer my assistance only to be rebuffed again.

"Alright then. You know where to find me." Without waiting for a response, I step into the hallway, walking quickly down the hallway toward the exit.

Before he'd interrupted me, I was about to tell Detective Mulhaney that Orla from the bookstore might know if anyone had a grudge against Jack. From what she'd alluded to earlier, Jack knew things about the matchmaking festival that the locals might prefer to keep hidden.

It's a tip I would have been only too happy to share with the detective. But since he's not interested in anything I have to say, I'll be making the trip to Prose and Cons on my own.

CHAPTER TWELVE

I shove open the door of the Garda station and stomp out into the early evening air, my cheeks burning with frustration. Detective Mulhaney's dismissive attitude sticks in my craw like a popcorn kernel lodged between my teeth.

There have been moments—fleeting as they may be—when the detective actually seems open to my insights. He might not be *thrilled* to discuss murder cases with me, but at least he grudgingly considers my theories. When he's not being an obnoxious pain, I even catch glimpses of someone witty and kind. Someone I might actually like. But the second he goes into full detective mode? It's like flipping a switch. He becomes as stubborn as a mule.

As I march down the main street, which is unnaturally quiet now that most of the shops have closed for the night, I try to shift my thoughts away from Detective Mulhaney and onto what secrets Jack might have been harboring about the matchmaking festival. It must be something juicy if it's made him persona non grata with the guards and some of the villagers. But that still doesn't explain why he would have reported a murder that—to all appearances—never happened.

I'm hoping Orla can answer some of my questions, but when I round the corner on the side street, I catch sight of the darkened windows and a "Closed" sign hanging on the glass door of Prose and Cons.

"Darn it!" My voice echoes down the empty street. "What do I do now?"

As if in answer to my rhetorical question, my stomach rumbles. It hits me that I haven't had a bite to eat since that meat pie at the Knot & Lantern. I suppose I could go back to the pub for dinner or try out the restaurant at the Abbey Wood Manor. Then, I remember that—before being distracted by a murder investigation—I had planned on going to the welcome dinner hosted by the festival organizers.

That probably explains why all the shops in town closed so early on a Friday night.

I look at my watch. It's quarter to six. The dinner doesn't start until seven, but with nothing else to do in the meantime, I decide to head straight there. In addition to being a free meal, the welcome dinner could be a good opportunity to get quotes for my article and see if any gossip is circulating about Jack's murder.

With renewed purpose, I set off down the main street toward the field outside the village. As I walk down the deserted country road, the sky stretches wide above me, a soft, pale blue fading into streaks of gold and pink as the sun begins its lazy descent. It's quiet except for the rustling of the bushes and the distant call of birds settling in for the evening.

Up ahead, I spot a huge white tent set up in the field with strings of twinkling lights draped along its edges like fireflies on a summer night. The aroma of sizzling meat and spices wafts towards me, making my mouth water.

Inside, the tent is still relatively empty, with only harried staff and a handful of early arrivals milling about. I make my way to an empty table near the back of the tent, trying to avoid drawing attention to myself.

With some time to spare before the festivities kick off, I pull out my phone and type "Irish Fetch folklore" into the search bar. I'm curious to know more about this legend that several locals seem to think is true. My fingers fly across the screen as I scan through the results.

"The Fetch," I murmur under my breath. "A supernatural double that appears as an omen of death."

Though the thought still sends a shiver down my spine, the information isn't new. It's the same thing Detective Mulhaney already told me. I want to know more. And, sure enough, the further down I scroll, the more unsettling the details become. Apparently, seeing someone's fetch is a sure-fire sign that their days are numbered. Some stories even say the Fetch can lure you to your doom, like a ghostly pied piper.

But nothing I read says anything about witnessing a fetch *being killed*. From a surface level understanding of the legend, fetches only wander around harmlessly, like they're going about their day. Though, apparently, marks on their body can give indications about how their double will die. If they're headless, for example.

My mind drifts back to Jack's claim about witnessing Molly Jenkins's murder. Was what he saw just a premonition? I mean, I'm not one to buy into supernatural mumbo-jumbo, but there's no denying the eerie timing of it all.

I chew on my bottom lip, lost in thought. If Jack really did see what he thought was Molly's death, does that mean he saw her Fetch? And, if so, shouldn't Molly have been the one to die...not Jack?

Shocked that I'm even willing to entertain the thought of a mystical explanation, I lean back in my chair. My gaze sweeps across the tent as more guests begin to arrive. From the number of place settings on the tables, I figure tonight's dinner will be even busier than the orientation ceremony this afternoon.

It dawns on me that this could be my last opportunity for a while to check and see how my friend Debra's getting along with Fergal, my precocious Irish wolfhound. It wouldn't surprise me if he'd torn my cottage apart in the twelve hours I've been away.

Stepping out from under the tent's canopy, I spot two large buses pulling up on the dirt road nearby. This place is about to become a zoo.

I dial Debra's number. She answers on the second ring, but it's clear her attention is elsewhere.

"Fergal, no! That's *my* dinner, you big eejit," Debra cries, her voice sounding far away. There's some ruffling on the line, and when she finally speaks again, her voice is much clearer. "Savannah? Sorry about that. Everything's under control."

A smile plays at the corner of my mouth. "You sure about that? It sounds like my dog just cheated you of your meal."

"It's grand," Debra assures me half-heartedly. "Sure, I wasn't that hungry anyway. But how's everything with *you*? Are you enjoying your time in Carrigaveen? I've never been, but I've heard it's lovely."

I consider mentioning the murder, but Debra will only ask me a bunch of questions, and I'm currently short on answers. There's plenty of time to fill her in on the details later. "Everythin' is fine here. I'm more worried about you.

Did I leave enough food in the fridge? Is there somethin' else you can eat?"

When my friend had kindly agreed to stay at my house and dog sit Fergal while I was away, I did my best to stock the place with everything she might need. I didn't plan on Fergal swiping her meals, though, in hindsight, I probably should have. Fergal's like an unruly teenager, always testing the fences, seeing how much he'll be allowed to get away with.

"Stop worrying. There's enough food here to feed an army. Though I might need to start locking Fergal out of the kitchen while I'm eating." Debra laughs. "But enough about us. How's the festival? Any hot guys there?"

An image of Detective Mulhaney flashes in my mind. I quickly push it away. "I wouldn't know. I'm here to write an article, not find a husband."

"Yeah, well. There's nothing to stop you from having a bit of craic, right?" Debra teases. "Oh! Have you heard the news?"

"You're gonna have to be more specific." I brace myself for whatever she's about to say.

"The president is coming to Ballygoseir!" she exclaims.

"The president of what?"

"Of the United States, silly!"

I frown, thinking I must be hearing her wrong. "Daniel Kilpatrick is comin' to West Cork?"

"He sure is," Debra confirms. "You know Peter Kilpatrick? He and his wife own the Tidewater Grill. Anyway, Peter is the president's cousin. So, they're having a bit of a family get-together."

"Did Peter tell you that?" I ask while my eyes follow a silver Range Rover pulling off the main road into the field.

"Sure, he didn't need to. I saw the Secret Service agents with my own eyes. You can't mistake a bunch of lads with earbuds, wearing suits with American flag pins on the lapels. Especially in a place like West Cork."

"Yeah, I guess they would stand out, alright," I agree. "So, when's all this happenin'?"

"Not for a few weeks. You should be back by then. I imagine we'll all get roped into cleaning up the village. Planting flowers and painting houses. The locals will all be wanting to put their best foot forward..."

Debra continues talking excitedly about the president's upcoming visit, but I'm no longer paying attention. The silver Range Rover has pulled up next to the tent, and Maeve McKeown is climbing out. I need to get back inside.

"Debra," I interrupt her chatter. "I'm sorry to cut you off, but I gotta get back to work. Can we talk about the president's visit later?"

"No bother. I'm sure we'll all be hearing plenty about it in the next few weeks, as it is," she says, good-humoredly. "Don't work too hard."

"Thanks. Give Fergal a big hug for me, and don't let him steal any more of your meals."

"I won't. Talk to you later, so. Bye, bye, bye, bye."

I can't help chuckling as I hang up. I've noticed that one goodbye is never enough in Ireland. It's usually four. Sometimes, even five. I have no idea why, but it makes me giggle every time.

Reining in my amusement, I step back under the tent just as Maeve moves toward the makeshift stage at the opposite end. The tables have filled up in the short time I was on the phone. Nearly all the seats are full of hopeful romantics. The clatter of stainless steel against porcelain plates dies as Maeve ascends the dais with the assistance of the same young man I saw her with earlier.

People begin rising from their chairs. A few start clapping, and soon, the whole tent erupts into thunderous applause. Worry lines are etched into Maeve's face, but she's smiling as she adjusts the microphone with a thump that makes the sound system shriek.

"Mind your eardrums." Maeve's voice comes out of the speakers, sounding tinny and high-pitched. "The microphone seems to have a mind of its own this evening."

The handsome young man comes up on stage to manipulate some settings on the sound system. Seconds later, he gives Maeve a thumbs-up and steps off the stage.

"Thank you, Niall," Maeve says, her voice now perfectly pitched. "How about a round of applause for my grandson?"

Everyone claps again for Niall, whose face remains perfectly stoic.

"Let's get down to business, shall we?" Maeve continues. "Why are we all here? And, contrary to what my grandson, Niall, might say, I don't think you've come all this way for the free whiskey. Though you should give it a try. It's distilled right here in West Cork. An old family recipe. All the shops in town stock it if you want to take some home with you."

Polite laughter ripples through the crowd. A man sitting to my left snorts into his Guinness, foam clinging to his mustache.

Maeve holds up a hand, and silence descends. "No, the real reason we're all here tonight is to find love. To fill that place in our hearts that has been empty for too long..."

As Maeve carries on with her welcome speech, I find my attention drawn to her grandson, Niall. Or, more accurately, the person he's conversing with—Orla from the bookshop. And judging by her body language, she's furious.

From the other side of the tent, I watch as Niall grabs Orla by the elbow and pulls her outside. She jerks her arm free, her auburn hair coming loose from its ponytail. Orla says something that makes Maeve's grandson stiffen, his shoulders tensing beneath his starched, button-down shirt.

He leans forward, whispering something in her ear. Orla's eyes widen in surprise. Then, she steps back, shaking her head. With a look sharp enough to cut glass, Orla whips around and storms off across the field.

Part of me is tempted to chase after her, but I get the sense that, right now, she's too angry to answer my questions.

First thing tomorrow, I will head to Prose and Cons.

It's becoming clear to me that something is rotten in the village of Carrigaveen. And I intend to find out what it is.

CHAPTER THIRTEEN

Brrring. Brrring.

The shrill ring of the hotel phone pierces the quiet of my room, jolting me awake. I lunge for the phone, sheets twisting around my legs as my palm smacks the nightstand hard enough to knock over a glass of water.

I curse softly under my breath. I could have used that water right about now. My mouth tastes like a bog after heavy rain. I never should have had three glasses of wine on an empty stomach.

Squinting at the antique brass clock next to the bed, I see it's just past six o'clock in the morning. Only one person would be calling me at this hour. I pick up the phone just to make it stop ringing.

"Miss Audrey?" I croak into the receiver.

"Still alive, then?" my aunt's crisp voice echoes down the line. "I started worrying when you didn't answer your cell phone."

I groan. "I turned it on silent when I went to bed. Why are you callin' me so early anyway? Is everythin' alright?"

"You tell me," she replies. "After all, you're the one who found a dead body yesterday and didn't bother to call and mention it."

I sit upright in the bed and rub the sleep from my eyes. I should have known my aunt would find out about Jack O'Hara's murder. It had crossed my mind to call her last night when I got back from the welcome dinner, but I hadn't wanted to wake her.

She chose not to return the courtesy.

"Chances are, you know as much as I do," I surmise aloud. "So, why don't you start, and I'll fill you in on whatever you're missin'?"

"Fair enough," Audrey agrees. "In the meantime, why don't you make yourself a pot of coffee? It sounds like you're half asleep."

"I *was* asleep," I remind her, wishing I didn't have to wake up now. Sighing, I swing my legs out of bed, the rug tickling my toes as I pad over to the single-serve coffee maker.

"Sure, you're awake now. So, it's all grand," Audrey attempts to convince me. "Now, down to brass tacks. I heard that your man who reported witnessing a murder a few days ago has now become a murder victim himself. God rest him. You found him strangled in the woods?"

"Uh-huh," I grunt, focusing on how to put water into the machine.

Audrey goes silent for a minute. "Are you paying attention to what I'm saying, or are you trying to figure out how to use the coffee maker?"

Does she have cameras in my hotel room? How could she possibly know that?

"Yeah, yeah. I'm listenin'." Even to my own ears, my voice sounds petulant. "I can do two things at once."

"You can, of course," Audrey says. She doesn't sound

convinced. "As I was saying, a friend in the guards tells me the fellow who was murdered is called Jack O'Hara. Now, I couldn't find a whole lot of information about him at first. He's very secretive, like."

She has my full attention now. "At first? Does that mean you were able to find somethin' out? Detective Mulhaney had nothin' on him."

"I'm not surprised. No disrespect intended to the good detective. More like Jack O'Hara went to great lengths to keep himself and his business out of the public eye."

"What kind of business would that be?" I ask, giving up on the coffee maker and settling for a packet of instant.

Audrey's excitement practically fizzes down the phone line. "He was a private detective. And a pretty well-known one, at that. In certain circles, anyway. His clients knew him only by his internet handle—Alias Hunter."

Whatever I'd been expecting, it wasn't that. "Jack was a P.I.? What was he doin' in Carrigaveen? This hardly seems like the kind of place where people would be able to hide out. Everyone knows everyone."

"That I don't know. But I'd bet it has something to do with why he was killed. Do you know if he had any friends in the village?" Audrey pauses for a second, then speaks again. "You know what? Never mind. You're there to write an article on the festival. You really shouldn't get involved."

With my pre-coffee brain, I can't figure out if this is some kind of trap. "Are you tryin' to use reverse psychology on me or somethin'?"

"Not at all," Audrey insists. "I've had a change of heart. It's probably for the best if we let the guards handle the investigation."

I can't help thinking she would change her stance if I told her how Sergeant Sweeney trampled over evidence. "So, let me get this straight. You woke me up at the crack of dawn to share information about the dead guy that you now want me to ignore?"

"When you put it like that, I can see why you might be confused," Audrey admits. "Sure, look, I'm just worried about you. I called to make sure you were alright, and then I got a little carried away. It's hard for me to resist a puzzle. You know that. But I don't think it's wise to have you putting yourself in harm's way again."

There's a certain rationale to her words. In the past year, I've found myself in the crosshairs of killers on three occasions—once in Florida and twice since coming to Ireland. I don't care to repeat the experience.

That said, I can't imagine leaving the murder out of the article I'm writing. So, at the very least, I need to speak with people in the village about Jack and what impact his death will have, if any, on the matchmaking festival.

"I appreciate your concern, Miss Audrey. I really do. But I have a job to do. And, in order to do it, I have to ask some questions around the village."

"What kind of questions? And who will you be talking to?"

"Well, for starters, there's a woman named Orla Gallagher. She runs the local bookstore. I was plannin' to go talk to her this mornin' after the shop opens. You know, durin' normal people hours."

I can practically hear Audrey rolling her eyes. "What do you want to talk to Orla about?"

"I didn't find Jack at the river by accident," I tell Audrey. "Orla said I should look for him there. She also mentioned that he knew things about the festival. Things the locals didn't want bein' made public."

Audrey draws in a deep breath. "Just be careful. Jolene

would haunt me to the end of my days if I let anything happen to you."

At the mention of my mama's name, a bittersweet smile curves my lips. Not a day goes by that I don't miss her.

There's a tightness in my throat when I speak. "She's done a pretty good job of lookin' out for me so far. We wouldn't want her gettin' bored up there in heaven, now, would we?"

CHAPTER FOURTEEN

Downtown Carrigaveen is already packed when I make it into the village an hour later.

Main Street is an obstacle course of tourists from around the world clutching tea and pastries, their voices a lively hum above the sound of a fiddle played by a talented busker in the square. The scent of fresh bread and coffee drifts through the cool morning air. Any other day, I might be tempted to stop, grab a scone, and listen to the music.

Right now, I just want off this crowded street.

Turning onto the quieter lane that leads to Prose and Cons, I brace myself to find a darkened storefront. After seeing Orla so torn up last night, I half expect her to have closed up shop for the day. To my relief, the lights glow warmly inside.

The bell jingles as I step through the door for the second time in as many days. Orla looks up from behind the counter. Even from across the shop, I can see the telltale redness rimming her hazel eyes.

I approach her with a gentle smile, my heart aching for

her loss. "Hello, Orla. I don't know if you remember me. I came in yesterday—"

"How could I forget?" she interrupts me, her lower lip trembling slightly. "You're the writer who wanted to find Jack. I hope you know that when I sent you to the river, I never expected you would find..." She doesn't— can't—finish the sentence.

"Of course, you didn't," I quickly insist, not wanting to leave her sitting with that image. "I'm real sorry for your loss. And I know we're strangers and all, but if there's anythin' I can do to help, you just let me know, you hear?"

A bittersweet smile curves the corners of her mouth. "Careful now, or I might put you to work shelving books."

I return her smile. "I'd alphabetize this whole dang shop if it would make you feel better."

Orla's laughter is soft but genuine. "Thanks for making me smile. I needed that. It was a long night. I just can't believe he's really gone, you know?"

I nod. Poor thing looks like she's barely holding it together. I need to tread carefully here. The last thing I want is to cause her more pain.

"How did you two become friends anyway?" I ask, genuinely curious.

Orla sighs and wipes a stray tear from her cheek. "Believe it or not, he helped me with my divorce. Nasty business, that was. I hired Jack to prove my cheating ex was hiding assets. Jack was a godsend during those dark days. He cheered me up at a time when I thought I'd never get out of bed again."

I feel a pang of empathy for Orla. I know all too well how a single event can turn your entire world upside down.

"That's why I feel so bloody guilty," Orla continues, her voice catching. "I'm the one who suggested he offer his services at the festival. Doing background checks and the like. I thought he could help people. If I'd known..." Her voice trails off as she blinks back a fresh flood of tears.

"So, that's why Jack was comin' to Carrigaveen every year?" I ask gently. "He was rootin' out bad actors at the matchmakin' festival?"

Orla nods. "Times have changed. In the old days, the matchmaker knew everyone in the village, their families, their histories. But now, with people flying in from all over, it's not so simple.

"Jack and I both thought it was important to have some kind of vetting process in place at the festival. So if a person met someone they liked, there was a way to find out quick enough if that person was who they claimed to be. That there were no skeletons hiding in the closet."

"That's mighty smart, if you ask me," I say, meaning it. "But I reckon not everyone saw it that way?"

Orla shakes her head, a small, wry smile playing on her lips. "No, not everyone. We tried to keep what he was doing quiet. Jack liked his privacy. But in a village this size, sure, we couldn't keep it secret for long. And there were those who thought Jack was meddling where he shouldn't. But Jack just wanted to make sure that people weren't being taken advantage of."

I think about all the villagers who might have been impacted by Jack's little side business, and one face keeps coming to mind. "How did Maeve McKewon feel about Jack runnin' background checks on her clients?"

"She wasn't exactly in favor of the enterprise, if you catch my meaning." Orla's words are laced with disgust. "When she found out what Jack was up to, Maeve made it clear that she didn't want him snooping around, stirring up trouble. She had the local guards keep an eye on him. If he so much as jaywalked they were issuing him tickets. Maeve herself even tried to run Jack out of town a few times."

My eyebrows shoot up in surprise. “Run him out of town? That seems a bit extreme.”

“That's Maeve for you. She has a silver tongue and an easy smile, but make no mistake, she's a force to be reckoned with. And she doesn't take kindly to anyone threatening her livelihood,” Orla tells me, anger lurking behind her eyes. “But Jack stood his ground. He wasn't about to let anyone intimidate him.”

My mind whirls with the implications of Maeve's opposition to Jack's work. If she was willing to run him out of town, what else might she be capable of if he refused to leave?

“And what about Maeve’s grandson?” I ask, trying to steer the conversation toward the argument I witnessed last night. “Did he want Jack gone, too?”

“Niall? As if that boy ever had a thought in his head that was his own.” Orla doesn’t even try to hide her disdain. “He’s been riding Maeve’s coattails since he was in nappies. He’ll do anything she asks without question. I suspect he’s mostly in it for the money. Between the festival and all the branded products, that family is so flush with cash you’d think they were printing it themselves.”

Even though I’m worried it might put her off talking to me, I have to ask about what I saw the night before. “I hope you don’t mind me sayin’, but I couldn't help noticin’ your fight with Niall at the welcome dinner.”

Orla grimaces. “You saw that?”

“Yeah. Sorry. I didn’t know if I should step in. It seemed to get pretty heated.”

Orla waves a hand dismissively, but I can see the tension in her shoulders. "Oh, that was nothing," she says with a little too much nonchalance. “My blood was boiling when I got word about Jack, and I had to find someone to blame.”

“Do you think Niall or Maeve had something to do with Jack’s death?”

Orla holds her hands up. "It doesn't matter one bit what I think. And, sure, I wouldn't want to be pointing a finger at anyone without proof."

"I get it," I assure her. "But the guards will be tryin' to figure out who might've had a grudge against Jack. Can you think of anyone else he might have had a problem with?"

Orla snorts. "He wasn't exactly in the business of making friends. Not in his line of work. It's a fair bet he's stepped on more than a few toes over the years."

"What about recently?" I press. "Do you know if anyone at the festival had hired him?"

Orla breaks eye contact and starts rearranging some books on the counter. "Sure, I wouldn't know anything about that. He didn't like to talk much about what he was working on." She pauses, deep in thought. "Though I did notice that he seemed a bit on edge this year. Jumpy, like. Always looking over this shoulder."

"Any idea why?" I ask.

Orla shrugs and shakes her head. I get the sense she knows more about what Jack was up to than she's letting on, but I decide to let it slide. For now. "Did Jack have a partner?"

"Oh, no. Jack always worked alone."

"Can you think of anyone who mighta known what he was workin' on?"

Orla shrugs. "Not really. He kept himself to himself. Said it was safer that way."

Safer? What in tarnation had Jack uncovered that made him so spooked? "What about his files? Did he keep 'em on his computer? Or at an office somewhere?"

Orla's eyes widen, a sudden realization dawning on her face. "His notebooks!" she exclaims, snapping her fingers. "Jack was always jotting things down in this little leather-bound notebook."

I perk up like a bloodhound catching a scent. "Do you know where he kept it?"

Orla exhales thoughtfully. "If he didn't have it on him, it might be at my place. Jack always stayed at the coach house in my back garden when he came to the village. It's nothing fancy, mind, but he said it suited him just fine."

I open my mouth to speak, but a sudden realization hits me like a punch to the gut.

I'm standing at a crossroads.

I could take Audrey's advice. Cut my losses and walk away before getting pulled any deeper into something I can't control. Or I could chase the story and see where it takes me.

Part of me figures there's no harm in just *looking* for Jack's journal. It's not like the local guards are likely to find it. And if I do? I'll hand it straight over to Detective Mulhaney.

After I've had a peek inside, of course.

But I've been down this road before, where one seemingly harmless decision sent me straight into the line of fire. I can't help wondering if this is another one of those moments. Is it worth the risk?

In the end, I make the only decision I can live with. "I don't suppose there's any way I could take a peek inside the coach house? I hate to ask. But those notebooks could bring us a step closer to findin' out what happened to Jack."

I watch as a war of emotions plays out across Orla's face. "Jack always said he wouldn't trust the local guards to find saltwater in the ocean. So, I doubt he would have wanted *them* poking around in his things."

Seeming to have made her decision, Orla reaches for a notebook and a pen lying on the counter. She scribbles down an address, presumably to her property, rips the page loose, and holds it out to me. "The spare key is hidden in a plastic rock bordering the begonias."

I accept the paper from her hand. "Thank you so much, Orla. I'll let you know whatever I find."

"I'd appreciate it. Just be careful, won't you? It's possible that whatever Jack was working on got him killed. I couldn't bear it if…"

She doesn't finish the sentence. She doesn't need to.

My stomach knots with a mixture of anticipation and anxiety.

What secrets am I about to uncover in the coach house? And, more importantly, were they worth dying for?

CHAPTER FIFTEEN

The walk to Orla's house takes me away from the festival, in the opposite direction of the tents and my hotel. The further I walk down the country road, the quieter it gets. The chatter and music fade behind me, replaced by birdsong and the soft rustle of the breeze through the hedgerows. The road narrows, winding between fields so perfectly green they look fake.

Orla's house sits at the far edge of one of these fields, looking like something out of a postcard. A gravel path curves around the main house, leading to a cozy-looking coach house—all sturdy, weathered timber, sanded smooth and stained a warm honey-brown. Dark green trim outlines the doors and windows. Outside, a fire pit is surrounded by a neat circle of chairs, with a stack of split logs ready for the next chilly evening.

I scan the area, my eyes darting left and right to ensure no one else is around. Orla gave me permission to be here, but anyone passing by won't know that. And Lord knows I don't need any more trouble with the local guards. Satisfied that

I'm alone, I make my way towards the coach house, my heart thumping in my chest.

Orla said the spare key was in a plastic rock near the begonias. At the time, I thought it would be easy enough to find. That was before seeing the flower garden. It's a massive circle of red, orange, and yellow perennials surrounded by rocks. There must be fifty or more!

With a nervous glance over my shoulder, I drop to my knees and run my hands over the rocks, searching for one that doesn't feel like the others.

"Come on, come on," I urge, my frustration mounting with each passing second. Just as I'm about to resort to more drastic measures, like Googling how to pick a lock with a bobby pin, my fingers brush against something smooth and spongy. The hide-a-key!

I straighten up, dust off my jeans, and hurry to the coach house door. I slip the key into the lock, and with a satisfying click, the door swings open. Stepping inside, it takes a minute for my eyes to adjust to the dim light. The air carries the faint scent of wood smoke and something herbal, maybe tea.

The space is small but spotlessly clean. A loveseat in soft, neutral fabric sits in the center, loaded down with colorful knit throws and cushions. Against one wall, a built-in bed with a sturdy wooden frame provides a practical sleeping area, while across from it, a compact kitchenette features a Belfast sink and a mini-fridge. In the corner, a cast iron wood-burning stove stands beside a shelving unit filled with books.

I start my search in the obvious places. I examine the armoire next to the bed with Jack's clothes, all neatly folded. I scan the titles of all the books on the shelves. I rifle through the cushions like a mad woman on a treasure hunt. I comb through every nook and cranny but still come up empty-handed.

Once I've searched the living area, I turn my attention to the small bathroom. The space is as functional and spotless as the rest of the coach house, with a pedestal sink, a compact shower, and a mirror above the sink that doubles as a medicine cabinet. I hesitate for a second, then reach up and open it.

Inside, a few basic toiletries line the shelves, but what catches my eye are the pill bottles tucked neatly in one corner. I pick one up—*Co-amoxiclav*. Another bottle reads *Metoprolol*. I have no idea what either of them is for or why he'd need them.

Not wanting to waste time guessing, I pull out my phone and snap quick pictures of the labels. I can look them up later when I'm not in the middle of searching a dead man's bathroom. For now, I close the cabinet, leaving everything exactly as I found it.

Disappointment washes over me as I step back into the living room. Detective Mulhaney would probably arrest me for interfering in his investigation if he knew I was here, and it would all be for nothing. Not only have I not found Jack's journal, I haven't even gotten a better sense of who he was. The place is so pristine and sanitized it's almost like he was never even here.

I decide to take one more lap around the coach house, stopping when I notice something metallic peeking out beneath the curtain hem on the windowsill. Pushing the curtains aside, I discover a pair of binoculars.

"Somethin' tells me these weren't for bird watchin'," I mumble to myself. "Who were you spyin' on Jack?"

I raise the binoculars to my eyes, and the world beyond the window comes into sharp focus. I scour the landscape, searching for anything other than green fields and grazing sheep. Then, I see it. In the distance sits a large stone house nestled in a copse of oak trees. Ivy curls up the weathered walls, and smoke billows from the chimney.

Zooming in, I catch a flicker of movement behind one of the ground-floor windows. The sheer curtains make it impossible to tell who it is, just a shadow shifting behind the fabric. Still, it's enough to make me lower the binoculars, a prickling sense of guilt creeping in. Watching people through their windows is a little too *Peeping Tom* for my liking.

I return the binoculars to the windowsill, ready to call it quits, when I notice something unusual on the other side of the room. It's very subtle, so I'm not surprised I missed it during my initial search. The sheets are slightly untucked on one corner of the bed as if someone were rushing to straighten up. Normally, I wouldn't even give it a second thought. But Jack seems to have been borderline obsessive-compulsive about tidiness. I figure it can't hurt to check it out.

I step toward the bed, my heartbeat picking up with every step. Holding my breath, I grip the edge of the mattress and lift it slowly, carefully. And there it is—tucked between the mattress and boxspring—Jack's leather journal.

The paperback-sized journal bulges with loose papers and photos, and I am careful not to let any of them fall to the floor as I untie the leather strap holding everything in place. Gingerly opening the journal, I start to read—or try to, at least.

Indecipherable shorthand covers each page as I flip through, searching for some word or phrase I might recognize. But only one word, repeated a few times, stands out—Magdalene.

Making a mental note to ask Orla about this mysterious Magdalene, I jump to the photos and papers stashed at the back of the journal. The first two photos are of an attractive middle-aged man. Broad-shouldered and stocky, he has the build of someone who's spent years working the land. His tanned skin is lined from the sun, and streaks of gray run through his short, dark hair. In one photo, he's working in the fields. In the other, he sits with a toddler on his knee, his arm wrapped around a woman cradling a baby. He looks familiar, though I can't for the life of me remember where I've seen him before.

I have no trouble, however, identifying the woman in the next photo. The glossy, professional headshot features a smiling Molly Jenkins, her blonde hair falling in golden waves past her shoulders.

My eyebrows draw together in confusion. Why on earth would Jack have had a photo of Molly tucked away in his journal? Based on what he told the guards when he was reporting her supposed murder, he'd only met her once at the Knot & Lantern. Something definitely isn't adding up.

Hoping the folded papers behind her photograph will shed some light on the situation, I cradle the journal in the crook of my arm and unfold the stapled pages. I can't say for sure, but it looks like a balance sheet from last year's matchmaking festival. Several line items are highlighted in yellow, but their significance is just as perplexing as Jack's cryptic notes.

As I'm refolding the balance sheet, the sound of crunching gravel stops me in my tracks. I listen, hoping it was just my imagination, but then I hear it again. Louder this time. Someone is coming to the coach house!

In my panic, a piece of paper slides loose from the journal and floats to the floor. Bending to grab it, I see the words *Leave now or else* written in bold, block letters.

There's no time to inspect the threatening message further, so I shove all the papers back inside the journal, my fingers trembling as I wrap the strap around and secure it.

My mind races, trying to come up with a plan. Kicking myself, I realize that I neglected to lock the front door when I entered earlier. Maybe the person walking up the path won't try to come inside. If I keep quiet, with any luck, they won't know I'm here.

Then again, if anyone—aside from Orla and I—knows Jack was staying here, they will likely also be aware of the fact that he's dead and won't be able to answer the door.

The person outside could even be Jack's killer, come to make sure whatever secret died with Jack stays hidden!

A shadow passes over the front window, and I glance around, cursing whoever designed the coach house for not installing a back door.

Frozen in place, I can only watch in horror as the door to the coach house swings open and in steps...Detective Mulhaney. His dark eyes, blazing with the intensity of a summer storm, meet mine.

"Jeffers? What in the name of all things holy are you doing here?"

CHAPTER SIXTEEN

"Is there someone inside, Sir? Need some muscle?" Garda O'Dwyer's voice drifts through the open door, eager and full of youthful enthusiasm.

"That won't be necessary, O'Dwyer," Detective Mulhaney replies, his gaze still locked on me. His tall, athletic frame fills the doorway, arms folded across his broad chest like a human barricade. "So, Jeffers, mind explaining what exactly you're doing?"

The brief relief I felt at seeing him—and not a murderer—vanishes under his withering stare. I've been caught red-handed. Again. My throat goes dry. "I…uh…was just—"

"Interfering in a murder investigation?" he cuts in smoothly. "You do realize I could have you arrested for being here, don't you?"

I resist the urge to roll my eyes. He's made the threat so many times it's impossible to take him seriously. "Arrested for what? I'll have you know the owner gave me permission to be here. I'm not doin' anythin' wrong."

Detective Mulhaney steps into the room, his presence filling the small coach house with the electric energy of a gathering thunderstorm. "Permission or not, this is an active crime scene. You can't just go poking around, contaminating potential evidence."

"Oh, you mean destroyin' evidence like—" I lower my voice to prevent Garda O'Dwyer from overhearing, "—Sergeant Sweeney when he missed the chewed-up toothpick and then trampled footprints at the *actual* crime scene?"

Detective Mulhaney sighs and shakes his head.

Behind him, O'Dwyer pops his head into the coach house. "Who are you talking to, Sir?" His jaw drops when he sees me standing in the room. "Her again? First at the river, now here? I think we should take this woman down to the station."

Detective Mulhaney tilts his head and raises his eyebrows as if to remind me his threat is not an idle one. But to O'Dwyer, he says, "Stand down, Officer. I've got this under control."

O'Dwyer obeys, but he doesn't look happy about it. He moves a beefy hand to the butt of the baton hanging from his belt. In the process, his elbow connects with a lamp next to the door, knocking it to the floor, where it shatters into pieces.

Detective Mulhaney glares at O'Dwyer but says nothing. Instead, the detective turns his attention back to me.

"Well, Jeffers, you think you're so good at finding evidence. Tell me," Detective Mulhaney taunts, "what have you discovered during your unauthorized search of the dead man's rooms?"

I shrug, the hint of a smile curving my lips as I hold up the leather notebook in my hand. "Nothin' much. Just this journal with all of O'Hara's notes and a threatenin' letter tellin' him to leave now or else."

Shock registers in Mulhaney's eyes before he has the chance to collect himself. Then he pulls a pair of rubber gloves from his coat pocket and slips them on his hands with practiced ease. "Where did you find it?"

"Hidden under the mattress," I tell him with a touch of pride as I hand him the journal. "I almost missed it myself."

Detective Mulhaney carefully unties the leather strap and opens O'Hara's journal. As he flips through the pages, his brow furrows.

Unable to tolerate the silence, I blurt, "Are you havin' trouble understandin' the shorthand, too? There were only a couple of words in there that I understood, but I reckon someone must be able to translate it for us."

At the mention of the word 'us,' Mulhaney glances at me reproachfully before returning his attention to the journal. "You mentioned something about a threatening letter?"

"Yeah," I reach out to show him, but he moves the journal out of my reach. I take a step back, holding up my hands in surrender. "It's at the back with some other loose papers and photographs."

Detective Mulhaney pulls out the papers and quickly sifts through the photos and the anonymous note. He lingers momentarily on the note, then holds it out toward Garda O'Dwyer. "I'm going to need you to test this for fingerprints."

O'Dwyer removes his hand from the baton to reach for the paper.

"Gloves," Detective Mulhaney says with a hint of exasperation.

"Oh, right. Of course," O'Dwyer says, fumbling in his pockets for a minute before Detective Mulhaney hands him a pair from his own supply. O'Dwyer struggles to get them onto his sausage-like fingers. "Not a bother. I'll test it as soon as we're done here."

Detective Mulhaney keeps his expression neutral, but I can tell it's a struggle. "I'll be grand here on my own. You get going on the fingerprints and I'll meet you back at the station."

O'Dwyer's blue eyes widen. "You want me to go now?" He glances at me. "You sure you don't need my help here with your one?"

"I think I can handle her on my own," Detective Mulhaney replies. "But don't wander too far from the station. I might need your help later to take her fingerprints when I've finished with her."

I blink, taken aback that I could, once again, be considered a suspect. "My fingerprints? What do you need those for?"

"Because my guess is you've touched that note—and everything in this room—with bare hands," Mulhaney says as if he's explaining a difficult concept to a toddler. "We need to be able to exclude your prints from any others we might find."

I open my mouth to argue, but the wisdom of his statement stops me short. As much as I hate to admit it, he has a point. I probably should have brought gloves if I was planning to snoop around.

O'Dwyer, sensing my discomfort, shoots me a satisfied look before exiting the cottage. The crunch of gravel as he walks away gradually fades, replaced by the sound of an engine turning over.

Alone with Detective Mulhaney, I can't stop my thoughts from pouring out of my mouth. "Who do you think sent that letter to Jack? I think it'd be worth looking into Maeve McKewon—"

"Your one's over eighty years old!" Detective Mulhaney cuts me off with a frown. "I doubt she'd have the strength or the stamina to strangle a full-grown man before tossing his corpse into the water. And you, yourself, said it's men who strangle."

"That's true. I did," I concede. "But have you seen her grandson, Niall? He's built like a refrigerator with legs. And, from what I hear, he does just about anythin' his grandma asks him to do."

Detective Mulhaney shakes his head, unconvinced. "I grant you, Niall seems handy enough to have pulled off the job. But that doesn't explain why either of them would *want* to kill O'Hara."

"Runnin' him outta town hadn't worked so well for them," I point out. "Or don't you know that they were against his little side hustle runnin' background checks on festival attendees?"

An exasperated sigh escapes from between Mulhaney's pursed lips. "Oh, I knew about it, alright. I don't know how *you* figured out that Jack was a private detective, and, more likely than not, I don't want to know. But I'm not going to go jumping to conclusions without having all the facts. I can't even say for certain who that letter was intended for. Not yet."

I can't help but roll my eyes. "Oh, come on. A threatenin' letter hidden in the journal of a man who just got himself murdered? That's not exactly a coincidence, is it?"

"In my line of work," Detective Mulhaney replies, his voice dry as dust, "we tend to prefer evidence over speculation. Novel concept to the likes of you, I know."

I plant my hands on my hips and take a step toward him. "Alright, fine. Who do *you* think the letter might have been for if not Jack?"

"Were you not listening to me? I just said I wasn't going to speculate."

"Just name one other person who mighta got a letter like that."

"You're sorely testing my patience, Jeffers."

"And you're only sayin' that because you can't think of anyone."

He steps closer. "I can, indeed."

I have to tilt my head back to look him in the eye. "Well, don't keep me in suspense."

We're mere inches apart. I can smell mint on Detective Mulhaney's breath when he replies, "Molly Jenkins."

I blink in surprise. "Molly Jenkins? No. That doesn't make a lick of sense. Why would Jack have a letter that was sent to Molly? She didn't even know him."

"Well, you were just going on about coincidences. It seems like a mighty big one that he had a photograph of the woman he claimed to have seen murdered."

"Maybe he printed it *after* he reported what he thought he saw," I fire back. "It looks like it's from a website, doesn't it? He might have just wanted a better look at her."

"But you don't know for sure, do you?" he demands. When I don't respond immediately, he seizes on his advantage. "All I'm saying is, I need to be sure of the facts before I start making accusations against anyone. Including you, I might add."

"Me?"

"In case you haven't noticed, the local guards would like nothing more than to blame O'Hara's murder on an outsider. You fit the bill. And it doesn't help that you keep turning up at crime scenes," Detective Mulhaney says, his eyes softening. "Believe it or not, I'm just trying to look out for you."

The tenderness in his voice slices through my indignation, and it dawns on me how close his body is to mine. If I lifted my hand, I'd be touching his chest. I wonder if his heart is suddenly beating as wildly as mine. I'm tempted to find out. Instead, I take a step back and clear my throat. "I appreciate your concern, Detective. But I can take care of myself."

"You can, of course," he says, a husky twinge to his voice.

"Now, if you'll excuse me, I need to get to work. And you need to be...anywhere but here."

I nod, not entirely trusting my voice. He steps to the side, allowing me to pass. I take him up on the invitation and hurry for the exit. Only when I'm outside can I breathe again. I suck in a deep lungful of air.

I can't believe the thoughts I was just having about Detective Mulhaney. He's the most frustrating man I've ever met. Why would I even *think* about him in any sort of romantic way?

Not to mention, he's a distraction I don't need right now. Especially if he's right about the locals wanting to pin O'Hara's murder on a convenient scapegoat—like me.

I should be keeping my head down, but if I want to remove suspicion from myself, I need to give the guards somewhere else to look. To do that, I have to find facts and evidence that are undeniable—all while staying under the radar.

Lucky for me, I have the perfect cover. I still have an article to write. And the festival is the perfect place to learn more about Maeve, Niall, and Molly Jenkins.

CHAPTER SEVENTEEN

By the time I make it back to the center of the village, my pulse has finally settled—but my thoughts? Not so much. I can still feel the heat of Detective Mulhaney's stare. Still smell his sandalwood cologne.

Focus, Savannah.

There are far more important things to be thinking about. First off, I have an article to write. Second, and more importantly, Jack O'Hara is dead, and someone in this village—whether a villager or festival attendee—killed him.

I pull my phone out of my crossbody bag, determined to get back on track with work and my investigation. Thumbing through my schedule to see if I have anything lined up for the day, my stomach drops.

Eoman Scully—1:00 PM—Interview at The Whistling Kettle.

I groan under my breath. In all the excitement, I'd completely forgotten about my pre-scheduled meeting with the chief executive of the local council. He'd agreed to meet with me to do an interview about the festival's impact on the local community. I doubt he'll be willing to talk with me about the murder, but if I want to keep my editor happy, I can't afford to skip the interview.

That leaves me with about an hour to kill.

Glancing around the square, I spot a festival schedule pinned to the brightly painted door of Brennan's General Store. Striding over, I scan the list of events, searching for something to occupy me until the interview.

Sheep shearing demonstration at noon at O'Donnell's farm? Pass. I have no desire to spend my free hour watching some poor woolly creature get shorn like a freshly recruited army private.

Traditional Irish storytelling at Orla's bookshop? Intriguing, but between wanting to question Orla about Jack's shorthand and listening to the folk tales, I'd probably be late meeting Eoman.

Only one other event is happening in my timeframe: The Great Potato Peel-Off. It starts in just a few minutes in a tent at the end of the main street. If nothing else, I can get some good photos to include in my article.

The small tent is a hive of activity as I approach, with a steady stream of eager competitors and curious onlookers buzzing in and out. Long tables—rough-hewn and sturdy—span the length of the tent laden with baskets filled to brimming with potatoes of every size and variety—starchy, buff-colored maris pipers; round, crimson-skinned roosters; plump, purple rain tubers. Beside each basket rests a peeling station with two peelers, a bowl for the skins, and a bucket for the naked spuds.

Competitors mill about, some eyeing the potatoes like prize fighters sizing up their opponents, others trade jabs in good-natured competition. In one corner of the tent, an Irish folk band plays a lively jig on their fiddles, tin whistles and bodhráns. I don't recognize the tune, but it's a got a lively catchy beat.

Reaching into my bag, I grab my small digital camera. After playing with the settings for a minute, I begin snapping photos of the laughing crowd. But as I pan across the tables, searching for my next shot, my finger freezes over the shutter button. My heart skips a beat.

There, on the far side of the tent, is the same attractive middle-aged man from the photos in Jack's journal. My stomach does an odd little flip as another memory comes rushing back.

I've seen this man before. Not only do I recognize him from the pictures, but he's also the same man who spilled beer on me the night of the orientation ceremony. He'd started hitting on me until I'd mentioned I was a journalist, then he'd fled like a rabid possum that just heard a shotgun rack.

Senan, he'd said his name was. Just Senan. He didn't give a last name.

At the time, I'd brushed off his cagey behavior, figuring he was wary of the press because he didn't want his wife to find out where he was or what he was doing.

Now, I wonder if there was more to it.

I keep the viewfinder trained on Senan's face as he walks through the tent. As I watch, he makes a beeline for a blonde woman a few tables over—Molly Jenkins!

I don't care what Detective Mulhaney thinks. It can't be a coincidence that the two people from Jack O'Hara's photos are meeting up at the festival, can it?

Without taking my eyes off Senan, I reach up and switch the camera to video mode just as he approaches Molly. I watch as Senan touches her elbow, leaning in close to murmur something in her ear. Molly stiffens, her smile freezing on her face. I swear I see a flicker of something. Disgust? Fear? But it's gone before I can place it.

She says something, I'm too far away to hear what, and

then walks away. Senan stares after her, his expression a muddle of confusion and something else. Something darker. But then he pastes on a rigid grin and moves down the table, increasing the distance between them.

With my camera still rolling, I weave through the crowd toward Molly. I can't help feeling like she's the key to everything that's been happening, whether she realizes it or not. If I can just get her to open up, to trust me...

A sharp whistle pierces the air, cutting through my thoughts like a knife. I whirl around, my eyes darting to the small stage at the front of the tent. A man stands there with a microphone in hand.

"Alright, alright, settle down now, you lot! It's time for the main event!"

At the announcer's direction, the contestants start pairing off, each duo claiming a spot at the long tables. There's a flurry of activity as they settle in, picking up their peelers and rolling up their sleeves.

The crowd presses closer, jostling for a better view. I find myself being carried along with them, and I have to break free before I get so close to the tables that someone offers me a peeler.

Moving to one side, I find a space behind a table occupied by two women and three men, all in their sixties or seventies. One of them turns to whisper something to her neighbor, and I see she's wearing a green sash with the title 'Judge' emblazoned across it.

Then the announcer's voice barks out from the PA system: "On your marks. Get set. Peel!"

Participants dive in with enthusiasm, peeling potatoes as fast as they can. Skins fly through the air and land on members of the crowd, who just laugh and flick them off.

Figuring I should get some shots for the magazine, I lift my camera and begin snapping. Trying to get a better angle, I lean toward the judges and end up inadvertently eavesdropping on their conversation.

"...can't believe Senan O'Malley had the gall to show his face here. He doesn't even have the sense to lay low after what happened a few years back!"

My ears prick up, my pulse quickening. I sidle closer, keeping my camera trained on the competition, but my attention is laser-focused on the judges' chatter.

"If Maeve sees him, she'll have a right fit. The man has no shame," another judge replies, clucking her tongue. "That poor wife of his. What was her name again? Sally?"

"That's the one," the first judge confirms. "Though I heard she finally got fed up and left him. High time, if you ask me. A man like that."

The second judge shakes her head. I can see her gray hair bouncing in and out of frame in my viewfinder. "His poor father must be rolling in his grave."

"Aye, Thomas O'Malley was a fine man. The apple fell so far on that one, you'd almost be tempted to think it was from another tree."

The second judge chuckles. "Now, Moira. You know we're here to judge potato peeling, not other people's life choices. However questionable they may be. So, who do you think has the best form?"

While the two women ease into a conversation about wrist placement and blade speed, I try to put what they said in the context of what I already know.

I'd already suspected that Senan was a bit of a cad after our first run-in. The older ladies just confirmed my hunch. I also now know that Senan lives close enough to Carrigaveen for folks to know him—and his wife—by name. And I learned that he's been to the matchmaking festival before and was involved in some kind of incident when he last attended.

Is it possible that Jack—as a private investigator—was somehow connected to that past incident? Did he run a background check on Senan for a client and find a bigger skeleton than adultery in Senan's closet?

But even if he did, what does any of it have to do with Molly? She's only been in Ireland for a few days and doesn't seem particularly well acquainted with either man. Yet her picture had been right there, next to Senan's, in Jack's journal.

Why did Jack have her photograph? There must be a reason.

But the harder I search for a connection, the more confused I become.

Lost in thought, I jump when the speaker next to me booms with the announcer's voice. "Time's up, folks. Put your peelers down!"

At the mention of the time, I glance down at my watch and bite back a curse. I only have ten minutes to get back to The Whistling Kettle to meet with Eoman Scully.

As much as I want to stay to pull Molly aside and ask her some questions, I know I can't blow off the chief executive of the local council. Not if I want to keep my press credentials and access to the festival.

With a sigh of regret, I force myself to walk away.

As I step out into the sunshine, I can't resist one last glance over my shoulder. Through the crowd, I catch a glimpse of Senan, his gaze locked on Molly like a heat-seeking missile. Something about his expression makes my skin crawl.

CHAPTER EIGHTEEN

Even though my Vans sneakers are the most comfortable shoes I own, my feet are still aching by the time I get back to the center of the village. After all the walking I've done today, I can't wait to sit down in the coffee shop.

I wish I could order a coffee and have a solitary moment to think.

Information has been coming at me fast and loose all day, but I haven't had the time to piece it all together. Making connections on the fly is proving nearly impossible.

But reflection will have to wait. I have an interview to get through first.

I pause outside The Whistling Kettle, taking a moment to appreciate the café's teal cladding, the color of a lake reflecting clear, summer skies. Gold trim traces the windows like delicate lace, framing views of the homey interior. Above the entrance, a whimsical wrought-iron sign depicting a steaming kettle sways gently in the breeze.

Taking a deep breath, I push open the door, and I'm immediately wrapped in the warm, inviting scents of freshly brewed tea, rich coffee, and something buttery straight out of the oven. It reminds me of Sunday mornings back home in Alabama when my grandma would bake her famous peach cobbler.

The café hums with soft chatter and the clink of ceramic cups. The space is a cozy mix of rustic and quirky, with mismatched wooden tables and chairs scattered across the room. One wall is covered in a mural of rolling hills with tiny cottages and sheep dotting the landscape, while another sports shelves lined with vintage teapots and kettles. At the center of it all is a polished wooden counter, its glass display case overflowing with flaky scones, golden pastries, and perfectly frosted cakes.

My stomach grumbles. Maybe I can sneak in a pastry while I'm chatting with Eoman. But first, I need to find him.

My eyes scan the crowded café, roving over tables packed with locals and visitors, happily enjoying their cream teas and conversations. How in Carrigaveen's holy hills am I supposed to find Eoman when I'm not even sure what he looks like? I give myself a good mental kick for not Googling his picture before stepping inside.

Then, a man in an impeccably tailored navy suit rises from a booth at the back of the café. He waves, a practiced smile spreading across his face.

I return the smile and, dodging wayward chairs and servers with trays, make my way to his table.

"Miss Jeffers?" he asks, his Irish lilt rolling warmly off his tongue as he extends a hand.

I return the gesture. "That's me, but please, call me Savannah. It's a pleasure to meet you, Mr. Scully."

"Eoman, please," he insists, giving my hand a firm shake. His grip is firm, his skin cool and dry against my palm. "Would you like a coffee? And perhaps a slice of lemon drizzle cake? It's Sharon's specialty."

I rub at the corners of my mouth, just to make sure I'm not drooling. "That'd be great, thank you."

He nods and catches the eye of a passing waitress. He places my order with the casual ease of a repeat customer then slides into the booth and gestures for me to do the same.

After settling on the brightly colored cushion, I reach into my bag and pull out my phone, setting it on the table between us. "Do you mind if I record our chat?"

Eoman waves a hand in acquiescence. "By all means."

I tap the screen starting the recording. "So, Mr. Scully—"

"Please, call me Eoman."

"Sorry. Eoman, can you start by tellin' me a little about the history of the matchmakin' festival? I hear it's quite the tradition 'round these parts." I start with an easy question to put him at ease.

It seems to work. Eoman leans back, his posture relaxed, though his blue eyes remain sharp. "Indeed it is. The festival has been a lifeblood of our community, bringing people together for generations. It's been my privilege to help ensure its success, year after year."

"And y'all have been holdin' this festival for the past hundred and fifty years?"

He nods. "Give or take. In the early days, it was just a small affair. A few local families going to the village match-maker to arrange marriages for their sons and daughters. It only really started to grow in the last fifty years or so. I myself have been involved with arranging the festival for the past twenty-five odd years."

"I've bumped into people from all 'round the world since I've been here. What's the draw?" I ask, hoping he'll reference Maeve McKewon's obvious appeal to festivalgoers.

He shrugs. "In a world that moves so fast, the festival reminds us to slow down, to appreciate the simple magic of two hearts finding their way to each other. I think that's ultimately what attracts people here. Well, that, and the advertising campaign I personally launched. It really seemed to tap into people's hopes and dreams, if you know what I mean."

I nod politely, but I can't help noticing that, like a skilled politician, he keeps bringing the attention back to his agenda. In this case, himself. If I want to pump him for information about Maeve, I'll have to come right out and ask.

Just as I'm about to, the waitress arrives with two coffees and a generous slice of moist yellow cake. I push my phone to the side to make room for the plate. Unable to resist, I cut off a sliver of cake with my fork and pop it into my mouth. It's so delicious an involuntary groan escapes my lips.

"Didn't I tell you it was good?" Eoman muses, his smile revealing perfect white teeth. "Now, back to your question, there's a lot that goes into making the festival a success. We invest heavily in beautifying the village, ensuring it's picture-perfect for our visitors. And then there's the marketing. I personally see to it that we advertise far and wide to attract the kind of international attention we want."

I want to interrupt him to ask about Maeve, but when he was talking, I took another bite of lemon cake. With my mouth full, I can't speak.

My silence gives him leave to continue. "Of course, all of this comes at a cost. The beautification of the village alone costs upwards of €50,000. And don't get me started on the marketing budget for our international outreach. But the economic boost to Carrigaveen makes it all worthwhile. You see, the festival isn't just about celebration. It's about securing our community's future. That's a duty I happen to take very seriously."

In addition to continually bringing the conversation around to his own contributions, something else strikes me as odd about Eoman's behavior. Not only is he talking a lot about the festival's finances, which I never asked about, but he also seems very defensive about justifying the festival's importance. It's as if Eoman is trying to convince not just me, but himself, of the festival's value.

"You have to understand, Miss Jeffers," he continues, "that the festival is more than just a line item in a budget. Without it, many of our local businesses would struggle to stay afloat. The revenue it generates, the jobs it supports—it's all crucial to our village's economic health. And every single business owner shares in the profits."

I'm about to finally shift the conversation to Maeve and her cult-like following, but before I can speak, Eoman's phone buzzes loudly on the table. He glances at the screen, his brows furrowing.

"Forgive me, but would you mind giving me a moment?" he asks. "I'm afraid I need to take this."

"Of course," I say, scooting out of the booth and standing. "Do you know where the ladies' room is?"

"Through the swinging doors, down the hall, and to the right," he speaks quickly but calmly, his finger poised above the answer button on his phone.

After bobbing my head in thanks, I follow his directions to a door with the word "Mna" above a stick figure wearing a dress.

In the quiet of the washroom, I stare at my reflection in the antique mirror. Something is troubling me about this interview with Eoman, something beyond just his blatant self-promotion and defensiveness around festival expenses.

Then it occurs to me he's so focused on telling me how great the festival is, despite its not insignificant costs, he's completely avoided addressing the elephant at the event—Jack O'Hara's murder. It's almost like he's pretending it hasn't happened.

If he's head of the local council, he must have heard by

now that a redheaded American journalist found the body. Heck, if Carrigaveen is anything like Ballygoseir, everyone in the village knows. Is Eoman waiting for me to bring it up? Is he secretly hoping I won't?

Determined to start hitting him with harder questions, I exit the washroom and push through the double doors that lead back into the café. But a glance at the table stops me in my tracks.

Eoman is locked in a heated discussion with a portly, ruddy-faced man in a tweed jacket and flat cap. From a few feet away, I can only catch snippets of their conversation, but I hear words like "festival funds" and "chipped in."

As if sensing my presence, Eoman turns his head and spots me watching them. His expression changes from angry to agreeable in the blink of an eye.

"Ah, Savannah! You're back," he calls out, his tone as smooth as Irish whiskey. "Fergus here was just leaving. Weren't you, Fergus?"

The portly man nods stiffly, his face still flushed. "Aye, so I was. Don't forget, Eoman. End of the week."

As Fergus storms out of the café, I slide back into the booth across from Eoman. "I'm real sorry for interruptin'."

"Not at all," he says, his tone casual but his shoulders tense. "People are always coming up to me, asking questions. Just comes with the job, I'm afraid."

"Well, I can see you're a busy man, and I don't want to be takin' up too much of your time. But I do have to ask, are you worried about Jack O'Hara's murder impactin' this year's festival?"

He must be an excellent poker player because he doesn't even flinch. Instead, his eyes bore into mine, like he's trying to see straight through to my thoughts. "I understand you're the one found his body."

Well, on that score, at least, I was right. He did know. "That's right."

"Well, in answer to your question, no. Seeing as how the poor man's murder is completely unrelated to the festival, I don't think it'll have any impact whatsoever."

I open my mouth to protest, but he doesn't give me the opportunity.

"I'm sorry, Savannah," he says abruptly, standing up. "But that phone call was related to an urgent matter I must attend to immediately. Perhaps we could continue this another time?"

Stunned by this turn of events, I'm at a momentary loss for words. "Yeah, um, I guess. But I would like to speak with you some more. You know, for my article."

"Not a bother. I'll have my assistant get on to you about setting something up," he says, though I get the distinct impression he's planning to fob me off. "Enjoy the rest of your lemon cake, so."

As he hurries out the door, I'm left sitting there, my mind buzzing with questions.

What in the heck just happened? And why would he fabricate an emergency to get out of talking about Jack O'Hara's murder…unless he has something to hide?

CHAPTER NINETEEN

I step out of the Whistling Kettle, feeling annoyed by Eoman Scully's sudden departure. My mood is darker than when I went inside, but my wallet is quite a bit lighter. Eoman left so quickly he forgot to pay the bill for the sandwich, cake, and coffee he had before I arrived.

Thinking of lunch, my stomach reminds me that I've only had a slice of lemon cake since dinner last night. With nothing pressing to do, I figure I might as well grab a bite to eat at the Knot & Lantern. Since it's mid-afternoon, I'm hopeful there won't be too many people with the same idea.

I turn toward the pub, dodging tourists at every turn on the crowded streets. But I don't make it far. Out of the corner of my eye, I catch sight of Molly Jenkins slipping into a pop-up museum dedicated to the history of the matchmaking festival. I hesitate for only a second before changing course.

Lunch can wait.

If Molly's interested in the museum, maybe I should be too.

After waiting for a bus transporting dozens of festival

goers to go past, I cross the street and follow Molly into the old corner shop that's been converted into a temporary exhibit space.

It takes my eyes a minute to adjust to the dim lighting inside. The exhibit is jam crowded with people, and, at first, I don't see Molly. I worry that she might have wandered off while I was waiting to cross the street. Then, I spy golden blonde hair across the room. Molly is standing in front of a display with her back to me, her head bowed as if engrossed in one of the exhibits. I sidle closer, acting like just another curious tourist.

Pretending to study an early 20th-century faded black-and-white photograph of a young couple smiling shyly at the camera, I keep Molly in my peripheral vision. Now that she's in silhouette, I see that she isn't looking at an exhibit. She's staring down at her phone.

I take a few steps closer to Molly, landing in front of an exhibit about the legendary Cupid of County Cork, Eileen McKewon.

A large placard boasts that Eileen, Maeve's grandmother, could take one look at a couple and predict with startling accuracy how long they would stay together, how many children they'd have, even what they'd bicker about. An old wedding portrait shows Eileen, a knowing glint in her eye, standing between a pair of newlyweds.

The neighboring display features Maeve more prominently. After Eileen passed away some fifty years ago, Maeve took up the matchmaking mantle. But while Eileen focused on locals, Maeve had grander ambitions. She started reaching out to Irish expats and descendants in America, Canada and Australia, selling the month-long festival as a way to reconnect with their roots and find love in the process.

Her business savvy paid off. According to the sign in

front of me, the once-quaint local tradition now draws over 30,000 visitors a year from across the globe. That's over the course of the whole month, but it's no wonder the streets of Carrigaveen are packed to the gills.

Judging by the numbers and having previously researched how much Maeve charges to connect couples, it's clear that Maeve is sitting on a goldmine. And that's before considering the proceeds of her family's branded products and merchandise.

To my left, a flash of movement captures my attention. Molly holds her phone in front of her face and sighs in frustration. That gives me an idea of how to approach her without rousing her suspicion.

Closing the distance between us, I ask Molly, "Are you havin' trouble gettin' a signal in here, too?"

Molly glances at me in surprise. Her sapphire eyes widen briefly before her lips part in a sardonic smile. "I wish that was all it was. I dropped my phone and must have cracked the camera it uses for facial recognition. The blasted thing won't open."

"Can't you just type in your code?" I keep my tone light, like I'm offering a helpful suggestion and not pointing out the painfully obvious solution.

She rolls her eyes in response, but the smile remains on her face. "Honestly, it's been so long since I had to use it, I can't remember which code I used. I'm worried it'll lock me out if I keep trying."

As she's talking, her phone pings with an incoming text. Molly scowls. "And here's another message I won't be able to respond to. If I don't get this fixed soon, my family and friends are going to start worrying about me."

"I wish I could help you," I tell her. "But I don't know the first thing about fixin' iPhones. And the nearest Apple store is all the way over in Cork."

Molly sighs. “Ah, well. I guess that’s a problem for another day. And it’s probably for the best. I won’t find my soulmate with my head buried in my phone anyway.” She slips the device into her pocket and then brushes a strand of silky hair off her face. “My name’s Molly, by the way.”

“Savannah,” I say, shaking her hand. “Nice to meet you, Molly.”

“I’m kind of surprised there are so many Americans here. Did you come over for the festival, too?” she asks.

I consider pretending that I’m just another tourist seeking love, but lying isn’t really in my wheelhouse. “I’m actually a reporter here coverin’ the festival for a magazine back in the States. Care to do an interview?”

I sense a slight tensing of her shoulders, but then she chuckles softly. “Not really my cup of tea. And if this whole matchmaking thing doesn’t work out, I’d prefer to avoid the pitying looks from all my married friends when I go back home.”

“I hear ya.” I smile at Molly, drawn in by her effortless charm. “There’s nothin’ worse than married people askin’ you why you’re still single. That is precisely why I won’t ask you about your prospects so far.”

Light twinkles in her jewel-toned eyes. “Please don’t. I’d hate to have to tell you that suitors aren’t exactly beating down my door.”

“Come on, now. I know there’s at least one guy who’s got his eyes on you,” I tease. But when her brows draw together in a frown, I realize my mistake. She’s looking at me like I’m a stalker. I quickly try to explain myself, “I couldn’t help seein’ you at the potato peelin’ contest. It looked like Senan O’Malley was harassin’ you. I almost stepped in to help.”

The wariness in her eyes diminishes a little, but the frown remains. “Senan? You mean the Irish guy with dark hair? I thought he told me his name was George.”

"Huh. That's weird," I say, wondering why Senan would give Molly a fake name.

"But I'm probably just confused," Molly rushes to add. "I've met so many people. And to be honest, I wasn't really listening to the guy. He seemed like a bit of a creep."

It sure doesn't sound like they know each other very well. So much for my theory about them being connected. The mystery of why Jack O'Hara had both their pictures in his journal will remain unsolved. For now, anyway.

And speaking of Jack, this could be my chance to discover what Molly knows about the elusive private detective.

"Hey, I know this is kinda out of left field, but I was just wonderin'," I segue, "Did you hear that a man was murdered here the other day?"

She draws in a sharp breath, her eyes popping. "What? Really?"

I nod, trying to appear relaxed while carefully studying her reaction. "His name was Jack O'Hara. He was strangled out in the woods."

Molly stares at me for a minute. I can see wheels turning behind her eyes, but I don't have a clue what thoughts are powering them.

"Did you say Jack O'Hara?" she finally says, her voice lowered to a whisper. "He's dead?"

I try not to let my excitement show. "Yeah, did you know him?"

She breaks eye contact, staring off into the distance. "Not really. I met him once. But—and this is going to sound weird—he told the guards that he saw me being killed."

"What?" I say, hoping my feigned surprise sounds genuine. "Why on Earth would he do a thing like that?"

She shakes her head, returning my gaze. "I honestly have no idea. I thought he was just, I don't know, a little...

disturbed. But now you're saying someone killed him? That's awful. Do the guards know who did it?"

"Not yet," I tell her. "I think they're trying to keep it under wraps because of the festival and all."

Molly clucks her tongue, sadness dimming the brightness of her eyes. "You know, you hear about this kind of thing happening in America all the time. I guess I just didn't expect that kind of violence in a place like Carrigaveen. Especially not during a festival dedicated to love and new beginnings."

I nod. "It is hard to square the two things, isn't it?"

"It sure is," Molly agrees. Seconds later, she pulls her phone out of her pocket. "I guess I'll have to go and get my phone fixed after all. If the murder makes news in Boston, I need to make sure people back home can get in touch with me. I don't want anyone worrying."

I see the logic in her words, even if I am disappointed that she seems to be shutting down our conversation. "That's probably a smart move."

"Well, it was nice meeting you, Savannah. I guess I'll see you around."

"I'm sure you will," I tell her. "Good luck with your phone."

With a half-smile, she turns and walks to the exit. My eyes follow her across the room, but my mind is a million miles away.

Molly didn't shy away from any of my questions, she was honest, and she seemed genuinely surprised to learn that Jack had been murdered. I don't get the impression that she has anything to hide. Which only serves to confuse me more.

Is there some kind of connection to Senan that she doesn't even know about?

But that question seems insignificant in light of the bigger issues. I still don't know why Jack had her picture in his journal or why he claimed to have witnessed her murder.

CHAPTER TWENTY

After Molly departs, I linger in the museum for a few minutes, trying to decide what to do next.

There are plenty of events happening around the village, and I probably should go to one of them to get quotes for my feature article. In my pursuit of answers surrounding Jack O'Hara's murder, I fear I might be losing sight of the real reason I came to Carrigaveen.

At some point, I also have to swing by the Garda station to submit my fingerprints. But if the guards are already suspicious of me, it feels safer to wait to do that until I know Detective Mulhaney will be present. I tell myself it's a decision born out of good sense and not an excuse to spend more time with the handsome detective.

I almost believe it.

Resolving to re-focus my attention on the job I was hired to do, I push open the museum door and step out into the soft afternoon sunlight. As my eyes scan the area for one of the festival schedules that seem to be posted all around the village, a loud ringing sounds from inside my bag.

I pull out the device and see my editor's name in the caller ID.

"Hi there, Evelyn," I say after answering the call.

"Savannah, glad I caught you," Evelyn says, her voice a mixture of calm professionalism and harried New Yorker. "You know how we'd put in an interview request with Maeve McKewon? Well, her people just reached out and said she has a small opening in two hours. Can you be there?"

My heart skips a beat. "She's willin' to talk to me? That's amazin'!" Though a prominent figure at the festival, Maeve is notoriously media-shy. The last interview she did was more than five years ago. "I'll definitely be there. Can you send me the address?"

"I'll have my assistant ping it to you now," Evelyn replies. "Oh, and one more thing. I saw your message about the murder in Carrigaveen. We want to incorporate that into your article. A little intrigue and all that. Can you try to get in with the local police? See you what you can find out?"

It's on the tip of my tongue to tell her I'm already well acquainted with the guards here, but that could lead to admitting I'm currently one of their top suspects. So, instead, I merely say, "I think I can manage that."

"Great," Evelyn says, her attention already drifting to the next thing on her 'to do' list. "Send me some notes on how the interview with Maeve goes. And we'll chat again soon."

Before my lips can form the word goodbye, Evelyn is already gone. Seconds later, a text comes in with an address for my interview with Maeve. Evelyn is nothing if not efficient.

Tucking my body up against a nearby wall so I am out of the flow of foot traffic, I copy the address and pop it into my phone's map app. On foot, it will take me about twenty minutes to walk there. In fact, it looks like the location isn't far from Orla's house, where I was earlier this morning.

That leaves me with about an hour and a half to do last-minute research and draft some questions for the interview. Since the Abbey Wood Manor is a good twenty minutes away in the opposite direction, it doesn't seem worth the trouble to go back to my hotel. It makes more sense to stay close to town.

When my eyes land on the Knot & Lantern, my stomach tells me I should grab a late lunch while I do my work. My taste buds begin to salivate, thinking about Caroline's delicious steak and ale pie.

Decision made, I walk to the pub and step inside. There's an attractive young woman acting as a hostess today. She smiles at me as I approach her makeshift stand.

"Good afternoon. Table for one?" she asks with a smile.

"Yes, please." I look around, noting that many of the tables are already occupied. "If there aren't any tables, I don't mind eatin' at the bar."

She shakes her head, her blonde ponytail bobbing. "Not at all. There's a table just needs clearing that can be yours inside of five minutes."

"That sounds great. Thank you."

"Back with you in a tick," she says before bouncing off to chat with a lanky young man with red hair and a face full of freckles.

Still standing by the door, I have to step out of the way as an older couple walks toward the exit. As they pass, I hear the woman asking the man, "Did you remember to take your Nexium? Sure, you know how bad your heartburn gets after you've had fish and chips."

The man rolls his eyes. "I did, of course. I don't need you always reminding me, like."

Their lightheaded bickering continues as they open the door, but I'm no longer listening. Their conversation reminded me of the bottles I found in Jack O'Hara's medicine cabinet. While I wait, I might as well check and see what the pills were for.

After glancing at the photos I took, I open Google and type in *Co-amoxiclav.* The results come back that it's a kind of antibiotic. There are a number of different reasons he might have had those, so that doesn't tell me much. I clear the search bar and input the next name, *Metoprolol.* That turns out to be medication for high blood pressure. It strikes me that Jack was a bit young to need that, but otherwise, there's nothing particularly remarkable about it.

I continue scrolling through the results until the headline from a National Institute of Health study catches my eye: *Metoprolol-induced Visual Hallucinations: A Case Series.* I click on the article and begin reading. According to the research paper, several people taking Metoprolol reported seeing people in their bedrooms in the middle of the night. One person even claimed to be talking to dead people while on the drug.

Could Jack's medication have caused him to *think* he saw Molly being murdered? Was the whole thing just a pharmaceutical fever dream? That still doesn't explain why Jack had Molly's picture in his journal, but if she was already on his mind, it seems at least possible that his subconscious incorporated her into his hallucination.

Focused on the article on my phone, I don't even notice that the lanky redhead has approached me until he taps me on the shoulder. Involuntarily, I flinch.

The young man drops his hand to his sides, blushing. "Sorry, Miss. I didn't mean to startle you. I just wanted to let you know your table is ready."

I will my heartbeat to slow down as I give him a shaky smile. "Thanks. Lead the way."

He walks me past the bar—where I see Cian holding court to a group of out-of-towners—and across the restaurant to a table next to the fireplace. The young man pulls out a chair for me, but I get the impression that it's less for my benefit than to impress the pretty hostess. He hasn't taken his eyes off her.

"My name's Noah," he introduces himself after I'm seated. "I'll be taking care of you. Can I get you anything to drink?"

"I'd love a Diet Coke. And a glass of water," I tell him.

"No bother." He doesn't write it down. "Do you know what you'd like to eat?"

I glance at the table, then back up at Noah. "Um, would it be possible to see a menu?"

His cheeks redden with embarrassment, nearly camouflaging his freckles. "Did I not give you one? Lord, where's my head at?"

I smile. I have a pretty good idea where his head is. "You know what? I'll just take a steak and ale pie. I had one the other day, and it was real good."

Relief floods his face. "Sure, you won't regret it. That's Caroline's specialty. I'll get your order in right away."

He strides off and, with his head turned to look at the hostess, nearly trips over an empty chair. I chuckle at the power of puppy love and teenage hormones.

Settling into my seat, I take out my phone and open the notes app to write down some questions for my upcoming interview with Maeve. I plan to go easy at first, asking a few quick softball questions to put her at ease. But with the aborted interview with Eoman Scully still fresh in my mind, I'll need to proceed to the harder questions—things like Jack's unwelcome background checks business and his subsequent murder—pretty quickly. After all, Evelyn didn't specify how long Maeve would be willing to chat.

I'm tapping on the phone's touchscreen when Noah returns to the table, carrying a pint glass of soda.

"Here you are," he says, setting down the glass. His eyes

follow the hostess as she escorts two women to a table nearby. "Caroline's just heating a pie for you, so it should be out shortly."

"Thank you kindly. I'll take a water, too, when you have a minute."

He smacks his forehead with the butt of his palm. "Shoot. I knew I was forgetting something. I'll be right back with it. Two seconds."

Noah hurries away from the table, but between me and the bar, he crosses paths with the hostess. They stop to chat, and his face practically glows with a combination of nerves and excitement.

I make a silent bet with myself that he will forget all about my water. Again.

Taking a sip of soda, I return to my interview prep. If Jack had been doing background checks on attendees, it could be worth asking Maeve whether she's had any complaints about the matches she's made. I doubt she'll like the question, but that doesn't mean it's not a fair one to ask.

It could be five or fifteen minutes later when Noah returns carrying a plate loaded with fried fish and French fries. He sets it down in front of me.

I look at the plate, then up at him, then back at the plate. "I don't mean to complain, but this isn't what I ordered. I asked for the pie."

He closes his eyes, taking a deep breath. "So you did. Sorry, this is meant for table twelve. You're table twenty-one. I got the numbers confused. I'll be right back with your pie."

"Thanks," I say, calling out to his retreating back, "And that glass of water."

Another couple of minutes pass before Noah returns carrying my pie. But when I look around, I notice there's no cutlery.

I mention their absence to Noah as he sets down the

plate. "And while you're gettin' utensils, can you also grab me a glass of water?"

His green eyes widen. "Did I not bring you that?"

I smile, trying to lessen his discomfort. "Not yet."

"I am so sorry. I'll be right back." Noah scurries off again toward the bar.

Lucky for me, the hostess is on the other side of the room, seating a male customer. Without her presence to distract Noah, he promptly returns to the table, carrying a glass and a large bottle of water.

"Sorry again for the delay," he tells me, putting the glass on the table.

As he unscrews the top of the bottle, I am drawn to the sound of a woman's laughter off to my left. Glancing over, I see the hostess smiling at her attractive male customer.

I look up at Noah and see that he's also noticed the pair. What I don't see is that he's already started pouring water into my glass. I only realize when some of it, having overflowed from the glass, spills off the table into my lap.

I shove the chair back to avoid further dousing.

"Oh, my gosh. I am so sorry," Noah cries out. "Let me get you a serviette."

"You're fine," I try to reassure him. "A little water never hurt anyone. Where's your washroom?"

He points to the back of the bar. Without another word, I stand and make my way to the women's restroom. I have dark jeans on, so at least it doesn't look like I had an accident on myself.

I grab a paper towel from a dispenser on the wall and begin drying my leg. Only when I reach for a second towel do I see the words written in marker on the tiled wall:

Senan O'Malley is a stalker pig.

CHAPTER TWENTY-ONE

The paved driveway leading to Maeve's house seems never ending. I must have turned off the main road and gone through the filigreed gates a good ten minutes ago, but I'm still walking.

Shade from the large oak trees lining the private road blocks out the warmth of the late afternoon sun, making me shiver. Even in Spring, it's always best to dress in layers. You never know when the weather might turn. Rummaging in my cross-body bag, I find the light sweater I wore this morning.

I set my bag on the ground and pull the sweater over my head. Through a gap in the branches, I can see another house off in the distance. Slightly behind it sits a small wooden building with green trim. Even from about a mile away, I recognize it as the coach house where Jack O'Hara was staying.

It occurs to me that, as I was looking through the binoculars from his living room, I was staring at Maeve McKewon's house and didn't even know it. Had he been spying on the matchmaker? And, if so, why?

As I continue along the driveway, Maeve's house slowly comes into view. Correction: Maeve's mansion. The honey-colored stone building is not only ornate—with balconies, detailed window frames, and roses climbing up the walls—it's also enormous. There have to be at least six bedrooms upstairs, if not more.

The matchmaking business has been good for Maeve. It makes me wonder how far she'd go to stop someone threatening to take it all away.

Finally, I reach the house's imposing front door. There's a large brass knocker in the shape of a Claddagh, but before I can lift my hand to use it, the door swings open, revealing a petite maid in a crisp black uniform.

"Miss Jeffers?" she asks, her eyes smiling but her face stoic.

"That'd be me," I confirm.

She nods. "Right this way, please."

Walking through the foyer, my jaw nearly hits the polished marble floor. Crystal chandeliers drip from coffered ceilings, and priceless artworks adorn walls covered in pastel silk damask. The maid guides me to a sitting room with plush velvet sofas, a fireplace big enough to roast an entire pig, and floor-to-ceiling windows offering a panoramic view of the lush gardens at the side of the house.

Busy admiring the space, it takes me a minute to realize I'm not alone. Maeve McKewon sits perched on the sofa, an emerald shawl draped over her shoulders like a cloak. Beside her, Niall lounges against the sofa arm, his sturdy, athletic frame at odds with the delicate teacup balanced on his knee. They are a study in contrasts—Maeve's welcoming smile and Niall's guarded gaze.

Before I can even say hello, Niall barks, "You've got ten minutes. My grandmother is a busy woman."

Maeve frowns and swats her handsome grandson on the

knee. "Go away with you. Where are your manners, Niall? I know I raised you better than that."

Niall doesn't look the least bit put out by his grandmother's reprimand. "I'm not trying to be rude. But you have a meeting with—"

Maeve holds up a wrinkled hand. "Sure, I know my own schedule. You don't need to be reminding me all the time." Maeve turns back to me with a conciliatory smile. "Don't pay my grandson any mind. You're very welcome here."

"Thank you kindly. I won't take up too much of your time." Trying not to appear rattled, I pull my phone out of my bag, activate the recording app, and set the device on a large mahogany coffee table. "Why don't we start with somethin' simple? How's the festival goin' so far?"

Maeve leans back, the light catching her silver hair. "It's shaping up to be quite an interesting year, as it happens. We've already had our fair share of excitement."

I raise an eyebrow, wondering if she's referring to Jack O'Hara's murder. I'd be surprised if she wants to steer the conversation in that direction right away. "Excitement?"

"Well, for starters, someone made off with a stack of questionnaires. I ask everyone to fill them out, you see, to assist with the matchmaking process," Maeve explains. "I have my notes, of course, but the originals that attendees mailed in have just disappeared."

I'm surprised by her candor. I imagine there's a lot of sensitive and personal information on those forms. "Do you have any idea who woulda taken 'em?"

"None at all," she admits. "The guards are looking into it. And we'll have to let our festival guests know, of course, once we've figured out whose paperwork went missing. But we get thousands of application forms every year, it could be weeks before we know which ones were taken."

Niall scoffs, absently putting a toothpick in his mouth.

"I'll bet you a pretty penny they slap us with fines. All those new data protection regulations coming from Dublin are a bloody nuisance."

Maeve glares at her grandson. "Would you ever stop? People have a right to their privacy. It only seems fair we should compensate people for our mistake."

Out of the corner of my eye, I see Niall weighing me up.

I suddenly get the distinct impression the two of them are putting on an act for my benefit. If they plan to notify festival attendees about the data breach, they know I'll find out eventually. By addressing it upfront, they get to put their own spin on the story.

But since Maeve opened the door, I decide to press and see what else she might be willing to admit. "Has anythin' else out of the ordinary happened at this year's festival?"

I sense Niall tensing, but Maeve doesn't even bat an eyelid. "As a matter of fact, yes. One of my appointments, a lovely woman called Máirín, was a no-show. That's fierce irregular, I'll have you know. People don't generally pay for a service and then not turn up to collect it."

Niall glowers, but I notice the tension has gone out of his shoulders. "She better not come around looking for her money back. We have a strict no refunds policy."

As he speaks, my gaze snags on the toothpick in his mouth, a jolt of recognition coursing through me. I'd found a chewed-up toothpick next to Jack O'Hara's body. Could Niall be Jack's killer?

It's probably not the best course of action to taunt a potential murderer, but he wouldn't do anything with his grandmother in the room. At least, that's what I tell myself when I dive right in.

"Speakin' of bad things happenin', I'm sure you're aware that a man's been murdered in the village..." I let the sentence trail off.

Maeve doesn't shy away from picking up the thread. "I am, of course. Poor Jack. It's a horrible business, so it is. But Jack was the sort of man who went looking for trouble. Always sticking his nose where it didn't belong."

Niall's jaw clenches so hard I'm surprised he doesn't snap the toothpick in half. "Had a knack for ruffling feathers, that one."

"To be clear, I'm not saying Jack deserved what he got. God rest him. No one deserves that," Maeve makes a point of clarifying. "But I can see how Jack might have gotten under people's skin with all his meddling."

Going off a hunch that Jack had a photo of Senan because he was looking into him for some reason, I ask, "People like Senan O'Malley?"

For the first time, Maeve seems at a loss for words. Something burns behind her clever eyes. It looks like anger.

"Senan O'Malley," she finally says, "is no longer welcome at our festival. Sadly, even the most carefully vetted events can sometimes attract...unsavory characters."

So, there is something there after all. "Oh, my! If you don't mind my askin', what did he do?"

Maeve's lips purse. "I'd rather not say. But I will tell you this: at any large gathering, there are bound to be a few bad apples. But they are rare, Miss Jeffers. Very rare, indeed. And when we find them, we toss them right out."

It's on the tip of my tongue to mention that I've seen Senan at this year's festival, but then I see a red-faced Niall setting his teacup on the coffee table. He clearly doesn't like the direction this interview is taking and plans to put a stop to it.

Maeve stills him with a glance, but when she speaks, her words are directed at me. "I'm worried all of our talk here might give you the wrong impression about Carrigaveen and the festival. And it'd be a right shame if you left here without a better sense of the good that comes out of what we do. You've seen the wall of medallions at the Abbey Wood Manor, have you?"

An image of the hotel's foyer flashes in my mind. I nod. "I have. I don't know what it's all about, though."

Maeve smiles, her eyes shining brightly. "Let me be the one to tell you, so. All those medallions represent matches we've made at the festival over these past decades. Thousands of couples from all around the world have come here to find love, and we have given them that gift. That's what's important. And I hope *that's* what you'll be focusing on with your magazine article."

I nod, moved more than I expected to be by her passionate words. I watch as she twists her two-carat wedding ring on her finger. Her husband, I had read, died more than twenty years ago. Before I can stop myself, I ask, "Have you ever thought of doin' any matchmakin' for yourself?"

Maeve blinks, surprised, and then throws her head back with a laugh. It's a rich, throaty sound filled with genuine amusement.

"Oh, good Lord, no!" she says, wiping at the corner of her eye. "I've no need for another man around the house, tracking mud on my carpets and leaving whiskey tumblers on my antique end tables!"

Then, as if catching herself, Maeve's expression sobers. "But I suppose I shouldn't poke fun. My Thomas was a good man. God rest him. And when you've been married to your soulmate, you just aren't willing to settle for anything less. It'd be like trying to light a candle next to the sun."

"On that note," Niall says, standing, "that's all the time we have for you. Collect your things, and I'll be happy to show you out."

Annoyed by Niall's curt behavior, I ignore him

completely as I stop the recording and slip my phone back into my purse. "It was real nice meetin' you, Miss McKewon. Thank you so much for your time."

"Not a bother, dear," she replies, rising slowly from the sofa. She takes my hand in hers and gives it a gentle squeeze. "Do enjoy the festival, dear. And you never know; you just might find someone who catches your eye."

An image of Detective Mulhaney, once again, pops into my head. I shove it roughly away. "I don't think so. But thanks, all the same."

As Niall ushers me toward the door, something in my peripheral vision catches my attention—a room filled with boxes stacked to the brim. Everything from whiskey to scented candles to lotions and even Irish crystal, all bearing labels with the McKewon name.

I can't help but marvel at the business savvy behind it all. Maeve may speak of love and magic, but it's clear that the festival is also a well-oiled machine, a commercial enterprise as much as a romantic one.

And as I step out into the sunshine, I know one thing for sure: the McKewons are a force to be reckoned with, in matters of both the heart and the pocketbook.

CHAPTER TWENTY-TWO

The sun sits low on the horizon as I make my way back from Maeve's house, my thoughts darker than the sky at dusk. There are things about my meeting with the legendary matchmaker and her grandson that aren't sitting well with me.

To all outward appearances, Maeve appears to be a warm, caring grandmother who believes in love above all else. Yet, I can't get past the feeling that part of her demeanor, at least, is a carefully crafted façade that hides less noble entrepreneurial ambitions.

And then there's the toothpick Niall had in his mouth. Just like the one I found by the river. It wouldn't be a stretch to imagine him killing Jack to protect the family business. It might have been possible to either prove or disprove my suspicion if only Sergeant Sweeney hadn't made such a mess of collecting evidence at the crime scene. Without the toothpick I saw, there's nothing tying him to Jack's murder.

I'm fuming in frustration. Each breath I take thunders in my ears, the only sound breaking the silence of the winding country road. Even the village feels eerily subdued as I pass through the unnaturally quiet center of Carrigaveen. But just as I near Abbey Wood Manor, the evening's peace shatters—a discordant sound slicing through the calm.

"Check, one, two. Check, check."

The voice, amplified through speakers, echoes across the sprawling field next to the monastery-turned-hotel. At the far end of the grassy plot, butting up against the forest beyond, I see metal scaffolding forming a stage with crowds of people gathered around it. Food trucks line the perimeter, the savory scent of grilled meats and fried foods wafting on the evening breeze.

Then, it hits me—the concert! In the whirlwind of my day, traipsing all over the village, I'd completely forgotten about the musical event scheduled for tonight.

When I'd been looking over the festival itinerary from the comfort of my cottage in Ballygoseir, I thought the concert would make a great opening paragraph for my article. It was always my intention to cover it. But now, with my feet aching and my head spinning, the prospect of diving into a noisy crowd feels downright daunting. All I want is to retreat to my cozy hotel room, kick off my shoes, and climb into bed.

With a sigh that reaches all the way down to my toes, I tell myself I only have to stay for an hour. Just long enough to get a few interviews and some photographs. Squaring my shoulders, I cross the field and plunge into the crowd. I'm instantly caught up in a sea of people, all laughing and sloshing beer out of plastic cups.

As the opening act takes the stage, I try to chat with a few festivalgoers—all of us shouting to be heard above the music. My throat raw from the effort, I finally give up and retreat to the edge of the crowd, away from the blaring speakers.

It looks like someone else has the same idea. Leaning against a pole at the back of the tent, I see a broad-shouldered and ruggedly handsome man. There's an air of defeat about him as he scuffs the grass with the toe of his boot. He doesn't look up as I approach.

"Mind if I join you?" I ask.

He startles at my voice, his head snapping up. He looks at me blankly. "Wouldn't you prefer to be out there dancing?"

I shrug. "Wouldn't you?"

"I'm not really in the mood," he replies. Even his charming Irish brogue sounds deflated.

"I know what you mean. I've had a long day, too," I tell him, turning my body toward the crowd so that the man and I face the same direction. "What's got you feelin' lower than a snake's belly?"

"I was supposed to meet someone earlier today," he admits, shoulders sagging. "I paid for your one Maeve to set me up with a nice girl I'd be proud to take home to my mother. But it appears my true love got a case of cold feet."

"You're saying she didn't show up?" I ask, my mind drifting back to Maeve's complaint about the festival attendee who was a no-show.

"From what I was told, she didn't turn up for her meeting with Maeve. Never even checked into her hotel." He sighs deeply. "I feel like a right eejit paying all that money for nothing. The universe is clearly trying to send me a message."

"Come on, now. Don't be so hard on yourself," I encourage him. "I have no idea why she didn't show up. But I'm pretty sure it has nothin' to do with you."

"That's very kind of you to say." He raises his green eyes to my face and really looks at me for the first time. His mood seems to lift. Then, he smiles. "The name's Johnny, by the by. It's hard to believe a girl as pretty as you doesn't have a date. Can I buy you a drink?"

Is he...flirting with me?

The realization sends a strange mix of flattery and panic

fluttering through my stomach. I'm not used to being on the receiving end of casual male attention. I'm more accustomed to being threatened with arrest.

I'm also acutely aware of the power dynamic at play here. This man is vulnerable after a perceived romantic slight. The last thing I want is to give him the wrong idea, to lead him on when my interest is purely professional.

So, I do what any self-respecting woman would do. I lie through my teeth. "I have a boyfriend. But if I didn't, I would definitely take you up on that offer."

Johnny nods as if he'd been expecting to be shot down. "Where is the lucky guy, so?"

I hadn't expected him to ask that. "Oh! He, um, had to answer nature's call. I should probably go and find him."

He frowns. "In the toilet?"

My face grows hot. "I don't mean…I won't go *into* the toilets to look for my boyfriend. But he's been gone awhile. He might be lookin' for me. I don't want him to get worried."

"Sure, look, I'm sure this boyfriend of yours knows you're well able to look after yourself." The achingly familiar voice comes from behind me.

I whirl around to see Detective Mulhaney standing with his hands in his jacket pockets and a mischievous smirk on his lips.

For a moment, I just stare at the detective, my mouth opening and closing like a landed trout. Johnny glances from me to Detective Mulhaney and back again. He quirks an eyebrow.

Knowing I will probably regret this, I slap on a smile and slip my arm through Detective Mulhaney's elbow. "There you are, um, darling. I was just about to come find you."

There's a twinkle in Detective Mulhaney's eyes. "Not a bother, sweetheart. We always seem to bump into each other, sooner or later."

My face feels like it's on fire when I turn back to Johnny. "It was real nice meetin' you. I hope you find what you're lookin' for."

Without waiting for a reply, I practically drag Detective Mulhaney away, deeper into the crowd. He doesn't resist. Once we're out of Johnny's line of sight, I stop and turn to face the detective.

His lips twitch as if they're aching to break into a smile. "Are you sure your boyfriend won't mind you manhandling me like this?"

I immediately release my grip on his chiseled arm. "Oh, don't you start. I was just tryin' to let the poor man down easy. You know how it goes."

He raises one dark eyebrow. "Do I, now?"

My eyes narrow. "What are you doin' here anyway? I thought you were allergic to fun. Don't you have someone to be arrestin' or somethin'?"

Detective Mulhaney grimaces. "Well, that just goes to show how well you *don't* know me. Sure, I love a good craic."

I place my hands on my hips. "So, you're tellin' me you're only here because you wanted to listen to the band?"

"The Fenian Saints are class," he says, feigning a wounded expression. "Who doesn't sing along to 'Raise Hell & Raise a Pint' when it comes on the radio?"

"I've never heard it," I tell him, not buying this off-duty version of Detective Mulhaney in the least.

"Ah, well. You're in for a treat," he says. "It looks like the band is just about to start."

A ripple of anticipation spreads through the audience. Then, the floodlights blast on, bathing the stage in a golden halo, and the first low hum of an electric guitar rolls through the speakers like distant thunder.

A voice booms over the mic. *"Alright, Carrigaveen, let's make some feckin' noise!"*

The frontman, rugged and wild-eyed, throws a fist in the air before launching into the first song. I don't recognize the tune, but everyone around me seems to. They're all smiling and singing along.

I glance around at the crowd and see a familiar blonde head off to the left of the stage. It's Molly Jenkins. But she doesn't appear to be listening to the band. She's deep in conversation with Senan O'Malley!

My first thought is that Maeve would be furious to see him here. That observation is quickly followed by a question: why does Senan seem to be following Molly around? Is he interested in her romantically? Or is there something more to his relentless pursuit?

The sound of Detective Mulhaney's rich baritone draws my attention away from Molly and Senan. The normally uptight detective is singing along to the chorus. I'm a breath away from teasing him when, to my utter surprise, I realize I know this song, too.

My voice rises alongside his, "*You run, but I'm in your veins. Like whiskey, like thunder, like summer rain…*"

Just then, someone bumps into me, and I tumble forward, crashing into Detective Mulhaney's solid chest. Our gazes catch and hold. In that moment, I'm acutely aware of every detail of his handsome face—the crinkles at the corners of his eyes, the cleft in his strong chin, the way his lips part ever so slightly, like an invitation.

My heart does a little flip-flop in my chest, and I silently curse its betrayal. This is Detective Mulhaney, for heaven's sake! The man's been a thorn in my side since I arrived in Ireland. But as I look up into those dark eyes, one slightly more open than the other, I feel a pull I can't quite explain.

He leans in, and I find myself tilting my face towards his. I'm torn between wanting to close the distance and the urge to push him away and make a quip about his arrogance.

But before our lips can meet, a loud boom rips through the night.

We instantly pull apart. Detective Mulhaney's eyes, suddenly focused and alert, scan the crowd.

"Fireworks?" I suggest, though there are no telltale lights in the sky.

Before Detective Mulhaney can reply, a high, piercing noise shatters the sudden, fearful silence—the sound of people screaming.

"There!" I point, spotting a disturbance near the trees. "Looks like folks are runnin' from somethin' over there."

Mulhaney nods grimly. "We need to—"

"Check it out," I finish, already moving in that direction.

He grabs my hand. "Stay close," he orders.

Then we both start running, hand-in-hand, straight toward the danger.

CHAPTER TWENTY-THREE

The scene that greets us as we race across the field is one of pure chaos.

Just moments before, there had been laughter and dancing. Now, there is only blind panic. People are running in every direction, their faces pale and stricken in the harsh glare of the stage lights. Some stumble and fall in their haste, trampled by the relentless tide of fleeing bodies.

I catch snippets of terrified shouts rising above the din like fragments of a nightmare.

But as we draw closer, our progress is halted by a kind of human barricade. Some onlookers have remained behind in the confusion, gathered in a tight half-circle—a dense knot of bodies pressed together, their faces a mix of shock and uncertainty. I can't see past them, but I don't need to. The screams from earlier still echo in my ears.

Whatever happened, it was bad.

Though these people stayed behind, presumably to help, no one seems to know what to do. They murmur in low voices, their eyes darting between one another, waiting for someone—anyone—to take control.

Mulhaney doesn't hesitate. "Garda Síochána! Clear a path, now!"

His tone leaves no room for argument.

The crowd parts to let him through. I move in close behind him, slipping through the narrow space before it closes up again.

The smell hits me first—sharp, acrid, chemical. Smoke hangs in the air, making me cough. And then I see them. Two figures sprawled on the ground hurt and bleeding.

My blood runs cold as I recognize them.

Noah, my waiter from earlier this afternoon, lies motionless, his ginger hair matted with blood. Beside him, Molly Jenkins clutches her left arm as she writhes in pain, her golden locks tangled and streaked with dirt.

"Jeffers, call 112," Detective Mulhaney barks.

"On it," I reply, fumbling for my phone. My fingers tremble as I punch in the numbers. As the line connects, I take a deep breath, willing my heart to slow down.

"Emergency services, how can I help?" The dispatcher's calm tone seems to downplay the urgency of the situation.

"We need ambulances at Abbey Wood Manor in Carrigaveen," I say, surprised by the steadiness in my voice. "There's been some kind of explosion. Multiple injuries."

"Explosion, you say?" the man on the other end of the line asks in surprise. "Alright, I'm sending two ambulances to you now from Bantry. But it will take them some time to reach you. Is there a doctor about?"

I put my hand over the microphone before calling out to the crowd, "Is anyone here a doctor?"

Blank faces stare back at me. A few of them shake their heads. Then, a tall, slender woman pushes to the front of the crowd.

"I trained as a nurse," she says with a Scottish accent. "It's been a while, but I might be able to help until the ambulance arrives."

Detective Mulhaney points her toward Molly, but the woman goes to Noah instead. "She's screaming, which means she's getting air into her lungs. I'm more worried about him," the woman explains as she kneels beside Noah.

"Is he breathing?" Detective Mulhaney asks.

The nurse, her fingers resting on Noah's neck, nods. "He's unconscious, but his pulse is steady."

I quickly fill the dispatcher in on the situation. He tells me that paramedics and the local guards are on the way but that I should call back if I need anything else before they arrive. I hang up the phone, wishing there was more I could do.

Adrenaline courses through my veins as I take in the scene around me. My eyes land on something glinting in the grass near Noah's outstretched hand. A twisted metal tube, charred and smoking, lies ominously close to the injured pair.

Catching Mulhaney's eye, I point to the tube. "You see that?"

He nods, his jaw clenched. "It looks like a dodgy firework."

I can't help thinking that if Maeve is the one who arranged the pyrotechnics, she's going to have more problems on her hands than a few missing questionnaires.

As if reading my mind, Maeve's grandson, Niall, shoulders his way to the front of the crowd.

"What in the name of all things holy is going on here?" he demands, his voice sharp as thunder.

"It's too soon to tell, but it looks like one of your fireworks malfunctioned," Detective Mulhaney icily replies.

"*My* fireworks? Absolutely not! We didn't authorize anything of the sort," Niall rages. Then he spots the band's lead singer hanging back at the fringes of the crowd. Niall takes a step toward him. "Did you do this?"

The singer holds his hands up and takes a step backward. "It wasn't us. Sure, you know yourself, fireworks are too much of a hassle with health and safety."

The answer seems to satisfy Niall, but his anger isn't appeased. He spots the smoking metal tube in the grass and steps toward it.

Detective Mulhaney stops Niall with a hand on his shoulder. "I'm afraid I'm going to have to ask you to stand back. This could be a crime scene, and I can't have you interfering with potential evidence."

A crime scene? Does the detective suspect this was intentional and not just a freak accident? I suppose it makes sense that he would think that, especially with everyone denying bringing controlled explosives to the concert.

But who would do something like this? And why would they want to hurt Noah or Molly? Then, it hits me. Molly was talking to Senan right before the firework exploded. But as I scan the crowd, I realize he's nowhere in sight. Did he leave before the blast? Or right after it?

Molly moans, and I drop to my knees beside her. Her left arm is badly burned. Blisters are already forming on the reddened skin. I take her uninjured hand in mine.

"Molly?" I ask. Her eyes are open, but there is no recognition in them. "Molly? Can you hear me?"

"Molly…" she mutters.

"Try not to talk," I tell her. "You've been hurt pretty bad. But the ambulance should be here real soon."

As if on cue, the wail of sirens cuts through the night air, growing louder by the second. I look up in surprise. It's too soon for the ambulance to be here. Then, I remember the dispatcher telling me the local guards had also been contacted. That must be them arriving.

Detective Mulhaney seems to have the same thought because he walks over to me and pulls me to my feet.

"Go back to your hotel, Jeffers," he instructs me. I open my mouth to argue, but he abruptly cuts me off. "The guards have already found you at two crime scenes. I'd rather they didn't find you at another."

The obvious concern in his eyes silences the protest forming on my lips. He does have a point. Not to mention, I was supposed to go to the station for fingerprinting today and never made it. I'd rather not spend the night handcuffed to the cot in the Garda station, or wherever else they lock up the people they've arrested.

I nod. "I'm not gonna fight you on this one. But, if I were you, I'd keep my eyes peeled for Senan O'Malley." Realizing the detective might not know who that is, I explain, "He's the guy that was in the photos we found in Jack O'Hara's diary. I noticed him talkin' to Molly right before the blast."

Detective Mulhaney fixes his eyes on the crowd and asks, "Have you seen him since?"

"Nope. He just up and disappeared in all the commotion."

Detective Mulhaney nods in understanding, his head swiveling to watch the Garda vehicle approach. "Leave it with me. Now, go away with you."

With a final glance at Molly and Noah, I cut across the field in the direction of Abbey Wood Manor.

Stepping into the lobby a few minutes later, the warmth from the fire blankets my chilled skin. But it doesn't bring me the relief I crave.

Before the concert, all I wanted was to crawl into bed and forget the day. Now, I don't think I'll be closing my eyes anytime soon.

CHAPTER TWENTY-FOUR

I jolt awake, my heart racing. The clock on my bedside table screams 5:47 in angry red digits. Groaning, I flop onto my back, staring at the ceiling of my room at Abbey Wood Manor. Yesterday's events replay in my mind like a bad country song stuck on an endless loop.

The explosion. The screams. The sheer madness of it all.

I shove the covers off and sit up, scrubbing a hand down my face. A hint of dawn creeps through the window, painting the walls in soft gold, but it does nothing to settle the uneasy knot twisting in my stomach. The rug feels frigid under my bare feet as I stand, the chill snapping me instantly awake. Maybe it's a sign—a not-so-subtle push to get up, get moving, do something.

Molly must be waking up in the hospital in Bantry. Having seen the burns on her arms, I can't imagine they would have released her already. The image of her last night—dazed and in pain—lingers in the back of my mind. It doesn't sit right, knowing she's all alone and hurt in a foreign country. There's nothing I can do for her, not really, but staying still doesn't feel like an option either.

I don't waste time second-guessing. If I'm going, I need to get moving.

I swap my pajamas for jeans and a sweater, tie my hair back in a quick ponytail, and grab my bag and keys. The morning air is crisp as I step outside, carrying the scent of wet earth, still damp from the overnight mist. My car's engine rumbles to life, and soon I'm pulling out onto the narrow country road.

The drive to Bantry is quiet, the roads empty aside from a few tractors. Fields stretch out on either side, dotted with grazing sheep and the occasional farmhouse. I pass through a few small villages, their shopfronts still shuttered.

As I reach Bantry, the streets are busier, the town already bustling with morning traffic. I follow the signs to the hospital, find a parking spot, and head inside, the automatic doors sliding open with a gentle whoosh. A receptionist points me toward Molly's room on the second floor, and I make my way up the stairs and down the stark white corridor, my sneakers squeaking against the linoleum floor.

I push open the door, and the sharp scent of antiseptic hits me immediately. Tucked under starched white sheets, Molly looks impossibly small and fragile, tethered to beeping machines by a tangle of wires. Her wide blue eyes land on me, flickering with confusion at first. Then, recognition dawns, and she sits up in the bed, wincing as she moves her bandaged arm.

"You're Savannah, right?" Molly asks, her voice hoarse. "We met at the museum."

"That's me. I hope you don't mind me poppin' by to check in on you."

"Not at all. But why are you here? At the hospital?" Her confused look morphs into one of sympathy. "Were you injured in the explosion, too?"

"Oh, no. Nothin' like that." I quickly reassure her. "But I

know what it's like being the new person in town. Just wanted to make sure you didn't feel alone."

Her expression softens. "That's...really nice of you." She exhales, sinking back into the pillows. "Honestly, it's nice to see a friendly face after being grilled by a detective for what felt like hours."

I arch a brow. "Let me guess—Detective Mulhaney?"

Molly groans. "That's the one. I didn't mind at first—he's easy on the eyes—but my gosh, he's relentless. And bossy."

I let out a knowing laugh. "Yeah, he can come on a bit strong when you first meet him. But once you get to know him, he's not so bad."

She gives me a skeptical look but doesn't argue. "If you say so."

Pointing to the cracked faux leather chair next to her hospital bed, I ask, "Do you mind?"

"No, please sit," she says with a shaky smile.

I take my time moving to the seat, trying to buy time. I have a million questions I want to ask Molly, but I doubt she'll be receptive to another grilling. Especially since she has just complained about Detective Mulhaney's interrogation. I have to take this slow if I want to find out what she knows.

The old, stained chair cushion exhales dust as I sit down. "How are you feelin'?"

Molly shifts slightly in the hospital bed, her good hand absently smoothing the blanket over her lap. "I've been better. But the drugs help. So, I guess that's a positive."

I nod. "Small blessin's. I'm just glad you're alright. I was there last night. I'm still havin' trouble believin' what happened."

"You and me both," she agrees. "One second, I was leaving the concert, heading back to my hotel. Then—boom. The next thing I remember, I was on the ground in awful pain."

I frown. "You were leavin' the concert?"

Molly tilts her head. "Yeah. Why?"

"Oh, it's nothin'. It's just, well, before the explosion, I thought I saw you talkin' to that guy from the potato peelin' contest."

"George?" she says, then shakes her head. "No, you said that wasn't his name, didn't you? I can't remember—"

"Senan. Senan O'Malley," I remind her.

"That's right. And yeah, he did come over and ask me if I wanted a drink. To be honest, he creeps me out a little. He's a bit too...intense. Anyway, I told him I was calling it a night. He left, as far as I know. I decided to stay until the end of the song, but—you know," she points at her bad arm.

I lean forward in the chair. "How long was it between him leavin' and the blast?"

"A couple of minutes. Why do you ask? You don't think he had anything to do with it, do you?"

"Oh, I have no idea," I settle back into the seat. "I just can't help thinkin' he's been followin' you around. If he's the type of guy who doesn't take rejection well..."

Molly lifts a perfectly manicured eyebrow. "You think he tried to blow me up because I wouldn't let him buy me a drink?"

"Yeah, I guess that does sound kinda silly." I give her a self-deprecating smile, not wanting to freak her out. "I'm just tryin' to find out if there's anyone in the village who might want to hurt you."

"Hurt me?" Her sapphire eyes open wide. "Why would anyone want to do that? I've barely been in Ireland for five minutes. I don't think I've been here long enough to make any enemies. No. I'm sure it must have been an accident. Right?"

She seems so desperate to believe that she's not being targeted. I don't have the heart to tell her I think there may be more to it than that.

"I'm sure you're right," I attempt to reassure her before changing the subject. "You were tellin' me at the museum that you're from Boston. How did you end up at a matchmakin' festival in rural Ireland?"

The worry lines on Molly's face melt away. "I actually found out about it while researching where I come from."

I tilt my head. "You're from Ireland?"

"Technically," she says, her fingers tracing the edge of the blanket. "I was born here. My mom died in childbirth, and I was adopted by my family in the States when I was just a baby. I never knew anything about my birth mother. Not even her name." Her voice softens. "I don't know if I have family here or if she was alone when she had me. But I thought coming here might make me feel closer to where I came from."

Images of Ian, the father I only recently found, and my aunt, Audrey, tug at my chest. "I understand. I came here to find my family, too."

Molly lets out a breathy laugh, but there's no humor in it. "I hope it's turning out better for you. This hasn't exactly been the kind of homecoming I'd imagined. First, someone falsely claims I've been murdered. Then I nearly get taken out by a firework." She shakes her head. "I'm starting to think Ireland and I weren't meant to be."

"You're not thinkin' of heading back early, are you?"

She hesitates, staring at the IV taped to her arm. "I don't know," she admits. "I came here looking for something. A connection. A sense of belonging. But maybe I was wrong to think I'd feel any more at home here than I do in America."

I grin. The way she said America sounds more like the way an Irish person would say it. *Amurrica.* "You might feel more at home in the States, but you're startin' to sound like a local. That accent's already creeping in."

She laughs, shaking her head. "It's infectious. You spend

enough time here, and suddenly you're saying things like 'grand' and 'sure look' without even realizing."

"I know the feelin'." I lean forward conspiratorially. "You don't even realize it's happenin'. But then I call my friends back home, and they tease me about how I'm startin' to go full Irish."

Molly chuckles, but before she can reply, the door swings open, and a nurse steps inside, her expression kind but firm. "I'm afraid visiting hours are up, " she says. "Sure, Miss Jenkins needs her rest."

Molly and I share an amused look over the nurse's use of the word "sure." Then I nod, standing. "Okay. I'll be on my way." Turning back to Molly, I flash her a reassuring smile. "Get some rest. I'll try to stop by again tomorrow to see how you're doin'. If that's alright?"

Molly nods, smiling. "Thanks, Savannah. I'd like that."

I step out of Molly's room, the door clicking shut behind me, and make my way down the quiet hallway to the elevator. When the doors slide open, I step inside, leaning against the cool metal wall as the numbers tick down.

The lobby is busier than when I arrived, with visitors reading in the waiting room and doctors in scrubs passing through with weary expressions. I'm nearly to the exit when a familiar figure catches my eye.

Senan O'Malley.

He strolls up to the information desk, a bouquet of flowers tucked under his arm, his free hand applying a swipe of ChapStick like he's getting ready for a date. The receptionist barely looks up as he leans against the counter.

"I'm here to see Molly Jenkins," he says, all casual charm. "Can you tell me which room she's in?"

My stomach tightens.

Then I remember. Visiting hours are over. Thank goodness.

I don't trust Senan, and until I know more about him, I don't think he should come within fifty feet of Molly.

CHAPTER TWENTY-FIVE

When I reach the automatic glass doors to exit the hospital, I stop, wondering what I should do.

Should I warn someone that Molly might be in danger?

Would they even listen to me?

My indecision vanishes the moment I spot Detective Mulhaney standing on the curb outside, looking like he hasn't slept in days. He's talking to a uniformed female guard I don't recognize. She must be from Bantry.

I hesitate, waiting for them to finish their conversion. Finally, the guard nods at her superior officer, turns, and strides past me into the hospital. Detective Mulhaney walks in the opposite direction toward his car.

I race to catch up to him.

"Mulhaney," I call out.

He turns, frustration adding to the fatigue already etched on his handsome face. "Jeffers? What the devil are you doing here?"

"I just wanted to check on Molly. Make sure she's okay," I tell him, not allowing myself to be cowed by his disapproval.

"And to be honest, I'm a little bit worried about her. Remember last night, I told you I saw Molly talkin' to Senan O'Malley right before all hell broke loose?"

"The guy from Jack O'Hara's photos," he nods. "Yeah, I remember."

"Well, I just saw him inside the hospital. He was carryin' flowers and askin' for Molly's room number."

Detective Mulhaney waves off my concern as if he's swatting away an irritating fly. "Would you ever stop worrying?"

From the look on the detective's face, I know I should probably let it go, but I can't. Not when Molly's safety could be at risk. If something happens to her, I won't be able to forgive myself. "Now, you look here, I know you think I'm just always gettin' in the way and 'interferin' in your investigation,' but I really think—"

"Please. Just. Stop." Each word is punctuated with exhaustion. He rubs a hand over his face, the shadow of stubble making him look even more tired. "Your stubbornness may very well be the end of me. I said not to worry because I already told the hospital staff—no visitors except the guards. And you."

I blink, convinced I've misheard him. "Me?"

His lips twitch into something almost resembling a smile. "Figured I wouldn't be able to keep you away, so why bother trying?"

"Oh," I say, at a momentary loss for complete sentences.

"And that guard I was just chatting to? She's been assigned to sit outside Molly's door to make sure no one slips in while the staff aren't looking."

I can feel my cheeks growing warm. I'd underestimated Detective Mulhaney. A twinge of guilt stirs in my belly. I know how much I hate it when he underestimates me. "I'm sorry I doubted you. You're good at what you do. I shouldn't have implied otherwise."

A look of genuine surprise washes over Detective Mulhaney's face, but he has the decency not to push the issue by teasing me.

I clear my throat. "So, you're thinkin' the explosion last night wasn't an accident?"

He shakes his head. "No. I went through every record the council had on last night's event. Nowhere were fireworks mentioned. Someone brought them in. Deliberately."

A chill runs through me. "You think they were meant to hurt someone?"

"I'm not sure. But I can't rule out the possibility." He exhales, rubbing his jaw. "Based on what we know, there is a chance Molly was targeted for some reason. Noah just happened to be in the wrong place at the wrong time."

Shame smacks me in the face. I'd forgotten all about the young, lovesick waiter. "How's he doing?"

Detective Mulhaney's mouth flattens into a grim line. "Still unconscious. They might have to transfer him to Cork University Hospital."

For Noah's sake, I hope the pretty blonde hostess goes to visit him. "I just can't believe no one saw anythin'."

"Everyone was either watching the stage or too busy snogging their partners to notice a thing." He raises one eyebrow suggestively.

Heat creeps up my neck as an image from last night flashes in my mind. We were seconds away from kissing when the fireworks exploded. I look away quickly, pretending to be very interested in a pebble on the ground near my feet.

Detective Mulhaney must catch the flush creeping up my neck because he mercifully lets me off the hook. With a sigh, he folds his arms. "This whole thing has to be connected to Jack O'Hara's notes and the festival somehow."

That snaps me back to reality. "You think so?"

"Everything seems to be pointing in that direction," he says. "I probably shouldn't be telling you this, but since you're the one who found Jack O'Hara's notebook, it seems only fair. I've had someone translating the shorthand."

My pulse quickens. "Have you found anythin' interestin'?"

"Now, don't go getting too excited. I don't know what any of it means yet," he cautions me. "But there's a lot in there about Senan. And quite a bit about Maeve and her grandson, Niall, too."

"What kind of things?"

He doesn't look entirely convinced that he should be telling me, and for a second, I think he won't. Then, he sighs and levels me with a look. "Don't go repeating any of this, like, but it seems that both Senan and the McKewons had filed lawsuits against Jack. Senan accused him of ruining his marriage, and the McKewons claimed he was damaging their business. Both had plenty of reasons to want him dead."

I chew on that for a moment, thinking back to the other things I'd found in Jack's journal. "What about the balance sheet? Or Magdalene? Have you figured out who she is?"

Mulhaney shakes his head. "Not a who. A what."

A groan escapes my lips, and my eyes roll skyward. "Oh, Good Lord. Is this another one of those fetch-type things?"

He lets out a low chuckle. "No, not like that. I wish the Magdalene Laundries were a myth. Sadly, they were all too real."

"Magdalene Laundries? Were they places to take your washin'?" I frown, not understanding the connection.

"After a fashion, I suppose. But that's not all. They were asylums for girls run by the Catholic church. Horrible places. You can't imagine," Detective Mulhaney explains, his jaw tightening. "Thankfully, they don't exist anymore. Shut down in the '90s. You should read up on them yourself. If you have the stomach for it."

I get the sense there's more he could say, but he doesn't.

Before I can think of a way to push him for more detail, the detective's phone buzzes in his hand. He glances at the screen, his expression darkening. "I should probably take this," he says, already stepping away.

I nod. "Yeah, of course. I'll see you later."

Detective Mulhaney lifts the phone to his ear as I turn and head for my car. Slipping into the driver's seat, I start the engine, but as I shift into reverse, my gaze catches on movement near the hospital entrance.

Senan O'Malley.

He strides out onto the sidewalk, still clutching the bouquet meant for Molly. His shoulders are tense, his jaw set. I can't hear his grumbling from here, but I don't need to. I know the look of a man who's just been turned away.

A feeling of satisfaction settles in my chest. Whatever his reasons for wanting to see Molly, he's not getting near her. Not today, anyway.

I ease out of the parking lot and onto the road back to Carrigaveen. The drive is smooth, the coastal scenery unfolding around me, but my mind is stuck on what Detective Mulhaney said.

The Magdalene Laundries. Asylums for girls. Places that haven't existed in decades.

What in the heck do they have to do with a modern-day matchmaking festival?

CHAPTER TWENTY-SIX

When I'm finally back in Carrigaveen, easing my car down the busy main street, I realize I've forgotten to eat. Again.

My mama's voice echoes in my head. *No one ever does their best thinking on an empty stomach.*

Making a quick decision, I pull into a parking spot outside the Whistling Kettle, drawn by the promise of caffeine, pastries, and a place to think.

It's midday, and the café is packed with festival-goers, their chatter filling the air. I squeeze past a group debating whether scones should be eaten with jam or butter or both. At the counter, I place my order and wait to be served before scanning the room for an open seat.

Most of the tables are full, but a plush armchair near the unlit fireplace sits empty. I settle in, placing my coffee and scone on the small side table, and pull out my phone. It's time to figure out what these Magdalene Laundries were all about.

I take a fortifying sip of coffee, wincing at the heat, and type "Magdalene Laundries" into the search bar. As the results load, I can't help but feel a mix of curiosity and dread.

From what Detective Mulhaney said, I know this isn't going to be pleasant.

A few taps bring up article after article, each one worse than the last.

My eyes flit across the screen, absorbing snippets of information. Words like "abuse," "unmarried mothers," and "forced labor" jump out at me, each one landing like a punch to the gut. I take another sip of coffee, barely tasting it this time.

As Detective Mulhaney said, the laundries were institutions scattered around the country, run primarily by Catholic nuns, where so-called "fallen women" were hidden away from the rest of the world. From what I'm reading, "fallen" covered a wide range of "sins"—everything from being an unwed mother to simply being too rebellious for her family's liking.

Girls as young as twelve had been locked away, forced into grueling labor, washing laundry for no pay under brutal conditions. The places were secretive, severe, and centered around penance, though the real punishment seemed to be existing in the first place. One article has a photo of women hunched over washboards, their eyes hollow as empty confessionals.

I swallow hard, suddenly having no appetite for the scone on my plate.

The last of these laundries finally closed in 1996. Survivors have been coming forward in recent years, sparking public apologies and reparations. As if any amount of money could buy back the women's stolen childhoods.

I exhale slowly, setting my phone down.

Jack had been looking into this. But why? And what did it have to do with everything happening now?

Lost in thought, I nearly spill coffee all over myself when

my phone rings. I know who it will be without even looking at the caller ID.

"Hello, Miss Audrey," I say after answering the call.

"Well, if it isn't my favorite little troublemaker," Audrey says in her usual wry tone. "How are you holding up, dear?"

I lean back in the armchair, running a hand through my unbrushed hair. "Oh, you know. Another day, another attempt on someone's life. I'm guessin' you've heard about the explosion at the concert last night?"

"I have, of course," she replies, a note of reproach in her voice. "I was disappointed not to hear it from you if I'm being honest."

I roll my eyes. Then immediately regret it. It's not beyond the realm of possibility that Audrey has spies in the Whistling Kettle, reporting back on my every move. "Sorry, Aunt Audrey. It's just been real busy 'round here the past few days."

"I'm sure it has," she acknowledges, still sounding put out. "But look, I'm glad you're alright, but that's not why I'm calling. I've been speaking with one of Jack O'Hara's old work buddies."

I sit up straighter. "Really? What'd they have to say?"

"Well, it turns out Jack wasn't always a private investigator. He started his career as a guard, then realized there was more money to be made in the private sector."

"How long ago was that?"

"A little over ten years ago. And in that time, Jack certainly has made his fair share of enemies."

"Do any of them live in Carrigaveen?" I ask.

Audrey pauses, and I hear papers ruffling over the line. "A handful, yes. First, there's the McKewon family. They weren't pleased about him meddling with their matchmaking business. Then, there was a farmer, Senan O'Malley. He was furious that Jack ruined his plans for a little extramarital fun."

I shudder at the thought, but so far, Audrey's not telling me anything I don't already know. "Anyone else?"

"I have one more person listed here. A council member suspected of dipping his fingers into festival funds."

That catches my attention. "Wait—who?" I already have a sinking feeling I know, but I need confirmation.

There's another short pause, then Audrey says, "A fellow called Eoman Scully."

In my mind, a few puzzle pieces slot into place. I'd thought it was weird that he kept bringing up the festival finances when I'd interviewed him—right here, in this very café. It had been almost as if he was justifying why he was spending so much money. And then there was the balance sheet I'd found in Jack's journal. Had Jack been investigating Eoman?

"Savannah? Are you still there?" Audrey asks. "Have I lost the bleeding signal again?"

"No, no," I quickly assure her. "I'm still here. I was just thinkin'."

"Ah, right, so. There's one more thing I got out of Jack's old friends at the Gardaí."

"Yeah? What's that?"

Audrey's voice drops slightly, the way it always does when she's about to say something important. "Before he died, Jack was working on a new case. But he was keeping it all very hush-hush. Even his friends in the business couldn't get a word out of him about it."

"Yeah," I say, drawing the word out to two syllables. "That doesn't really surprise me. I mean, I never met Jack or anythin', but from what I've heard, he was more the strong, silent type."

"That may be so," Audrey concedes. "But the people who

did know him thought it was strange. They said he was acting different, too. Excited, like. More excited than they'd ever seen him. But he wouldn't talk about it. Not to anyone."

Despite the heat in the café, a chill creeps up my spine. Whatever Jack was working on, he must have thought it was big. And now he was dead.

Before I can respond, Audrey continues, "One of his friends said he thought Jack was seeing someone—a woman—but I'm not finding any evidence of a romantic interest. Oh, and one final thing—Detective Mulhaney is on his way to Bantry right now. He finally got a warrant to search Jack's house."

I sit up so fast my knee knocks against the table. My eyes dart to my bag, already searching for my car keys. "Send me the address," I say, not even bothering to ask if she knows it. Of *course,* she does.

Audrey exhales, the kind of sigh that makes it clear she thinks I'm making a mistake but knows I won't listen. "Be careful, Savannah. Jack was most likely killed to keep something a secret. If you keep digging, you might be putting yourself in the same danger."

I pause for half a second, fingers curled around my keys. Then I stand, already moving toward the door. "I appreciate your concern," I say.

But we both know what happens next. I'm going anyway.

CHAPTER TWENTY-SEVEN

The steering wheel vibrates under my palms as I speed down the winding road to Bantry for the second time today. According to my GPS, it'll only take me about half an hour to get to Jack's house. I hope Detective Mulhaney isn't in a hurry to search the place. I'd hate to arrive after he's already finished.

I can't help thinking there must be something—anything—inside that will help explain why Jack was killed.

When I finally reach Jack's quiet street on the outskirts of town, I pull into an open space behind Detective Mulhaney's car and kill the engine. The neighborhood is unassuming, lined with aging buildings that have stood firm against the Atlantic's relentless wind and rain. Jack's place is a modest and weathered duplex, the kind of building that blends into the background.

I step out of my car and take in the details. The façade is worn but sturdy, its white-washed exterior dulled by time. The pine green window shutters are cracked and peeling, exposing the raw wood beneath.

My sneakers crunch on the cracked concrete path. Through the front window, I see Detective Mulhaney look up, drawn by the sound of someone approaching. His expression darkens like the sky overhead when he spots me.

The door swings open before I can climb the two steps that lead to the front porch. Detective Mulhaney's body blocks the entry, his arms crossed over his chest, making it clear he has no intention of letting me inside.

"You've got a nasty habit of showing up where you're not invited, Jeffers," Detective Mulhaney mutters, his voice as icy as the wind that cuts through the narrow street. "Sure, I don't even want to know how you tracked me down here."

"That's probably for the best," I say breezily before looking pointedly at the empty driveway and deserted street. "Where's the cavalry? You're not searchin' Jack's place all by yourself, are you?"

"My partner's on his way from Cork," he replies dryly. "But after the events of last night, I didn't want to waste time waiting for him."

I don't bother pointing out that he could have asked some of the guards from Carrigaveen to help with the search. We both know they'd be more likely to destroy evidence than to find it. "Well, lucky for you, I turned up. Sounds like you could use an extra pair of eyes until your partner arrives."

"I need that like I need a hole in the head," Mulhaney quips. "This is an active investigation, and you're not part of it."

I roll my eyes at him. "Oh, please. You let me into Molly's hospital room, and now you're drawing the line at searchin' the dead man's house? Either you trust me, or you don't."

He scowls, clearly weighing his options, then rubs a hand over his face. "You're a pain in the arse, Jeffers."

I grin. "So I've been told."

Reluctantly, he pulls a spare pair of disposable gloves from his pocket. "Fine. But put these on. And don't touch anything."

I take the gloves and slide them onto my hands. "You do realize that makes no sense, right? Why would I be needin' gloves if I'm not touchin' anythin'?"

"One more word out of you, and I'm rescinding my offer," he threatens.

I press my thumb and forefinger together, then draw them across my lips as if zipping them. With a heavy sigh, Detective Mulhaney disappears into the house. I follow him in.

Jack's home is a study in controlled chaos. The leather armchair near the wall is well-worn, its armrests darkened by years of use. A small gray sofa sits across from it, functional but forgettable. The plain wooden coffee table is marked by the ghostly rings of a lifetime's worth of coffee cups.

I scan the walls. Maps of Ireland hang in a haphazard array, tacked up rather than framed, with red strings anchored by pushpins crisscrossed over them. A low shelf along one side of the room holds a jumble of books and binders, their spines cracked from frequent use. A few case files are stacked neatly alongside a pile of unopened mail.

I'm examining the files, searching for a name that rings a bell, when the faint sound of wood scraping against metal pulls my attention to the corner of the room. I glance over and see Detective Mulhaney fiddling with a desk drawer, his fingers testing the edges before something gives with a quiet pop. With a grunt of satisfaction, he pulls the drawer open and begins stacking files from inside onto the desktop.

I continue my own search.

"Jeffers," Detective Mulhaney calls a few minutes later. "Come take a look at this."

Something in his tone has me holding my breath as I cross the room. When I reach the desk, Mulhaney taps an open file folder, and the second I see what's inside, my breath catches.

Photographs. Dozens of them. All of Molly Jenkins.

I flip through the candid snaps, which show Molly boarding a plane, sipping coffee at a café, stepping out of what looks like a hotel lobby. Some of the pictures are grainy as if they were taken from a distance, but others are uncomfortably close. Beneath the photos, there are pages and pages of notes that detail Molly's life in precise, clinical detail—schools, jobs, social media connections, even her flight itinerary to Ireland.

I glance up at Detective Mulhaney, my stomach twisting. "This feels a tad...obsessive."

"Maybe. But I also found this." He holds up a crisp, white document that appears to be an invoice of some kind. "Turns out Jack wasn't doing this on his own. Someone hired him to look into Molly's background. And they didn't want their name attached."

"But who would want to do that?" I ask. "Molly's never even been to Ireland before. None of this makes a lick of sense."

Detective Mulhaney shakes his head, his confusion mirroring mine.

I shift my focus back to the notes Jack had made on Molly. Her entire life is laid out in black and white, but it's the section on her career that makes me pause.

"She's a watchdog," I murmur, my eyes snagging on a paragraph about her job back in the States. "She writes a blog that's dedicated to exposin' fraud."

Detective Mulhaney leans closer. "What kind of fraud?"

"All sorts," I say, skimming faster. "Investment scams, shady charities, politicians pocketin' donations." My stomach twists. "She told me she came here for the festival, but what if it wasn't for the matchmakin'? What if she was workin' on a story? A scam?"

A thought slams into me. I remember the balance sheet tucked behind Molly's photo in Jack's journal. And what Audrey said about Eoman Scully being furious with Jack for sniffing around missing festival funds.

"What if she was looking into the festival's finances?" I say, lifting my gaze to Detective Mulhaney. "If you ask me, there's somethin' fishy about Eoman Scully. He seemed real anxious to justify the festival's expenses when I was interviewin' him the other day. And then I saw him arguin' with a local business owner who said Eoman owed the villagers money."

Detective Mulhaney rubs his jaw, his expression unreadable.

I press on. "If Jack was diggin' into missin' money and Molly was too, maybe they both got too close to somethin'. It's possible, right?"

Detective Mulhaney considers what I've said for a second, then starts rifling through papers on the desk. "I was just reading something about Eoman Scully. Where did it go? Ah, here it is. It looks like Jack was hired a while back to look into Eoman's finances as part of a divorce case. The wife claimed Eoman was hiding money so he could cheat her on alimony. The judge agreed with her."

All of this sounds very familiar. "What's the wife's name?"

Detective Mulhaney consults the paper in his hand. "Orla Gallagher." When I suck in a sharp breath, he frowns and asks, "Do you know her?"

I nod. "She runs Prose and Cons. The bookstore in Carrigaveen. She told me about Jack helpin' her with her divorce. But she didn't say that Eoman was her ex."

Detective Mulhaney's shrewd dark eyes narrow. "Do you think there's a reason she kept that to herself? Could she have been helping Jack—or possibly Molly—investigate her ex-husband? A way to get revenge, maybe?"

I consider his question. "I honestly have no idea. I mean, there are probably a million reasons why it wouldn't have come up."

It looks like Detective Mulhaney is about to ask me something else when his cell phone buzzes with an incoming text. He takes the device out of his pocket and reads the message.

"That's my partner. He's fifteen minutes out." His eyes flick to me. "You probably shouldn't be here when he arrives."

Fair enough. I'd rather not get chewed out by another detective today. "Yeah, yeah, I'm goin'. But before I take off, do you mind tellin' me what you're plannin' to do next?"

Detective Mulhaney exhales, slips his phone back into his pocket, and surveys the papers spilled out across the desk. "I'd say there's plenty to keep me busy here for the next few hours. But then, I need to have another chat with your one from America. Until I do, I'd be much obliged if you kept your distance. For your own safety."

My eyebrows knit in a frown. "You think Molly might be dangerous?"

"I think her name keeps coming up in ways that don't make sense," he says. "And I don't like things that don't make sense." He leans his elbows onto the desk. "I want to run a full background check on her. See if she's got any connections to people in Carrigaveen that she's not sharing. We're missing something, and I need to know what it is."

I nod slowly, chewing on my lip. Detective Mulhaney's words have bothered me more than I care to admit.

I like Molly. And I felt like she was being honest with me.

But when I asked her if she knew of any enemies, she said no. That seems unlikely, now, given the nature of her job.

And if she didn't tell me about her blog exposing scams, what else could she be hiding?

CHAPTER TWENTY-EIGHT

I step out of Jack O'Hara's house into the milky afternoon sunlight. The scent of a brewing Spring shower hangs in the air as I make my way to my car. My thoughts churn, but I force myself to push aside the questions about Molly. Speculating about why she lied—if she even did—isn't going to get me anywhere right now.

Besides, Mulhaney made it clear he doesn't want me anywhere near her. Even if I was inclined to ignore his warning, he's probably already called the hospital to make sure I don't get past the front desk. That road is closed, at least for now.

Which means I need to shift focus.

Eoman Scully seems like the logical second choice. If Jack was onto something about him skimming festival funds, maybe that's the thread I need to pull on to unravel this whole case.

I slide into the driver's seat of my car, shutting out the brisk wind picking up outside, and start the engine. The car rumbles to life, and I'm about to shift the vehicle into gear when a thought occurs to me. I have the next thirty minutes to kill while I'm driving back to Carrigaveen. It could be worth listening to the recording I made of my interview with Eoman. Just to see if there are any clues I might have missed.

I pull up the recording on my phone, connect it to the car's Bluetooth, and hit play. As I reverse out of my parking space, another vehicle swings into Jack's driveway. Mulhaney's partner, no doubt. It's probably for the best that I left when I did.

I pull onto the road, the sound of distant voices and clanking silverware from the café filling the car. Then, I hear my own voice.

"So, Mr. Scully—"

"Please, call me Eoman."

"Sorry. Eoman, can you start by tellin' me a little about the history of the matchmakin' festival? I hear it's quite the tradition 'round these parts."

I keep listening, my fingers tapping idly on the steering wheel as I navigate the winding country roads. The interview plays out exactly as I remember. No slip-ups, no obvious red flags.

But then—

"Do you know where the ladies' room is?"

My voice echoes back at me, and suddenly, I'm gripping the wheel tighter.

My pulse spikes as realization dawns. I never turned off the recorder when I went to the washroom! I left my phone sitting on the table, and it must have kept running. Excitement surges through me, chasing away the frustration that had been creeping in. I have a recording of Eoman's fight with the businessman—the one he tried to play off as some kind of misunderstanding.

I crank up the volume, trying to drown out the racket from loose stones in the road hitting the undercarriage of my car.

Static crackles for a moment, and then I hear voices.

"Go away with you, Eoman. I'm done with the excuses. You give us the money you promised, or I go to the guards. Simple as that."

The man's voice is sharp with anger, the kind of mad that only comes from frustration that's been building for a long time. I hold my breath, waiting to see how Eoman will respond.

"Fergus, calm down," Eoman finally says, his voice a study in patience. "You're making a big deal out of nothing."

"Nothing?" Fergus scoffs. "You promised that local business owners would get a generous cut of the festival earnings. But we still haven't been paid from last year's festival. Where's the money, Eoman?"

There's a brief silence. I can picture Eoman's easygoing mask slipping, his mind working overtime to spin a new excuse. Then Fergus speaks again, and his words nearly make me swerve off the road.

"I won't be fobbed off again," he snaps. "You pay up, or I tell the guards exactly where you were the day Jack O'Hara was killed. Someone saw you, Eoman. In the woods. With Jack."

My breath catches. I stare at the road ahead, but my mind is reeling.

Eoman met with Jack in the woods? The same day Jack was killed?

I fumble with the volume button, cranking it even higher, my pulse hammering as the conversation continues.

On the recording, Eoman lets out a short, nervous laugh. "Fergus, whoever told you I was in the woods that day was feeding you a line. Sure, I wasn't anywhere near—"

"Cut the crap," Fergus snaps. "The whole village knows you've been skimming from the festival funds for years. We just never had the proof. That's why we all chipped in this year. Hired someone who could go through the books properly, like."

I nearly slam on the brakes. The locals hired Jack to look into the festival's budget? That's a twist I didn't see coming.

"Jack had the numbers," Fergus's angry voice blares from the car speakers. "He had proof. You knew that. But before he could report what he found, he ended up dead. Now, how do you think that looks, Eoman?"

I can't help wondering if Jack had really found some kind of proof that Eoman was a thief or if Fergus was just bluffing. Either way, it's clear Fergus thinks Jack was murdered because he uncovered something big.

As my thoughts race in circles, one thing sticks out, tugging at the edge of my mind. If the locals were the ones investigating Eoman, there's a good chance Molly really did just come to Carrigaveen for the festival. She might not be working on an embezzlement story at all.

The sound of Eoman's voice, low and dangerous, draws my attention back to the conversation. "I'm warning you, Fergus—"

There's silence for a beat. When Eoman speaks again, his angry growls have been replaced by the dulcet tones of a practiced politician. "Ah, Savannah! You're back. Fergus here was just leaving. Weren't you, Fergus?"

Eoman had abruptly ended our conversation soon after Fergus left, but I listen to the brief exchange anyway. Eoman brings up the fact that I'm the one who found Jack's body, before trying to convince me that Jack's death is completely unrelated to the festival. Then, Eoman cuts short the interview, saying he'll answer my questions some other time.

That's it. That's all I've got. But it's more than enough.

There's enough smoke to consider the possibility that Eoman started the fire. It sounds like he had a motive for wanting Jack dead. He's also in shape, likely strong enough to strangle a full-grown man. So, he had the means. And if he was spotted chatting with Jack in the woods that day, he had the opportunity.

It hits me that I ought to let Detective Mulhaney know what I've found.

Once I find a shoulder on the road, I pull over just as small raindrops begin to dot the windscreen. With quick, practiced movements, I tap out a message to Mulhaney.

You should have a chat with a local businessman named Fergus. Someone told him they saw Eoman with Jack right before Jack was murdered. I figure you want to talk to whoever that was.

I press send, watching the screen for a moment before starting another message. This one isn't as urgent, but, given the events of the past few days, I'll feel better having someone know where I'm headed.

Going to speak with Eoman's ex-wife. In case you need me.

I send the text, drop my phone into the cup holder, and take a steadying breath.

If I hurry, I can be back in Carrigaveen before Prose and Cons closes.

Orla must have known her friend, Jack, was digging up dirt on her ex-husband. I'd had the sense she was holding out on me when I asked about what cases Jack had been working on. But she's only met me twice, so a case could be made she didn't want to hang out all the village's dirty laundry for me to examine right away.

I only hope she's willing to open up to me now.

Because if anyone knows whether a man is capable of murder, it's his ex-wife.

CHAPTER TWENTY-NINE

I pull into Carrigaveen just as the late afternoon light casts long shadows across the brightly colored buildings. Parking down the street from Prose and Cons, I cut the engine and take a moment to collect my thoughts.

The day has been one revelation after another, and my mind is still reeling from the recording I've just listened to. I'm hoping Orla can tell me more about Eoman and what exactly the villagers hired Jack to do.

Stepping out of the car, I glance at the bookshop—and do a double-take. The line spilling out the door and down the street definitely isn't what I was expecting. People are chatting excitedly, gripping tote bags, and snapping photos of the storefront, the kind of buzz that means something big is happening inside.

As I get closer, I spot a sign near the entrance in bold, cheerful lettering: *Today Only! Bestselling Author Saoirse Callahan Signing Her Latest Romance Novel!*

Well, that explains it. I've never heard of Saoirse Callahan, but judging by the size of the crowd, she's a big deal. And honestly, it tracks—what better place for a romance author to make an appearance than a matchmaking festival?

I hesitate on the sidewalk, weighing my options. If it were earlier in the day, I'd come back later when things quieted down. I really don't want to wait until tomorrow to talk to Orla, but this book signing looks like it'll be going on for a while. Orla is bound to be busy until closing time rolls around.

Just as I decide to put off my visit until tomorrow, movement in the narrow alley beside the bookshop catches my eye. I pause, peering down the dimly lit passage, and spot Orla leaning against the brick wall, a vape pen balanced between her fingers. She exhales slowly, a curl of vapor dissipating into the evening air. Her shoulders are tense, and she looks exhausted.

I step into the alley, pleasantly surprised that my arrival happened to coincide with her break. "Looks like you hate crowds just about as much as I do," I joke.

Orla startles, then gives me a half-smirk as she tucks the vape into her pocket. "Well, I suppose it's a bit of a double-edged sword. Crowds are great for business but dreadful for my poor nerves. Luckily, I've got an energetic, young helper who comes in a few days a week. Otherwise, I would lose my mind altogether."

I chuckle, then nod toward the bookshop entrance, where the crowd is still giddy with excitement. "Judgin' by that line, I'd say tonight will be real good for business at least."

She scoffs, rubbing a hand over her temple. "Yeah, a roaring success. Nothing like selling fantasies about love when your friend's just been murdered. Feels a bit sordid, if I'm honest."

I nod in sympathy. I imagine the last thing she wants to do right now is sell love stories to a horde of avid romance readers. At the same time, she'll probably make more money selling books tonight than she will the rest of the year.

"I'm real sorry," I tell her, meaning it. "It's hard pretendin' everything's normal when it's not."

Orla lets out a breath slowly, her gaze drifting to the ground. "Sure, what can you do? I just needed a minute to myself. But I should be heading back inside. Poor Naomi will be run off her feet."

After witnessing her vulnerability, I'm hesitant to press her with questions. But I also know the only thing that might bring her peace now is figuring out what happened to Jack.

I swallow a lump in my throat. "Listen, Orla, I hate to bring this up, but I need to ask you somethin'. It's related to Jack's murder."

She inhales sharply, bracing herself. "Go on, so."

"Do you know if Jack was trying to uncover some kind of scam at the festival?" I ask. "Maybe even one involving your ex-husband, Eoman?"

Her jaw tightens at the mention of her ex, and for a long moment, she doesn't say anything. I half expect her to shut me down completely. Demand to know why I've been asking around about her marriage. Then, her shoulders sag, and she looks me in the eye.

"He was," Orla admits. "Jack told me some of the business owners in the village hired him to get to the bottom of Eoman's financial shenanigans. See, the locals were starting to think Eoman was skimming money from the festival. And not just a few quid here and there. Serious money."

This must be what she was hiding from me in our earlier conversation, but now she's not telling me anything I don't already know. I'd heard Fergus say as much on the recording. Still, as a journalist, I know better than to rely on just one source. Now I have confirmation from Orla. Jack wasn't just poking around out of curiosity. He was working for people who wanted answers.

And if Eoman found out that Jack was getting too close to the truth?

"Orla, do you know if Jack had any proof that Eoman was stealin' festival funds?"

Orla retrieves her vape from her pocket and puffs. "I've been wondering about that myself. I can't remember him saying anything to me about it. But then, having proof wouldn't have made much of a difference in my mind. Or Jack's, for that matter."

I tilt my head. "What do you mean?"

Orla takes a long drag from her vape, the tip glowing briefly in the dim alley before she exhales a plume of smoke. "Jack and I both knew Eoman was a crook. It wasn't exactly a revelation," she says, her voice edging between bitterness and exhaustion.

"Jack caught him trying to hide assets during the divorce," Orla continues. "Thought he was being clever, moving money around, making it look like he had nothing. Told a judge that I was the one who needed to support *him*. He just wanted to get his hands on a chunk of *my* inheritance. The dirty old thief."

Anger rises in me on her behalf. "Sounds like a real jerk. Had you ever seen him do anythin' like that before? Try to cheat people outta money?"

Orla shrugs. "I suppose he's always been that way. For a long time, I just didn't want to see it. But deep down, I think I've always known. If there's money on the table, Eoman's the first to grab it. And he'll always make sure he gets more than his fair share."

I remember how Eoman stuck me with the bill after our meeting at the Whistling Kettle. At the time, I thought he was just in a hurry to leave. I'm beginning to suspect otherwise.

"If Jack *did* have proof that Eoman was stealin', what do you think Eoman woulda done?"

Orla assesses me with her shrewd hazel eyes. "Are you asking me if I think my ex-husband is capable of murder?"

Heat rises in my cheeks. "I'm sorry. It was rude of me to ask that."

"Not at all. It's a fair question." Orla's face tightens. "I never thought he'd be capable of that sort of thing. He's a 'cute hoor,' you know—always working an angle, always charming his way out of trouble. But violent? No, that was never his style."

I watch her carefully. "Would that change if he knew he was about to be exposed? In front of the whole village?"

"I really want to say no." She swallows, eyes dark with something close to regret. "But people change, don't they?"

Orla checks her watch. She probably needs to get back inside to help with the rush of customers. But there's one more person on my suspect list I need to ask her about.

"I have one more question, if you don't mind?" I wait for her to nod before proceeding. "It's probably none of my business. But I'm only askin' because I want to find out who killed Jack."

"Alright," Orla says.

Without giving her time to change her mind, I ask, "Why were you fightin' with Niall the night of the orientation dinner?"

She takes a moment to think before answering. "To be honest, my first reaction when I heard Jack was dead was anger. I wanted to be mad. Niall and the festival were an easy target."

"But do you think Niall had somethin' to do with Jack's death?"

Orla raises her hands, palms up, in a questioning gesture. "Ach, I don't know. I'm of two minds about it. On the one hand, murder's not a good look for a matchmaking festival. I can't imagine Niall doing anything to jeopardize the brand."

"And on the other hand?" I press.

"Well, he and his grandmother did make life hell for Jack, particularly after he exposed that Maeve had matched a woman with a married man a few years back. It was quite the to-do," Orla tells me. "As you'd expect, Maeve was fierce upset about the negative publicity. She didn't like anyone questioning her matchmaking prowess. And Niall? His first concern has always been the bottom line. He'd protect that at all costs. That's why they tried to run Jack out of town."

Something she said catches my attention. "Do you know the name of the married man? The one Maeve matched at the festival."

Orla nods. "Not personally, like. But I did hear his name being tossed about. Senan. Senan O'Malley."

It doesn't come as a huge shock to hear his name. I vaguely remember the judges at the potato peeling contest referring to an incident at the festival. What I don't understand is why he'd come back to the festival after being blackballed. And why does he seem obsessed with Molly Jenkins?

Orla takes another glance at her watch and straightens up. "Sorry to cut this short, but I really do need to get back inside."

"Of course, I'm sorry to be takin' up so much of your time," I say, standing aside to let her pass. "If you had to guess, who do you think killed Jack?"

"I'm sure I've no idea," she replies. "I will say this, though. People have all sorts of ideas about the kind of things they deserve in life. I think Jack was killed because he was standing in someone's way of that. Find out who, and you've found your killer."

CHAPTER THIRTY

I step out of the alley, my mind still turning over everything Orla just told me. My stomach, however, has other priorities, growling loudly enough to remind me I've barely eaten all day. Deciding I need a break—and maybe an adult beverage—I head to the Knot & Lantern.

As soon as I step inside, I know I won't be getting a quiet meal. The place is packed, the hum of conversation and clinking glasses filling the air. The smell of sizzling meat and freshly baked soda bread makes my stomach tighten in anticipation. A group of tourists crowd near the entrance, scanning the room for an empty table, but I already know better. There won't be one.

Instead, I make my way to the bar, where a few stools remain open. Sliding onto one, I take in the décor that gives the pub its name. Knotted rope accents twist along the wooden beams, and behind the bar, a mural stretches across the wall, a tangled mess of knots that forms a lantern.

I don't have to wait long before Cian Byrne, the bartender

I met my first day in Carrigaveen, approaches me from the other side of the bar, carrying a shandy.

"Welcome back, Georgia," he winks as he slides the drink in front of me. "You're wearing the day on your face. I thought you could use a cold one."

I rub my hands over my face. "That bad?"

"Nothing a perfectly blended shandy won't fix," Cian points to the glass. It's the drink I ordered the first time I came in.

"That's real nice of you. Thanks." I take a sip. "Do you remember what all your customers like to drink?"

"Only the ones who ask too many questions," he teases. "And, seeing as how I'm not above a little bribery, I'm hoping to get a nice little mention in that article you mentioned you're writing."

I fight to rein in the smile threatening to break out on my face. "Well, that depends. Any good gossip you can send my way?"

"I'd have thought you'd have plenty of that after what happened at the concert last night," Cian replies. "But to be honest, I'm a bit worried about your one. The other American. You know, the dead woman who didn't really die."

It takes me a second to realize he means Molly. My stomach clenches, wondering if something has happened since I saw her at the hospital this morning. "What do you mean?"

Someone at the other end of the bar signals for a pint. Cian grabs a glass and starts filling it from the tap. "First, someone saw her fetch. And then, just days later, she nearly gets turned into a human sparkler. That's no coincidence. She's been marked."

I resist the urge to roll my eyes. Folklore lives very close to the surface at times here. "You're seriously thinkin' she's cursed?"

Cian lifts a shoulder in a half shrug, but his face is serious. "I think death doesn't like being cheated. Have you never seen the film *Final Destination*?"

I let out a short laugh before I can stop myself. "You're tellin' me you think Molly's in some kind of horror movie situation? If fate doesn't get her one way, it'll try again another?"

He doesn't laugh. "Stranger things have happened. But if I were her, I'd be sleeping with my eyes open. Just in case."

Cian steps away to deliver the pint he pulled, leaving me with a queasy feeling in my stomach. Not because I believe in vengeful spirits or inescapable death, but because, for all the talk of legends, I know one thing for sure—someone tried to kill Molly. And whether Cian's right or not about fate, I don't doubt for a second that whoever did it could try again.

To protect Molly, Jack's killer needs to be caught. And fast.

When Cian returns to my end of the bar, I decide to pick his brain about my top suspects.

"Hey, Cian. I wanted to ask you about somethin'. A little birdy told me about financial shenanigans with the festival." I tilt my head, observing Cian. "Can you tell me anythin' about Eoman Scully?"

Cian lets out a slow breath, rubbing the back of his neck. "There've been rumors about Eoman pocketing festival proceeds for years. But no one's ever been able to prove anything." He pauses, then adds, "Not yet, anyway."

The way he says it—casual but pointed—makes me think he knows more than he's letting on. I study his face, wondering if *he* was one of the locals who chipped in to hire Jack. Either way, Cian doesn't seem to be very friendly with Eoman, which makes me feel better about asking my next question.

"I also heard someone spotted Eoman in the woods the

day Jack died," I say, my eyes focused on Cian's face for any reaction. "Any chance you know who mighta seen him there?"

Cian tilts his head, thinking. "I don't recall anyone mentioning anything like that. When was Jack killed again?"

"Sometime Friday afternoon," I immediately reply. "Why do you ask?"

Cian scratches his chin. "Are you sure about that?"

"A hundred percent." That day, my first in the village, will be seared into my memory for years to come.

"Well, then, I don't see how anyone could have seen Eoman in the woods," Cian pulls out a rag and wipes imaginary spots from the shiny bar. "He was with my wife, Fiadh, down at the orientation tent all day. They were part of the welcome wagon, taking videos of all the new arrivals for the festival's social media something or other."

My hopes for wrapping up this case in a neat little bow rapidly deflate. "Is there any chance he snuck off for half an hour or so? I mean, they can't have been together *all day*, right?"

A smirk appears on Cian's face. "Oh, no. It was the whole day. Trust me. I got an earful from my wife about how she didn't have two minutes to herself away from Eoman's boasting."

Before I can press him further, Cian's phone rings. He glances at the screen, frowning. "Sorry, I've gotta take this. Give me a holler if you want to order some food."

As Cian disappears into a room behind the bar, I'm left thinking about the implications of what he said. If Cian and Orla already knew about Jack's investigation, how many others did? The more I think about it, the more it seems like Jack's investigation is the worst-kept secret in Carrigaveen. And if everyone already suspected what Eoman was up to, what did he stand to gain by killing Jack?

Not to mention, if what Cian says is true, Eoman didn't have the opportunity to kill Jack.

I'm so lost in thought that when a hand lands on my shoulder, I nearly knock over my shandy. I whip around, half-expecting to see Detective Mulhaney with another warning about keeping my nose out of police business.

Instead, I see my Aunt Audrey, with my father, Ian, standing beside her.

For a split second, my brain short-circuits, skipping right past *Why are they here?* and straight to *Did something happen to my dog?*

"Is Fergal okay?" I demand, my voice sharper than I intend. I'd been texting with Debra, and she hadn't mentioned anything being wrong, but my aunt showing up unannounced has alarm bells ringing in my head.

Audrey waves a dismissive hand. "Easy there, love. He's perfectly fine. Probably dragging poor Debra on another walk. She can't resist those big eyes of his."

I know exactly what she means. Fergal has perfected the art of "the look." When he turns those big, soulful eyes framed by shaggy fur on you, it's impossible not to reach down and scratch behind his ears, reassuring him that, yes, he is the best boy, and, yes, he will absolutely be getting a treat.

I exhale, relief washing through me. "If you're not here to bring me bad news, what are you doin' here?"

"Isn't it possible we just missed you and wanted to see how you were getting on?" Ian asks a little too enthusiastically.

Audrey and I both stare at him, making it clear his performance isn't convincing anyone. Red splotches appear on his cheeks.

"You shouldn't lie, Ian. It doesn't suit you," Audrey finally tells him. Then she turns her attention to me. "We heard about the little fireworks demonstration last night. We've come to make sure you don't put yourself in harm's way. *Again.*"

It's on the tip of my tongue to ask Audrey how she found me at the Knot & Lantern, but then I think better of it. My aunt could find a drop of whiskey in a rain barrel.

"We just wanted to make sure you're safe, that's all," my father chimes in. But the concern on his face is soon replaced by a sheepish look. "But there is one tiny problem. Since no rooms were available, owing to the festival, we'll have to crash with you."

I blink. "With me?"

Audrey gives a little shrug. "Afraid so. But at least we'll be able to keep our eyes on you at all times."

Before I can even open my mouth to address the inevitable battle over sleeping arrangements, Cian appears on the other side of the bar. Anxious energy practically radiates off him.

Something in his demeanor compels me to motion for Audrey and Ian to hang back. But I know Audrey will still be listening. She has ears that would put a bat to shame.

Cian leans his elbows on the bar and gestures for me to come closer. When our faces are mere inches apart, he speaks in a low voice. "You were just on to me about wanting a scoop. And I've got a big one for you. What do you say we make a little deal?"

I raise an eyebrow. "You tell me what it is and I write somethin' nice about the pub?"

He smiles. "If it wouldn't be too much trouble. Sure, establishments like mine live and die by reviews."

I'm tempted to point out to him that, with the crowds in here during the festival, he doesn't really need my endorsement. Also, I'd already planned to include the quaint little pub—with its charming bartender and delicious meat pies—

in my article. But part of me suspects he doesn't even care what I write. I think he just likes the banter and the illusion of subterfuge.

I decide to play along. "I don't know, Cian. I guess it depends on how good of a scoop it is."

Cian scratches his head in an exaggerated show of deep thought. "Ah, you're right. It's probably not that interesting to you anyway."

"Oh, no you don't. You brought it up. That means you have to tell me now."

"Well, I suppose I'll trust you with what I know." Cian glances down the bar, making sure no one is listening. "So, every day, like clockwork, my cousin takes his dog for a walk in the woods behind the Abbey Wood Manor. Now, he likes to vary his route. Stray off the path and the like. Just to keep things fresh."

I nod, wondering if he ever plans on getting to the point.

"Only today, he got the surprise of his life," Cian continues. "He called me straight after he was onto the guards."

A knot forms in my gut. "Why did your cousin call the guards?"

Cian's eyes reflect excitement and a healthy dose of what looks like fear.

"To report a murder. He found the body of a woman in the woods."

CHAPTER THIRTY-ONE

I turn to face Audrey and, for a split second, we just stare at each other, the weight of Cian's words settling between us. Then, as if guided by the same unspoken thought, we move.

My chair scrapes against the floor, and we hurry toward the exit, weaving through the packed pub without a word. Audrey leads the way, her pace brisk.

My father, who probably couldn't hear my conversation with Cian, trails behind us. "Uh, guys. Anyone want to tell me what we're doing?"

"Just keep up, Ian," Audrey barks. "We'll explain in the car."

Outside, the cool evening air hits me like a splash of cold water, but there's no time to stop and take a breath. Audrey unlocks her car with a sharp click, and the three of us pile in without hesitation.

Audrey's car peels away from the curb before I even have my seatbelt on, the tires spitting up gravel as she speeds toward the woods behind Abbey Wood Manor.

As Audrey fills Ian in on where we're going and why, I

yank my phone out of my bag and jab the touchscreen to call Detective Mulhaney's number.

Ring. Ring. Ring, Ring.

The line clicks, and I think the detective has answered. But it's just the phone redirecting me to his voicemail. I hang up.

"Come on, Mulhaney," I mutter, redialing as the car bumps along the uneven road. "Pick up."

Once again, my call goes to voicemail.

When we finally reach the outskirts of the hotel grounds, flashing blue lights pierce the dusk. A small group of curious onlookers mill about, their voices swallowed up by the music playing from a nearby festival event. I push open my door before Audrey has fully stopped the car, my legs moving before my brain catches up.

Audrey and Ian aren't far behind.

Following a pair of guards into the woods, we weave through the undergrowth, stepping over gnarled roots and ducking beneath low-hanging branches. I catch a glimpse of something bright—a shock of orange that turns out to be a forensics officer pulling on gloves—and then, suddenly, we walk right into a strip of fresh crime scene tape strung between the trees.

"Whoa, there. This is as far as you go," a guard says, blocking our path.

I exhale sharply, frustration knotting in my chest. Somewhere beyond that tape lies another victim, another unanswered question. And Detective Mulhaney still isn't answering his phone.

I squint to see in the gathering darkness, and that's when I spot him. Detective Mulhaney is here, on the other side of the barricade. I'm about to call out to him when he glances in my direction.

He immediately starts shaking his head. Taking his sweet

time, the detective ambles over to where we're standing. "I should've known you'd show up," he says, voice dry as dust. Then his gaze flicks past me, landing on Audrey and Ian. "Though I can't say I expected you to turn it into a family outing."

Audrey snorts. "It's nice to see you again, too, Detective Mulhaney. I heard your poor mother had a spot of bother with the new hip. Please give her my best when you see her next."

A frowning Detective Mulhaney opens his mouth—no doubt to ask Audrey how she knew about his mother's hip replacement surgery—then thinks better of it. Instead, he sighs, then says, "She's doing much better now, thank you."

Having addressed Audrey, Detective Mulhaney turns next to my father and gives him a tentative nod. It's more of a formality than a greeting. Ian returns it just as stiffly, the tension between the two men as thick as the mist curling through the treetops.

It's no wonder my father feels a bit uneasy. It's not every day you come face-to-face with the man who once slapped handcuffs on you and accused you of murder. Ian was cleared, of course, but that doesn't make their meeting now any less awkward. Mulhaney, to his credit, looks just as uncomfortable as my father.

I clear my throat, eager to get back to the body found in the woods. "We heard you're after findin' a woman dead. Do you know who she is?"

Over Detective Mulhaney's shoulder, I see Sergeant Sweeney hovering above what must be the body. The earth is churned up around his feet, and the air smells of damp leaves and something sharper—something acrid that makes my stomach turn.

Mulhaney shakes his head, jaw tight. "Not yet. Someone

poured lye on her face and hands. Destroyed any identifying features."

A chill runs down my spine. "So there's no way to tell?"

"If we're lucky, we might get a dental match," he says, rubbing the back of his neck. "But even that's not a guarantee."

"Where would someone even get lye around here?" I ask.

Before Detective Mulhaney can answer, my father speaks. "Sure, every cattle farmer in the county keeps some on hand," Ian says. "They use it to treat feed for livestock."

His words barely register before a memory slams into me. That first morning in Carrigaveen, when I was standing in line to check in at the hotel, I'd seen a story on the front page of the local paper. *Cattle Farmer Reports Theft of Grain Chemicals Overnight.*

I suck in a breath. "The newspaper. There was an article the day I arrived. Someone stole grain chemicals from a farm not far from here."

Detective Mulhaney's eyes darken with understanding. "Which means either she was already dead before you got into town..."

"Or someone was plannin' this well in advance," I finish for him.

We all let the thought hang between us for a minute.

Audrey is the first to find her voice. "If she's been out here a few days, how is it no one's found the body until now?"

"She'd been buried. Not very deep, mind," Detective Mulhaney explains. "A local man was walking his dog, and the dog wouldn't stop scratching at a mound of dirt. The man went over to fetch him and saw a hand sticking up out of the ground."

"Poor fellow probably won't be taking his dog into the

woods again anytime soon," my father says. "Can't say I'd blame him."

An image of a skeletal hand rising from the earth flashes in my mind, and I push it away. Who was this woman? And more importantly, why did someone go to such lengths to make sure she couldn't be identified?

Then, a thought occurs to me. "I wonder if this is the woman who was MIA at the festival?"

Detective Mulhaney, Audrey, and Ian all turn to look at me, identical questions in their eyes.

I realize they have no idea what I'm talking about. "A woman paid to come to the festival but never showed up. Maeve was tellin' me about it, and I heard it from a couple of other people, too. What if that's her?" I nod toward the crime scene. "Does the woman you found have blonde hair? Maybe Jack confused her for Molly. Maybe he wasn't hallucinatin' from his meds after all."

Detective Mulhaney's frown deepens. "What meds?"

I blink. "The ones in the medicine cabinet at Orla's coach house. Didn't you see 'em?"

His jaw tightens almost imperceptibly. "I need to talk to Maeve. See what she can tell me about this missing festival-goer before I go jumping to any conclusions."

I narrow my eyes. He's dodging the question about Jack's pills, which can only mean one thing. I found something he didn't, and he doesn't want to admit it.

Audrey interrupts my gloating to bring herself up to speed. "What do we know about this Molly person?"

"We haven't figured that out yet," I tell her. Then turn, once again, to Detective Mulhaney. "You were fixin' to run a background check on her. Did you find anythin' out?"

He shakes his head. "Nothing suspicious. We checked with immigration. She's never been to Ireland before, and she's only made a handful of calls here. All of them seem tied to this trip. No hidden connections, no red flags."

I chew on the inside of my cheek. "What about texts? If she's used to investigatin' scams, she'd know how to cover her tracks. She could've been usin' an encrypted app to communicate."

"Fair point," Detective Mulhaney acknowledges.

"Forgive me for interrupting," Ian says. "I'm still trying to catch up. And I certainly don't know who this Molly person is. But if Savannah's right and the killer was after her, that means Molly could be in serious danger. Do you know where she is so we can warn her?"

"She's at the hospital, restin' after bein' injured in the explosion last night," I explain to my father. To Detective Mulhaney, I ask, "Do you still have a guard at the hospital?"

"I do," Detective Mulhaney confirms. "But it's best not to take any chances. I'll call and have a second guard posted outside her door. Just until we can get this mess sorted."

As I stare past the crime scene tape to where a woman lies dead and disfigured, I can't help thinking we're running out of time to catch the killer before they strike again.

CHAPTER THIRTY-TWO

The buzzing of my vibrating phone drags me out of a sleep so deep it feels like I've been yanked from the bottom of the ocean.

Groping blindly for my cell on the nightstand, I crack open one eye to glare at the clock. Not even six in the morning. I groan as my fingers finally land on the device. After spending half the night listening to my dad's snoring, I'd barely gotten any sleep.

How does one man make that much noise?

I glance at the phone's display. The screen reads *Arrogant Arsehole*. I probably should change Detective Mulhaney's name in my contacts.

Worried the ringing will wake up my aunt and father, I answer in a croaky whisper, "This better be important."

"Jeffers." Detective Mulhaney's voice is sharp, cutting through the last remnants of sleep like a cold splash of water. "I thought you'd want to know. Molly's gone."

My eyes fly open. I'm suddenly wide awake, hoping it's all just a bad dream. "Gone? Are you sayin' Molly's dead?"

"No, no. Sorry, I probably could have phrased that better," Detective Mulhaney tries to reassure me. "She disappeared from the hospital sometime overnight. The guard outside her door was knocked out."

"You said you were gonna be postin' two guards!" I remind him in a harsh whisper.

"Come here to me, I'm just as upset about this as you are," he says, short on patience. "And, so you know, I *did* request a second guard. The eejit left his post to run to the chippy for a takeaway."

"Jeez Louise, haven't they ever heard of Uber Eats?" I grumble, even though I know it won't make a darn bit of difference. "And no one at the hospital noticed someone knockin' out a guard and walkin' out with an injured woman?"

Detective Mulhaney. "Apparently not. And the guard that did stay at his post told me he didn't see a thing. He'd been hit from behind. He's fine, like. But his head will be smarting worse than a hangover for a few days."

"Are you at the hospital right now?" I ask.

"I am. Sure, someone had to check the room and see if whoever did this left any clues behind. And, at the moment, I don't have much confidence in the local guards."

It's a fair point. "Have you found anythin'?"

"Just Molly's hospital gown, lying on the floor," Detective Mulhaney says.

So, whoever took her must have dressed her in her street clothes to avoid suspicion. "Is that it?"

"Pretty much. Just the gown and a stick of ChapStick on the floor next to her bed."

I sit up so fast that the covers tangle around my legs and, in the process, I accidentally yank the blanket off Audrey, who's sleeping on the other side of the large bed. She stirs with a grumble, blindly tugging the fabric back over her shoulder before settling again.

I keep my voice low, barely above a whisper. "Did you just say *ChapStick?*"

"Yes. Why?" There's a pause. "And why on Earth are you whispering? Am I interrupting something?"

I exhale, rolling my eyes toward the ceiling. "Yes, you're interruptin' my *sleep*," I whisper-hiss. "And if I don't keep my voice down, we'll also be interruptin' my *dad's* sleep. And my *aunt's* sleep."

Mulhaney snorts out a laugh. "You're having a slumber party?"

I close my eyes and pinch the bridge of my nose. "Only because there are no other rooms in town," I mutter. "Which means I got stuck sharin' a bed with my aunt while my dad's snorin' away on the sofa."

"Sounds cozy."

"Sounds like they didn't want to let me outta their sight, more like," I counter.

I slip out of bed as quietly as I can and tiptoe toward the washroom. The floor creaks under my weight, and I wince, pausing to make sure I haven't woken anyone. Audrey shifts but doesn't stir. My dad lets out a snore loud enough to rattle the windows.

I slip inside the washroom, shutting the door gently behind me. "Okay," I say, still keeping my voice low. "Back to the point, you said you found *ChapStick*."

"I did indeed." There's a beat of silence from Detective Mulhaney. "Do you think that has some kind of significance?"

"Maybe. I saw Senan usin' some when he was in the hospital lobby yesterday," I tell him. "I remember thinkin' it looked like he was gettin' ready for a date or somethin'."

Mulhaney exhales heavily. "Okay, let's say you're right. And the ChapStick I found was his. That still doesn't explain *why* Senan would want to hurt Molly. I can understand why he had a problem with Jack for busting his cover at the festival, but what could he possibly have against a woman he only met a few days ago?"

It's a good question. One I don't have an immediate answer for. "I don't know," I admit.

I rub my eyes, wishing I had a cup of coffee—or an entire pot—before being expected to string coherent thoughts together. Instead, I have nothing but my own exhaustion and Detective Mulhaney's skeptical silence on the other end of the line.

"Look," I say, trying to formulate a theory. "Maeve told me someone stole some of the matchmakin' questionnaires. They're these forms everyone has to fill out before they arrive. What if Senan took 'em?"

Mulhaney lets out a noncommittal grunt. "And why would he do that?"

I lean against the sink, thinking. "From what I've heard, Senan fancied himself a real ladies' man. Maybe he wanted a sneak peek at who'd be showin' up at the festival. Get a jump on the competition."

Mulhaney still doesn't sound convinced. "That's a stretch, Savannah."

"Is it?" I push back. "Molly's a good lookin' woman. It's not out of the realm of possibility that Senan got a little *too* interested. Maybe even obsessed. And I did see some graffiti in the ladies' room at the Knot & Lantern the other day. Someone called Senan a *stalker pig.* That's not exactly a glowin' review of his character, now, is it?"

"You're basing your theory on bathroom graffiti?" Detective Mulhaney doesn't sound convinced.

I shake my head, even though he can't see me. "Not only

that. You don't think it's suspicious that he was talkin' to Molly right before the blast went off? Or that you found ChapStick where Molly disappeared? Right after I saw Senan usin' some in the lobby?"

That shuts him up for a second.

"Alright," he says finally. "I'm not saying I think you're right. But I'll grant you that it's worth looking into."

It's not the ringing endorsement of my theory I'd been hoping for, but it'll have to do. I hear the faint rasp of Mulhaney scratching his beard through the phone line, a sound I've come to associate with him trying to piece together a puzzle that refuses to fit.

"I suppose it's too much to ask that you would let me speak with Senan alone and fill you in afterward?" he finally asks.

"Considerin' I'm the one who brought him to your attention? Yeah, that'd be too much to ask," I tell him, my voice firm.

Detective Mulhaney releases a long-suffering sigh. "Might as well take you with me, so."

I bite my lip to keep from laughing. "Admit it, you know I can help you."

"I know no such thing," he quickly counters. "But I know if I don't take you, you'll just go talk to him on your own. If you're determined to stick your nose in, I'd rather be there to make sure it doesn't get broken."

"How chivalrous."

He groans. "Just do me one favor. Leave the family at the hotel. It's bad enough having to take *you.*"

"Rude," I say, but I'm already nodding. As much as I appreciate Ian and Audrey's protective instincts, I know Mulhaney's right. If we want Senan to talk, we don't need an audience getting in the way.

"I'll pick you up at the hotel in thirty minutes," Detective Mulhaney says. "And Savannah?"

"Yeah?"

"Try not to do anything reckless before I get there."

He hangs up so quickly he doesn't hear me reply, with a smile, "No promises."

CHAPTER THIRTY-THREE

Detective Mulhaney's car pulls up outside Abbey Wood Manor just as dawn begins to light the horizon.

I've been waiting outside the hotel's grand front entrance alongside my aunt and my father. They'd insisted on coming downstairs with me, saying they didn't want me waiting alone in the dark.

"Thanks for keepin' me company. I'll see y'all in a couple hours," I say, stepping toward the car's passenger seat, but before I can reach for the door handle, Audrey sticks out an arm, restraining me like a human seatbelt.

Audrey leans over until she's eye level with the car window and indicates for the detective to roll down the window, which he promptly does.

"You listen to me, Detective," Audrey says once the window is all the way down. "You bring my niece back in one piece, or you'll be answering to *me*."

The corners of Detective Mulhaney's lips twitch as if he's resisting the urge to smile, but he says somberly, "I'll protect her with my life."

I roll my eyes and reach again for the door handle. "Alright, you two. Let's not get carried away. We're goin' to talk to a suspect, not stormin' an enemy stronghold."

Audrey raises a whitish-blonde eyebrow. "Oh, really? Sure, you know yourself, you don't have the best track record of staying out of harm's way."

"She's not wrong, dear," my father unhelpfully supplies.

I can't argue with either of them, so I don't even try. I just open the car door and slide into the passenger seat. "We'll be fine. See you in a while." Then I turn to Detective Mulhaney and mouth the word *drive*.

Unable to stop himself, he smiles as he shifts the car into drive. As we pull away from the hotel, I glance in the side-view mirror and see Audrey and Ian watching us drive away.

"You know," Detective Mulhaney muses as he pulls out onto the main road, "I think I might be more afraid of your aunt than the murderer."

"Smart man," I tell him with a grin. "But, naw. She means well. She just wasn't happy about bein' left behind."

Detective Mulhaney snorts. "The apple doesn't fall far, I suppose."

I scowl at him, but he keeps his eyes focused on the road, navigating the twists and curves with practiced ease. The journey takes longer than I'd expected, each turn revealing nothing but endless hedgerows and the occasional stone cottage.

Finally, after passing through two tiny villages, we pull onto the road leading to Senan O'Malley's farm. The place is quiet. Eerily so. A weathered farmhouse sits at the top of a small rise, flanked by a sprawling barn and a few rusted-out pieces of farm equipment that look like they haven't been touched in years.

After parking in front of the house, we climb the few steps onto the porch. Detective Mulhaney knocks on the front door. No answer. He tries again, louder this time. Nothing.

Concern for Molly twists my insides. "If Senan abducted Molly, we need to find him before..."

I don't finish the thought, but one look from Detective Mulhaney tells me I don't have to. The same thought has crossed his mind, too.

Mulhaney steps off the porch, glancing around. "Come on. Let's check the barn."

The barn doors are ajar, just enough for us to slip inside. The air is thick with the scent of hay and something earthier, a mix of damp wood and animal musk. A few cows regard us lazily from their stalls, utterly uninterested.

Then, movement. A figure emerges from the shadows, climbing up through a square opening in the barn floor.

Senan.

Holding a gallon jug labelled "Caustic Soda Lye."

He sets the container on the ground before hauling himself out of the barn's basement. He freezes when he sees us. For a split second, his face betrays something—surprise, maybe? Guilt? But it's gone before I can pin it down. Then his eyes rake over me with a puzzled expression on his face, as if he knows he's seen me before but can't remember where.

"Jaysus," he grumbles, wiping his hands on his shirt and grinning at me. "Bit early for house calls, isn't it?"

I exchange a glance with Detective Mulhaney before flicking my gaze back to the open hatch in the floor. A cellar. A dark, ominous-looking cellar. And just like that, my mind starts spinning through every horror movie I've ever watched. Does Senan have Molly trapped underground like in some serial killer film?

I consider asking to take a look down there, but Detective Mulhaney is already opening his mouth to speak. He doesn't waste time with pleasantries. "When's the last time you saw Molly Jenkins?"

Senan blinks, clearly caught off guard. He recovers quickly, squaring his broad shoulders. "Couple nights ago. At the concert," he says. "Why?"

Detective Mulhaney tilts his head slightly, watching him the way a cat watches a mouse. "So you weren't aware she was injured not long after speaking with you at the concert?"

I keep my expression neutral, but I know exactly what Detective Mulhaney is doing. He's trying to trip Senan up. We both know Senan was at the hospital yesterday. So, if he pretends he doesn't know anything about the fireworks accident, we'll have him in a lie.

Senan hesitates just a second too long. I see it in the way his mouth presses into a firm line. He's deciding whether to lie or come clean. Finally, with a small exhale, he shrugs. "I heard something happened, yeah," he admits. "Some kind of accident with the fireworks, wasn't it?"

Mulhaney's expression doesn't change. "Would it surprise you to learn that it might not have been an accident?"

Senan shifts his weight from one foot to the other and crosses his arms over his chest. He doesn't ask for details, doesn't feign shock. He just stands there, staring Mulhaney down, as if willing the detective to make an accusation.

The silence stretches. Finally, Senan asks, "Is that why you're here, so? You think I had something to do with it?"

"I think you're not denying it," Detective Mulhaney replies smoothly.

Senan lets out a dry chuckle, but there's no humor in it. "Well, you'd be wrong."

"Alright. We'll come back to that in a moment," Detective Mulhaney says. "How about you tell me where you were overnight?"

Senan frowns. "What?"

"Where were you?" Detective Mulhaney repeats.

Senan's wary eyes flick between us. "I was here all night. What's this about?"

Detective Mulhaney doesn't answer. Instead, he fires off another question. "Did you go by the hospital in Bantry?"

Senan stiffens, then shakes his head. "No. I didn't."

"So, you didn't go there to visit Molly Jenkins?"

Senan's eyes harden into slits. "I did try to stop by yesterday. But the staff turned me away. Why are you asking that? Has Molly been saying I was there?"

Mulhaney tilts his head. "Cut the act, Senan. Things will go a lot easier for you if you help us find her."

"What are you talking about?" Behind the bluster, Senan looks genuinely confused. "Are you saying that Molly's missing?"

I study him closely, watching how his brows knit together, the slight widening of his eyes. Either he's an incredible liar, or he truly has no idea what's going on. A whisper of doubt begins to grow in my mind. Is it possible I was wrong about Senan? I mean, there's no denying he's a creep and a womanizer. But a killer?

And if Senan killed the woman in the woods, why did he need to steal lye from another farm? He already has some. He just brought it up from the cellar.

If Detective Mulhaney is beginning to share my doubts, he doesn't let on. "Do you use ChapStick, Mr. O'Malley?"

Senan scoffs, dismissive of the apparent non sequitur. "I do, of course. I always have it on me. The ladies don't like kissing cracked lips. Why?"

"Would it surprise you to hear we found a tube of ChapStick in Molly's hospital room after she went missing?" Detective Mulhaney asks.

"What's that got to do with me? Sure, you can't think I'm

the only person in Ireland who uses a bit of lip balm now and again." Senan's hands ball into fists and he shakes his head. "No, no. You're not pinning this on me, Detective. I would *never* hurt Molly. Never."

I've stayed quiet so far, not wanting to interrupt Detective Mulhaney's line of questioning, but I can't resist asking, "Do you like Molly, Senan?"

Senan's lips twist into a self-satisfied smile. "We like each other. It's hardly a one-way street, darlin'."

"But you've only known her a coupla days, right?" I press.

"That's right. Sometimes that's all it takes."

"So, you're tellin' us you had no idea who Molly was when you met her a coupla days ago and, after talkin' to her a few times, you felt close enough to take her flowers at the hospital?" Surprise flickers in Senan's eyes, prompting me to add, "I saw you in the lobby."

"What's she getting at?" Senan demands of the detective before turning back to me. Seconds later recognition dawns in his eyes. "Hold up a minute now. I remember you. You're a journalist! Why are you even here? What kind of fake news story are you two cooking up?"

I exchange a look with Detective Mulhaney before turning back to Senan. "Someone stole a bunch of match-makin' questionnaires," I say. "We were wonderin' if *you* took 'em to see who was at the festival this year."

Mulhaney picks up the thread smoothly. "Molly's a pretty woman. Did you see her photo? Decide that she belonged with you?"

Senan's jaw tightens, his voice cold. "That's ridiculous. I didn't steal any bloody questionnaires. And I wasn't stalking Molly, if that's what you're implying. And I think I've had just about enough of your questions."

Senan slams the cellar door shut and pushes past us toward the exit.

"Senan," Detective Mulhaney calls after him. "I'd start talking if I were you. Right now, you're a suspect in Jack O'Hara's murder *and* Molly's disappearance."

"And possibly the death of the woman found in the woods," I add.

Senan flinches like I've just struck him. "What woman in the woods?"

Before I can respond, Detective Mulhaney places a hand on my arm. He's silently asking me to let him handle this one. He probably wants to withhold some details of the crime scene that only the killer would know. I've seen detectives do that in some of the crime shows I used to watch with my mama.

"The body of a woman was found behind the Abbey Wood Manor yesterday," Detective Mulhaney says slowly, carefully. "We're considering the possibility that the woman was mistaken for Molly Jenkins when she was killed."

Senan raises his hands as if in surrender. "I—" He shakes his head. "I had nothing to do with that. With any of it. Sure, I hated Jack for ruining my marriage when he ratted me out for straying. But I didn't *kill* him. Or the woman in the woods. And I certainly didn't have anything to do with Molly's disappearance."

As dislikable as he is, I'm tempted to believe him. Then I remember Molly's dismissiveness toward him whenever I saw them together. I narrow my eyes. "Didn't it make you mad that Molly was rejectin' you?"

His mouth tightens, one side raises in a snarl. "You've got it all wrong. Molly was the one coming on to *me*."

"Oh, come on," I say, knowing my disbelief is spelled out across my face. "I saw you two together a coupla times. She looked like she wanted nothin' to do with you."

Senan's jaw twitches. "That's just how she is, sure. Standoffish in public, but behind closed doors? Whole different story. She's all over me. In a way, it's like a game."

"Are you sure it's one she wanted to play?" Detective Mulhaney asks.

Senan's expression shifts, anger taking root in the lines of his weathered face. "You know what I think? I think if you *actually* had anything on me, you'd already have me in the back of your car on the way to the station. So, unless you're arresting me, we're done talking."

Detective Mulhaney opens his mouth to reply, but his phone buzzes sharply in his pocket. With a sigh, he pulls it out and glances at the screen before answering.

"This better be important," he hisses into the phone. As he listens, his irritation is replaced by something sharper, more focused. "Right. We're on our way."

Ending the call, he tucks the phone back into his pocket and turns to Senan. "We'll have to finish this conversation later, so. In the meantime, don't leave town."

Senan scoffs. "Where exactly do you think I'd go?"

Mulhaney doesn't dignify that with an answer, already pivoting toward the door. I follow, glad to be out of that barn with the creepy cellar.

As we walk toward the car, I glance over at Mulhaney. "What's goin' on? Why'd we rush outta there so fast?"

He doesn't slow his stride. "You know the young lad who was injured by the firework?"

"Yeah. Noah," I say, remembering his name from when he spilled water on me at the Knot & Lantern. I'm not sure I can handle any more bad news, but I can't resist asking, "Is he alright?"

"You can ask him yourself. He just woke up."

CHAPTER THIRTY-FOUR

Noah Kehoe is propped up against a stack of pillows when Mulhaney and I step into his hospital room in Bantry later that morning.

It has taken us over an hour to get here. Detective Mulhaney had to drop me at the hotel first so I could pick up my own car, but I get the sense Noah doesn't mind having had a little extra time to rest. He's been unconscious for a day, but he still looks exhausted.

Tufts of wild red hair poke out from beneath the bandage wrapped around his head, and his right arm, resting stiffly atop the thin hospital blanket, is in a cast. His blue eyes follow us warily as we enter.

The room itself is sterile but functional. There's a wall-mounted monitor, a stainless-steel IV stand, and a compact en-suite bathroom in the corner. The only bit of personality is a framed photograph of Michael Collins hanging on the wall, his steely gaze fixed over the room.

Sitting beside Noah in a well-worn armchair is a man who, judging by the similar pale, freckled skin and fiery red hair, must be his father. The older man is broader than his son, with a shock of gray at his temples and the deep lines of a man who's spent most of his life outdoors.

He stands as soon as we enter, his chair creaking as he rises. His sharp eyes flick to Mulhaney first, then to me, taking our measure like a man used to sizing people up. He gives Mulhaney a curt nod and extends a hand.

"Callum Kehoe," he introduces himself. "I imagine you have some questions for my son. Since he's not yet eighteen, I'd like to stick around while you're having your chat."

Detective Mulhaney nods. "Not a bother." Then, the detective walks over to the foot of the bed to face Noah. "How are you feeling, lad?"

Noah lets out a breath, managing a small, wry smile. "I've had better days," he says, shifting slightly against the pillows. "But at least the drugs help with the pain."

I hang back, not wanting to crowd the poor kid. He already looks like he's been through hell. His face is bruised, and his arm is swaddled against his chest like a baby bird with a broken wing.

"I need to ask you about the night of the concert," Detective Mulhaney says, flipping open his notebook. "Do you remember the fireworks going off?"

Noah nods, his expression serious. "Yes. Sir. I remember pretty much everything before the explosion."

"I'm going to need you to tell me everything that happened. In as much detail as you can remember," Detective Mulhaney speaks gently to the young man. "But first, do you recall seeing a woman called Molly Jenkins right before the blast?"

Noah frowns, clearly taken by surprise by the line of questioning. "Who?"

I pull out my phone, quickly scrolling through the pictures I took at the potato peeling contest. When I find a clear shot of Molly, I turn the screen toward Noah. "Her."

He squints at the image, then nods slowly. "Yeah. I remember your one." He exhales, like dredging up the memory is an effort. "She was talking to some guy. I thought he was her boyfriend at first. But I think he was just trying his luck, if you know what I mean."

That gets Detective Mulhaney's attention. "No, I don't. What do you mean?"

"The way she was talking to him, like," Noah explains, his forehead creases as he struggles to find the words. "She was saying really awful stuff to him. Like, calling him a sap."

"How did your man react?" Detective Mulhaney presses Noah.

Noah's face scrunches up as he thinks. "That's the weird part. He didn't seem put off by it. It was like—" He pauses, searching for the right words. "Like he thought it was all some kind of joke or something."

Detective Mulhaney doesn't miss a beat. "A joke? How so?"

Noah hesitates, glancing at his father. Then, lowering his voice, he leans a little toward Mulhaney. "I got the impression they were playing parts in some kind of..." He swallows. "Some kind of weird sex game or something."

The room goes quiet for a beat. My face feels warm, and I'm sure there's a blush reddening my cheeks. Callum, who's been watching the exchange with a clenched jaw, suddenly looks down at his hands, his fingers lacing together tightly.

A smile tugs at the corner of the detective's lips, but his voice is steady when he asks, "Did you get any sense that the man wanted to hurt her?"

Noah's eyes widen. "Not at all. Why?" he asks. Then, after a second, the color in his face fades to an even paler shade of white. "Wait, was she hurt?"

Detective Mulhaney nods. "She was injured in the blast, though not as badly as you were."

"But…but she's going to be alright?" Noah asks, a hint of desperation in his voice.

While I find it a bit surprising that Noah would be so concerned about a woman he claims he doesn't know, I'm more focused on how Detective Mulhaney will answer Noah's question. After all, Molly is still missing, and we have no clue about where she might be. As much as I don't want to admit it, there's a very good chance Molly is far from alright.

Detective Mulhaney seems to wrestle with the same dilemma because it takes him a minute to answer. "She had some pretty serious burns on her arms, but nothing life-threatening."

Noah exhales, some of the tension in his shoulders easing. "I'm glad she's okay. Was anyone else hurt?"

"No, just the two of ye," Detective Mulhaney tells him. "Now, I know this is hard, but can I get you to think back to that night. Did you see who planted the firework in the field? Or anything at all that looked suspicious?"

The air in the room shifts. Noah's throat moves as he swallows hard. His gaze flicks to his father.

Callum, who's been silent for the entire conversation, meets his son's eyes. A quiet understanding passes between them before Callum gives a slow, deliberate nod.

Noah licks his lips. "I know who set the firework."

"Who?" Detective Mulhaney demands.

Noah takes a shaky breath, then looks Mulhaney square in the eye. "It was me," he says. "I did it."

I blink. "You?" The word shoots out before I can stop it.

Noah's face turns red, and he shifts uncomfortably. "No one was supposed to get hurt."

Detective Mulhaney lets out a slow, controlled exhale, pinching the bridge of his nose. "And why, exactly, would you do something as bleeding stupid as setting off dodgy fireworks in the middle of a crowded concert?"

Tears well up in Noah's eyes, threatening to spill down his cheeks. "I wasn't thinking. It was just supposed to be cool, like."

Callum lets out a heavy sigh. "He wanted to impress the girl he likes."

I hazard a guess at the object of Noah's affection. "The hostess from the Knot & Lantern?"

"That's the one," Noah admits sheepishly. "She loves fireworks. I thought...I don't know, maybe if I did something big, something crazy, she'd notice me." He glances at Detective Mulhaney, then quickly adds, "But no one was supposed to get hurt! I swear, I didn't mean for any of this to happen."

Detective Mulhaney doesn't say anything right away. He just stands there shaking his head. Finally, he speaks. "Well, lad. I hope it was worth it. Your little stunt has impeded a murder investigation. I hope you think twice before doing anything so reckless again in the future."

Noah nods frantically. "You have my word I'll never do anything like this again."

Callum rises from his chair. "Are you going to charge him, Detective?"

Shaking his head, Detective Mulhaney says, "If your son does face any charges, they won't be coming from me. I was young and stupid once, too. But the woman you injured is now missing. So, Noah, if you think of anything else you saw —anything at all that might help us find her—please ring me."

Detective Mulhaney hands Callum a business card, then storms out of the hospital room.

I follow him out into the hallway, weighted down by the knowledge that we're no closer to finding what happened to Molly. Or where she might be.

CHAPTER THIRTY-FIVE

As we step into the corridor, the door to Noah's room clicks shut, muffling the sounds of Callum quietly scolding his son. The scent of stale coffee overwhelms me as we pass by the nurse's station. And, tired as I am after the early wake-up call, I'm tempted to stop and ask for a cup.

But Detective Mulhaney is striding toward the elevator, and I have to quicken my pace to keep up. He seems lost in thought. I can almost see the gears turning in his head.

I wait a beat, then another, before finally breaking the silence. "So, if the firework explodin' was really an accident, does that mean we've been wrong this whole time? Maybe Molly's *not* in any danger. Maybe she just panicked and ran, thinkin' someone was after her."

Detective Mulhaney reaches the elevator bank and presses the down arrow. "It's possible. Either way, we need to find her. If she's in hiding, we need to reassure her she's safe. And if she's not..." His voice trails off, but the implication is clear.

The problem is, I don't know Molly well enough to have

any ideas about where she might have gone. "How do we even go about lookin' for her?"

"I'll check with the rental car companies," Detective Mulhaney says as the elevator doors slide open, and we step in. "If she rented a car, we can put out an all-points bulletin. Have the guards on the lookout for her vehicle."

We ride down to the lobby in silence with Detective Mulhaney checking his phone for any missed messages while we were speaking with Noah.

Detective Mulhaney pockets his phone with a sigh as we exit the elevator. "Right. I need to go meet with the coroner. See if there are any updates on the body we found in the woods."

I perk up. "Great, I'll come with—"

He cuts me a look so sharp it could pierce Kevlar. "Oh, no you don't. I brought you along this morning because talking to Senan was your idea, and because my partner's busy trying to identify our Jane Doe."

"But don't you think—"

"The answer is no."

"You didn't even let me finish the question," I argue.

"I didn't need to," Detective Mulhaney says sternly. Then, he seems to take pity on me. "Look, I admit you're not the worst when it comes to solving murders. And I *am* learning to value your input. But there's no way you can go with me to the coroner. End of debate."

I hide the smile forming on my lips, especially since I can tell it took a lot out of the detective to admit I've been helpful. "Alright, alright. I'll leave you to it. Just please let me know if you find out anythin'?"

"I will, indeed," he assures me. With a quick nod of the head, he strides out of the hospital and into the parking lot. I watch him go.

As I'm contemplating my next move—because I am definitely not just going to sit around twiddling my thumbs—I feel my phone vibrate in my pocket. I pull it out to see a text from Audrey.

I'm sending you an address in Cork City. Meet me there as soon as you can.

I frown at the screen. No explanation, no pleasantries. Just straight to the point. Classic Audrey.

A moment later, another message comes through, this time with an address.

I don't bother asking for details. If Audrey had wanted me to know, she would've told me. Instead, I tap out a quick reply, a simple thumbs-up emoji, before heading to my car.

The drive to Cork is long and tedious, seventy miles of winding roads and occasional stretches of highway where I can finally pick up speed. By the time I reach the city, the overcast sky has given way to a pale afternoon sun, casting a warm glow over the rows of semi-detached houses.

The one Audrey directed me to is a classic red-brick home from the mid-20th century, with a neatly trimmed front lawn bordered by hedges that have been shaped with military precision. I spot Audrey's car parked across the street and pull in behind it.

Shaking off the stiffness in my legs, I step out of the car, slinging my purse over my shoulder as I cross the road. Before I can even reach the front stoop, the door swings open, and Audrey beckons me inside.

With only a nod of greeting, my aunt leads me into a bright and airy living room. A fire crackles in the hearth, casting flickering shadows on the whitewashed walls. The room is cozy yet elegant, with a well-loved sofa and armchairs arranged around a coffee table stacked with books. A wooden mantel above the fireplace is lined with framed photographs—smiling faces from different generations, a wedding portrait in black and white, and a faded picture of a girl in a school uniform.

Standing near one of the armchairs is a woman in her seventies, her white hair swept up into a neat chignon. She wears a dark skirt, a pale blouse, and a soft gray cardigan that matches her eyes.

Audrey gestures toward her. "Savannah, this is Eithne Clancy."

Eithne steps forward, her smile kind but reserved. "It's lovely to meet you, Savannah," she says, her voice carrying a gentle lilt, musical and soft.

"Nice meetin' you, too," I reply, shaking her offered hand.

Eithne asks us to sit and offers me a coffee, which I gratefully accept.

Audrey clears her throat. "I know you're wondering why I brought you all the way here."

The thought did cross my mind, but I keep my mouth shut.

"For the last several years, Eithne here has been researching and cataloguing the stories of the lost women of Ireland's Magdalene Laundries," Audrey continues, putting particular emphasis on the last two words.

I'd mentioned that the laundries were in Jack O'Hara's journal, but I hadn't realized Audrey had been actively pursuing leads on them.

I quickly try to remember what I'd read about the so-called homes for 'fallen women.'

"My great-aunt died in one," Eithne says, her voice steady but filled with something deep and personal. "For years, no one in my family spoke of her. She was simply, well, gone. When I finally began searching for answers, I realized how many other families had the same questions, the same silence. After I retired, I dedicated myself to uncovering as much as I could about the women who were housed in the Galway, Limerick, and Cork laundries."

Audrey leans forward, her voice brimming with quiet urgency. "Eithne's records are some of the most meticulous I've ever seen. She's uncovered information that even the official archives don't have. Including details on a woman named Máirín Teirny."

I frown, the name meaning nothing to me. "Should I know who that is?"

Eithne smiles as she lowers into an armchair and rests her hands gently in her lap. "I can't imagine why you would. You see, Máirín Teirny was a resident of one of the Magdalene Laundries when she was in her late teens. She had fallen pregnant, and her family sent her away." A shadow flickers across her face. "She was worked to the bone, barely given a moment to rest, let alone prepare for childbirth. It shouldn't have come as a surprise to anyone that she wasn't strong enough to survive it."

A quiet tension settles over the room. I shift slightly in my seat, trying to absorb the weight of what she's saying.

Eithne exhales softly before continuing. "After Máirín's death, God rest her, her daughter was adopted by an American family. A couple with the surname Jenkins."

My breath catches. "Jenkins?" My mind spins, trying to make sense of it. "You mean—"

Audrey nods solemnly. "Molly Jenkins."

I stare at her, my stomach tightening. "Molly was Máirín Teirny's daughter?"

"Yes," Eithne confirms. "But not her only daughter. There were two wee girls. Identical twins."

For a second, the words don't register. "Twins?"

"The second baby, a girl named Bridget, wasn't adopted," Audrey says, her voice grave. "She remained in the Magdalene Laundry until it shut down a few years later. After that, she was placed in an orphanage."

"She likely had a hard life," Eithne picks up the thread of the story. "No real family, no place to truly belong. It's a tragedy, really. Two sisters, separated at birth—one given a new life in America, the other left behind, abandoned."

I lean forward, gripping the edge of my seat. "What happened to Bridget?"

Eithne shakes her head, her eyes clouded with sorrow. "Your guess is as good as mine, I'm afraid. There are no records after she turned eighteen. But with a girl like that, with no family, no real support system, if something did happen to her, there was no one to even report her missing."

I don't know what I had been expecting when Audrey invited me here, but it certainly wasn't this. "Do you think Molly knows she had a twin sister?"

Audrey shrugs. "That's the million-dollar question, isn't it?"

I press my lips together, trying to corral my racing thoughts. If Molly had known about Bridget, would she have tried to find her? Is that the real reason she came to Ireland? To track down her long-lost sibling?

Audrey's voice pulls me from my thoughts. "What's the latest on Molly? Have ye found her?"

"Not yet. But Detective Mulhaney and the guards are lookin' for her."

Audrey gives me a pointed look. "They'd better find her soon."

I nod, my stomach twisting. Because now we had one more thing to ask Molly about when we find her. If we find her.

CHAPTER THIRTY-SIX

By the time I arrive back in Carrigaveen, night is settling in, wrapping the village in the warm glow of streetlights and shop signs. The air is weighted down with the rich aroma of sizzling meat and sugary fried dough, drifting in through the car's open window.

Up ahead, the guards are already at work, setting up roadblocks along the main road to keep traffic away from the heart of the street fair scheduled for tonight.

My foot is light on the gas pedal as I pass by the square, where a row of food trucks is already drawing eager crowds. Somewhere down the street, a chorus of voices—some in tune, most not—belts out a classic rock song. No doubt the night will be one to remember—or, for some, one to piece together in the morning.

All I want to do is park my car so I can get out and stretch my legs. The drive back from Cork had taken even longer than the trip there, mostly due to a tractor going five-miles-an-hour hogging up three-quarters of the two-lane road.

Finally, I pull up to the Abbey Wood Manor, but all the parking spots up front are taken, forcing me to park near the forest at the far end of the lot. There's a side door to the hotel not far from my car, but it's locked, so I have to walk around to the front, through the lobby, and up to my floor.

The lights are off, and my room is surprisingly silent when I step inside. I knew Audrey wouldn't be here. After leaving Eithne's, my aunt had stayed behind in Cork, saying she wanted to visit an old friend. The way she said it had me raising an eyebrow.

An old friend.

With Audrey, that could mean a lot of things. She might be meeting with a former colleague, someone who could help track down what happened to Bridget Teirny. Or maybe —just maybe—she is taking some time out to enjoy herself.

I secretly hope it is the latter.

But even though I knew not to expect Audrey to be here, I can't imagine where Ian might have gone. Then, my eyes land on a folded note sitting on the small writing desk near the window. Recognizing my father's handwriting, I pick it up.

Gone to get a bite at the Knot & Lantern before the village is overrun. Join me if you'd like.

He's wise to be thinking ahead. No doubt, the pub will be wall-to-wall people in a few hours, the air thick with laughter and the scent of whiskey.

Reaching into my purse, I pull out my phone and shoot off a quick text.

Heading your way. Save me a seat.

As I step into the hallway, a thought nags at the back of my mind. If Molly is scared and anxious to get out of town, she'll have to swing by the hotel to pick up her things before leaving.

It could be worth checking to see if she's there. Just in case.

It's a long shot, but I can't shake the feeling that if I don't at least try, I'll regret it. With a sigh, I take the stairs up one floor, my footsteps silent on the plush carpet.

Stopping in front of Molly's door, I knock. The door swings open an inch, revealing a sliver of the dimly lit room beyond. Someone must have left it unlocked.

"Molly?" I call out, keeping my voice even.

Silence.

"Molly?" I say again, pushing the door open just enough to see inside.

No answer.

Every instinct tells me I shouldn't be here. I have no right to enter Molly's room uninvited. But the door was open. Either she left in a hurry, or someone else has been in here.

Maybe the maid accidentally left it ajar? No. I doubt that. A mistake like that could get someone fired.

Which means…

I swallow, convincing myself I'm not snooping. I'm looking for a missing woman.

Steeling myself, I step inside.

At first glance, nothing seems amiss. The bed is made, the curtains are drawn, and everything looks neat and orderly. Walking deeper into Molly's room, my eyes search for anything out of place.

The closet doors are slightly ajar, and when I peek inside, all of Molly's clothes are still hanging neatly. Her suitcase sits in the corner, zipped shut and undisturbed.

A creeping unease settles in my chest.

I check the nightstand next. Aside from a pad of paper and a pen, there's nothing on the surface aside from a few books. I'm about to turn away when something catches my eye. Sitting beside a hardcover daily planner is a small navy booklet. I freeze.

Molly's passport.

I stare at it for a second, trying to process what I'm seeing. If she were planning to run, there's no way she'd leave this behind.

My fingers tremble slightly as I reach for the planner and flip it open. I scan the pages, looking for any clues about her life or where she might be now. Most of the entries are ordinary—meetings, reminders, a note about a lunch reservation from a few days before she left Boston.

Nothing jumps out at me.

I set the planner down and slide open the top drawer of the desk, expecting to find little more than a hotel-issued bible. Instead, I see a scuffed plastic folder. Unlike the rest of Molly's things, which are all expensive and pristine, this folder looks out of place. The edges are bent, and the plastic is cloudy with wear, as if it's been handled over and over again.

Curious, I pull it out and flip it open. Inside is a thick stack of papers. The first page is a printout of an old newspaper article from the local paper, dated three years ago. I skim the headline: *Festival Brawl Turns Ugly as Private Investigator's Findings Cause Uproar.*

My stomach tightens as I scan the article. It details a major fight at the festival between a local farmer, Senan, and an unnamed private investigator. The investigator had dug up some dirt on Senan, revealing embarrassing secrets that had the whole town whispering.

The private investigator has to be Jack. But why would Molly have this?

I set the article aside and pull out another sheet—a printout of an email. My breath catches as I recognize the sender.

Jack O'Hara.

The email is addressed to *phoenixofeire@anonymail.net*. An alias, no doubt. In it, Jack details Molly's travel plans to Ireland: dates, flight information, and even where she'd be staying.

Why would Jack send this to an anonymous email? And more importantly, who was on the receiving end?

The next few pages are filled with handwritten text I can't make heads or tails of. The letters look familiar, but the words make no sense. I frown, my eyes scanning the unfamiliar script. I can only assume it's Gaelic, but if Molly has never been to Ireland before, I doubt she speaks the language.

Flipping to the next page, it takes me a minute to figure out what I'm looking at. When I do, the air vacates my lungs. It's one of the missing festival questionnaires! I thumb through the subsequent pages and find several more questionnaires. A photo stapled to one of the pages chills my blood.

The name under the photo is Máirín.

My hands begin to shake. The folder slips from my grasp and papers scatter across the floor. I crouch to pick them up, and that's when I see it.

Something large and plastic peeks out from under the bed. It's a large plastic case, the kind you'd expect to hold musical instruments. But something about it gives me pause.

After a moment, I reach for it, pulling it out into the dim light. My fingers find the latches, and before I can second-guess myself, I flick them open.

Inside, nestled in thick foam, is a crossbow.

A sharp gasp escapes me, and I drop the lid as if it's burned me. My heart thunders in my chest. What in the heck is Molly doing with a weapon like this?

I shove the case back under the bed, my heart pounding

in my throat. My mind is racing with questions, but before I can fully process what I've found, a shift in the air makes the hairs on my arms stand up.

Then, a sound. The soft creak of a door hinge.

I freeze.

The bathroom door is open. And I'm no longer alone.

CHAPTER THIRTY-SEVEN

Molly steps into the room, a gun in her good hand leveled at my chest.

For a long beat, neither of us speaks.

Then, I let out a breath and say, "Hello, Bridget."

She falters. Just for a second. Her grip on the gun doesn't waver, but her expression flickers with something sharp and calculating. Then, slowly, she smiles. A humorless, knowing grin that makes me cringe.

"Well now, aren't you a clever girl?" she says, her voice smooth as silk. Gone is the American accent. In its place is a thick Irish brogue, full of quiet menace.

A chill runs down my spine.

She tilts her head, considering me like I'm an obstacle she hadn't planned for. Her eyes drift to the papers on the floor. "I see you've found my festival questionnaire. I had to steal it back from Maeve, of course. I couldn't very well leave behind a trace like that, now could I? Even if I did use my mother's name instead of my own."

Pieces of the puzzle finally slot together in my mind. But

I'm too frightened by the gun pointed at my chest to chastise myself for not figuring out the truth sooner.

"It's a shame, really," Bridget muses. "You seem like such a nice girl. If you'd come by half an hour later, I'd have been long gone, and things might've been...much different."

The unspoken implication hangs heavy in the air between us. I swallow hard, my mind racing. Trying to figure out how to get out of the situation I was foolish enough to stumble into. I force my voice to remain steady. "What are you plannin' to do?"

Bridget sighs, almost regretfully, as she keeps the gun trained on me. "You see my problem, don't you?" she says. "Sure, I can't have you calling the guards the second I walk out that door."

My heart pounds, but I force myself to stay calm. If she wanted me dead, she wouldn't bother talking. "You don't have to hurt me," I say, trying not to sound like I'm begging. "Tie me up. I won't be able to do anythin' until someone finds me. Could be hours before that happens."

Bridget lets out a short, humorless laugh. "Clever ploy, but no. That's not going to work." She gestures vaguely toward the door. "The hotel is fully booked. People are wandering the halls at all hours. You could scream, kick at the walls. Someone would come. No, that won't do at all."

I press my lips together, trying to think.

Bridget lifts her chin. "I need to be on a plane, halfway across the Atlantic before anyone even thinks to look for me. Starting fresh, just like I should have been able to do all those years ago."

So that's the plan. She wants to vanish into Molly's life. Start over in America. But she must realize that won't solve her problems, right? There's an extradition treaty between Ireland and the U.S. Even if she makes it stateside, she would probably be sent right back. She'll be running for the rest of her life.

I bite my tongue, swallowing the urge to point that out. The last thing I want is to make her think there's no way out. Because if that's the case, then killing me might start to look like her best option.

Bridget exhales slowly, the sound heavy with a weariness that doesn't match the steel in her eyes. "I suppose we'll have to go for a little drive."

My stomach tightens. "Where?"

"Does it matter?" Bridget's lips twitch into something that might have been a smirk under different circumstances. She dips the barrel of the gun to point at the papers littering the floor. "Be a good girl and pick those up. And grab the passport on the nightstand. I'll be needing that."

Moving slowly to buy time, I kneel and collect all the loose papers, stashing them inside the plastic folder. Turning my back for a brief moment to grab Molly's passport, I don't see Bridget creeping up behind me. In one smooth motion, she grabs my free hand and wrenches my arm behind my back. Pain shoots through my shoulder, and I let out a sharp gasp.

She is strong. Much stronger than I would have expected. Especially since one of her arms is still injured from the burns she sustained in the fireworks explosion.

The cold press of metal finds the small of my back. "Hold onto those papers and keep your mouth shut," Bridget orders me, her voice smooth but firm. "Unless you don't mind me making a mess of this fancy hotel."

I swallow hard and nod.

"Right then. Off we go." With a sharp push, she steers me toward the door, her grip unyielding.

The hallway is quiet. Too quiet. Each step we take toward the back elevator makes my pulse hammer harder. Someone could step out of a room at any second. A maid could round the corner. If I scream, would I have a chance?

The gun nudges against my spine, as if Bridget can hear my thoughts. "Don't do anything stupid, Savannah."

I straighten my spine and keep walking. Even if I could somehow break free, where would I go? The hallway stretches out before us, long and empty, devoid of any sign of life. No staff bustling about, no distant chatter of guests.

Bridget must have chosen to come back now—when all the guests are down at the festival in the village—on purpose. She didn't expect anyone to be around as she gathered her things to flee.

With each step, my hope of rescue dwindles. At the end of the hallway, Bridget shoves me toward a door marked "Employees Only."

"Open it," she commands.

With shaking hands, I twist the knob, the door swinging open to reveal a utilitarian room. Laundry chutes line one wall, and there's a service elevator on the other.

"Call the elevator," Bridget orders, nudging me forward with the gun.

I obey, my finger trembling as I press the button. The hum of the approaching elevator sounds unnaturally loud in the stillness, a mechanical harbinger of my impending fate. The doors slide open with a pneumatic hiss, revealing a dimly lit interior that smells of metal and stale air.

"In," she says, the word clipped and hard.

The elevator's interior is a dim, cramped box. The flickering overhead light casts long, distorted shadows across the dingy walls. Bridget stands beside me, the gun pressed into my ribs, as the elevator begins its very slow, very creaky descent.

Knowing that I'm running out of options for rescue, I make one last-ditch effort to summon help. As slowly and stealthily as I can, I slide my hand into my crossbody bag and feel for my phone's cool, smooth surface. Finding it, I slide my fingers to the volume button and hold it down, hoping it's now turned all the way off.

The elevator jolts, and Bridget's gun digs into my side. I nearly let go of the phone, but somehow manage to hold on long enough to, hopefully, activate the emergency call function.

I clear my throat, the sound unnaturally loud in the confined space. "Where are you takin' me?"

I'm not really expecting an answer—I just need to keep Bridget talking, in case, by some miracle, my call went through, and the guards are listening on the other end of the line.

"Would you ever be quiet? I need some time to think," Bridget snaps at me. "Kidnapping you wasn't exactly part of my plan."

The elevator shudders to a halt, the doors sliding open to reveal the loading dock. Bridget pushes me out of the elevator and through the loading dock to a nearby car, which I assume is hers. She yanks open the driver's side door and shoves me in, the gun never wavering from its aim at my head.

As she walks around the front to the passenger side, I glance down, wondering how long it would take me to hotwire the car.

Too long. Even if I knew how.

Seconds later, Bridget slides into the seat next to me. She grabs the folder and passport and hands me the keys. "Drive."

My hands shake as I grip the steering wheel, steering us out to the main road. I feel my hope fading faster than the hotel lights in the rearview mirror.

CHAPTER THIRTY-EIGHT

The car jostles as I navigate the winding country roads, my knuckles white against the steering wheel. The only light comes from the headlights cutting through the darkness and the occasional glint of silver as Bridget's gun shifts in my peripheral vision.

My pulse thunders in my ears, but I force myself to stay calm. If I can keep her talking, maybe I can come up with a way out of this.

"So," I say, keeping my voice light despite the fear clawing at my throat, "how long have you known about Molly? About havin' a twin?"

Bridget doesn't answer right away. I steal a glance at her. Her eyes are fixed on the road ahead, her expression unreadable.

"About a year," she finally says.

I wait, letting the silence stretch, hoping she'll fill it. She obliges.

"For most of my life, all I knew was that my mother died in a Magdalene Laundry, and I was put in an orphanage." Her voice is laced with bitterness. "No one ever told me anything more than that. No family came looking for me. I grew up thinking I was alone in the world."

I swallow, resisting the urge to glance at her again. "How'd you find out?"

Bridget exhales sharply, like she doesn't particularly want to answer, but does anyway. "Last year, I started looking into the records. I figured if no one was going to tell me about my mother, I'd find out for myself. And eventually, I did. I found my birth certificate. And Molly's, of course. With a notation that the Jenkins had adopted her."

I risk a glance in her direction. Her jaw is set, her grip on the gun steady.

"I spent my whole life thinking I was nobody," she murmurs. "Turns out, I was just the one that got left behind."

"Did you ever think about reaching out to her?" My stomach twists with nerves, but I keep my tone casual, like we're just two people having a conversation.

Bridget lets out a short, humorless laugh. "No, not at first. I just watched."

"Watched?"

"Social media," she says. "It wasn't hard. Molly put her whole bloody life online."

The way she says it—so detached, like stalking her own sister was just another way to pass the time—sends a fresh wave of unease through me.

"At first, I just wanted to see what kind of life she had," she continues. "What kind of person she'd turned out to be. But the more I watched, the more I wondered why her? Why did she get the good life while I grew up in an orphanage?"

I keep my eyes on the road, afraid that if I look at her, she'll see the fear I'm trying to hide.

"But still, she was my sister. My only family. I wanted to get to know her," Bridget explains. "So, I made a fake profile. A woman from Dublin named Máirín with similar interests.

I made sure to be just interesting enough that Molly would want to talk to me."

"And she did?"

Bridget lets out a bitter chuckle. "Oh, she did. We talked for months. She told me about her childhood, her parents, her plans for the future. She had no idea she was telling it all to a sister she didn't know she had."

I swallow. "How'd that make you feel?"

Bridget's voice drops. "Angry. Furious, actually. Seeing what she had, what should have been mine. It ate away at me. She had everything. A nice home, a good education, people who cared about her. And me? I had nothing."

Her bitterness chokes the air like peat smoke. I don't dare speak, afraid of setting her off.

"I changed my surname after I turned eighteen," she mutters after a beat, almost as if she's talking to herself now. "I thought if I could just start over, I could build a new life. But it didn't work. No matter how far I ran, I was still the girl no one wanted."

Bridget suddenly goes quiet. In the silence, the sound of the tires bouncing over potholes roars in my ears. Without moving my head, I try to catch a glimpse of Bridget. Her expression, cloaked in shadow, is unreadable.

Finally, she speaks. "It all changed after Molly's adopted parents died. She told Máirín all about it in a Facebook chat. How, all of a sudden, she was alone in the world. No siblings, no parents. And it got me thinking. If she were gone, would anyone even notice?"

I grip the wheel a little tighter. "So, you reckoned you could just take her place?"

Bridget answers my question with a disgusted grunt. "If only it had been that easy. Sure, loads of planning went into it. First, I had to hire a private investigator to learn everything I could about her. Work history, medical records. Even what kind of shampoo she used. I needed to know it all if I was going to become her."

"So, you're the one who hired Jack?"

"I was, of course," she replies in a tone usually reserved for toddlers. "He didn't know who I was or why I wanted the information. And he never asked. Not that I would have told him the truth anyway. But he got me everything I wanted and more. I think he might have even fallen in love with her, the silly fool. All the while I was listening to the videos she posted online. Practicing her accent. I needed to make sure I could pass for her when I made it to the States."

The headlights catch the curve of a brick wall up ahead, and I ease up on the gas to navigate the bend.

"She'd been divorced for years. No kids. She had her own house. I could slide right into her life with no bother," Bridget continues. "All I needed was an excuse to draw her back to Ireland."

"The matchmaking festival," I whisper.

"Convincing her was almost too easy," Bridget says. "I already knew she was lonely after her parents passed. All it took was a few hints on social media from her good friend Máirín, and she was filling out the forms and buying her plane ticket. All I had to do was wait."

My throat is dry, and my heart is hammering against my ribs. I need to keep her talking until I can figure a way out of this that doesn't involve crashing the car and killing us both. But I can't get my mouth to form any words.

Fortunately for me, she seems eager to unburden herself. "Once Molly arrived in Carrigaveen, I sent her a message, posing as Máirín. I told her I was in town for the festival as well and staying in a little cabin in the woods. I invited her to come visit me. She couldn't wait to meet me in person."

I grit my teeth. "That's when you killed her?"

"Shot her through the heart with a crossbow," Bridget

confirms coldly. "She went down fast. I thought I was home free. But then I saw your man high-tailing it through the trees like the devil was at his heels. I had to think fast. I tried to shoot him, but he was too far away, and I missed."

A sick taste fills my mouth. I want to scream, but with a gun pointed at my midsection, I know any sudden outburst won't end well for me. "So, you moved the body, tryin' to make everyone think Jack was just crazy."

Bridget shakes her head. "No, but that was an unexpected bonus. I'd already planned on moving the body. You see, I knew she'd be too close to the trail. So, I dug a hole in the woods in advance and stole some lye from a nearby farmer to make it harder to identify her if anyone stumbled across the body. But Jack almost ruined everything. I knew it wouldn't be long before he was back with the guards. I had to hurry. I wrapped her in a tarp and pulled her deeper into the woods, kicking leaves everywhere to cover the drag marks. I got away in time. But it felt rushed. Sloppy. And I had a loose end I needed to clean up."

"Jack," I say.

"Even if he didn't see who shot Molly, he knew too much," Bridget says as if trying to convince me of the necessity of another murder. "The problem was, how to get him on his own. And then it hit me, I could pass myself off as a festival goer wanting a background check on a potential suitor. I said I wanted to meet away from the village. Keep things private, like."

"He took the bait." I can hear the resignation in my voice.

"He did, of course. He showed up right on time, but I was already waiting with a syringe in my hand. He never saw it coming. I pumped him full of enough sedatives to knock out a small horse."

I frown, thinking about the official cause of death. "But he was strangled."

"So he was. I did it with my own bare hands." It almost sounds like she's bragging. "But I had to point the blame as far from me as possible. And sure, look, no one would think that a woman would have been able to get the jump on a man of Jack's size. Assuming the guards didn't spot the needle mark, they'd go on thinking a man must have killed him."

She's not wrong. I'd been fooled into thinking a man must have killed Jack.

"And the clues?" I ask cautiously. "Like the toothpick by the river? And the ChapStick in the hospital room?"

Bridget gives a small shrug. "Misdirection. There were plenty of sketchy people in this village already—Niall, Senan, Eoman. It was easy enough to point the suspicion their way. You see, I wanted the guards chasing their tails for a while, looking at the two of them. Anywhere but at me. I just needed to buy enough time to slip away, get on that flight, and disappear forever."

We're getting to the end of her story. I can feel myself running out of time to save myself. "So, why'd you end up runnin'?"

"I heard the guards talking outside my hospital room. They said a woman's body had been found in the woods." Bridget's voice is tight with frustration. "I couldn't take the chance that they might identify her. If they realized it was Molly…"

Her voice trails off, so I finish for her. "The whole house of cards woulda come tumblin' down."

"Something like that," Bridget acknowledges. "After all I'd done, I couldn't let it end like that. With Molly's money, I can start fresh in America. Build the kind of life I've always dreamed of."

She sounds so calm. Like all of this has been a game of chess, and she's only a few moves away from checkmate.

She sighs. "Looking back on it, I should have had Molly

meet me somewhere more remote. Far from any roads or hikers. Somewhere no one would have seen a thing." Bridget turns to look at me, her eyes gleaming with something cold and final. "I won't make the same mistake twice."

Panic rises in my chest. "Bridget, you don't have to do this—"

I don't get a chance to finish the sentence.

Just then, we round a bend and the headlights flash against something white and blue blocking the road. It's a Gardaí vehicle turned sideways across the narrow country lane.

I slam on the brakes, the seatbelt slicing into my stomach as the car screeches to a halt.

Bridget screams, "No." And the crack of gunfire splits the night.

CHAPTER THIRTY-NINE

My ears are ringing louder than church bells. Everything else sounds muffled and far away, like my head's underwater and the world's still turning above the surface.

The car jolts as it comes to a complete stop. Suddenly, the door flies open, and I feel someone reach across me, strong hands yanking the emergency brake before undoing my seatbelt.

Arms wrap around me, lifting me out of the driver's seat like I weigh nothing. The cold night air slams into me, making me shiver. Gravel digs into my spine as I'm gently placed on the ground.

"Savannah? Savannah, can you hear me?" The voice is urgent and panicked. "Talk to me, please. Are you hit?"

Still dazed, I blink until my vision focuses. Detective Mulhaney's face hovers above mine, pale as a ghost and lined with worry. His eyes scour the length of my body, checking for bullet holes.

"I'm okay. I—I think I'm okay," I stammer, struggling to sit up.

He sighs in relief, then places a hand on my shoulder, urging me to stay down. "Easy now. Don't move just yet. Are you sure you're alright? I thought—I thought she'd shot you."

"I don't think she meant to," I cough, tasting the burnt rubber emanating from the car's tires. "Or maybe she did. I don't know. She screamed when she saw y'all blockin' the road."

Detective Mulhaney looks over his shoulder and shouts something. With everything still sounding distant and hollow, I can't quite make out what he said, but I catch the blur of a guard's uniform running past us toward the other side of the car.

"She—she still has the gun," I croak, grasping at the fabric of Detective Mulhaney's coat. "We need to get somewhere safe!"

Still looking over his shoulder, the detective runs his hand absentmindedly over mine. "Don't you be worrying about that."

I push myself up to a sitting position. "What do you mean, don't worry? She's already tried shootin' me once!"

Detective Mulhaney shifts his gaze back to me. He seems to finally notice that he's practically holding my hand because he jerks away, embarrassed. "Your one has bigger problems to be dealing with at the moment."

"What's that supposed to mean?" I demand.

Detective Mulhaney doesn't answer me. He stands and shouts to the guard, who is kneeling on the other side of Bridget's car. "How's she doing?"

A disembodied voice replies. "Looks like she used the wrong size ammo. Gun blasted back in her face. She's passed out now, but she'll be grand. I've called an ambulance."

Whether from the cold or shock, a shiver races through me, intense enough to make my teeth chatter. Detective

Mulhaney strips off his coat, kneels beside me, and carefully drapes the garment across my shoulders.

Now that the adrenaline is ebbing and I'm relatively reassured that I'm not going to die on this lonely stretch of road, the questions practically burst out of me.

"Did you hear her confession? My emergency call must have gone through. That's how you found me, right?"

Detective Mulhaney's brows knit together. "Your emergency call? What are you talking about?"

"I dialed the guards. Or, at least, I think I did. I couldn't look at my phone, so I wasn't sure if my call actually went through," the words tumble out of my mouth in a rush. "But wait, if it didn't go through, how in the heck did you find me?"

The corners of Detective Mulhaney's lips tilt upward. "Your aunt called me. Told me she'd make my life a living hell if I didn't get out here and save her niece. Those were her exact words, I believe."

I grimace. "Sorry about that. But *I* don't even know where I am. How did *she* find me?"

Detective Mulhaney offers me his hand and helps me to my feet. "From what I gather, when you didn't meet your father at the Knot & Lantern, he got nervous. He tried ringing you. No answer. So, he called Audrey, who was halfway between Cork and Carrigaveen. She checked the tracker on your phone."

My back stiffens. "The what now?"

"The app on your phone that tracks your movements," he says. Then, after seeing the look on my face, he grins. "Let me guess, you had no idea she'd installed it."

"I most certainly did not!" I fume. "I can't believe my aunt's keepin' tabs on me like some delinquent teenager."

Detective Mulhaney tilts his head. "To be fair, we never would have found you without her. She noticed you were heading down some mad backroads toward Kerry. Thought it was odd enough to ring me. I hate to be the one to tell you this, but the nanny state might have saved your life."

I open my mouth to argue, but then quickly close it. Because, as much as I hate to admit it, he's right. Darn it. I hate that he's right.

I groan. "Miss Audrey's never gonna let me live this down, is she?"

"Not likely," he smirks. "But you mentioned a confession. Are you saying it was Molly who killed Jack O'Hara and the mystery woman in the woods?"

"No, Molly's been dead this whole time. Bridget killed her."

Detective Mulhaney looks at me like I just said the sky is green. "Bridget? Who is Bridget?"

I give the detective an abridged version of everything Bridget told me while I was driving to what I thought was my certain death.

When I'm finished, Detective Mulhaney lets out a low whistle and mutters, "Jesus, Mary, and Joseph."

"You can say that again." I rub my shoulder where the seatbelt bit into the bone when I slammed on the brakes.

Detective Mulhaney's eyes meet mine, and for a second, everything around me seems to fade away. "I'm glad you're alright, Savannah. I mean it. I don't know what I would have done if—"

His words catch. I see the raw concern etched on his face. Whether it's the adrenaline or the relief that I'm still alive, I don't know, but I find myself leaning toward him. Just slightly. Just enough. He lowers his head toward mine, closing the distance between us.

But in that half a second before our lips meet, we're interrupted by someone calling my name.

“Savannah!” My father’s voice rises above the wail of an approaching ambulance.

I barely have time to blush and back away from Detective Mulhaney before I’m swallowed in a double embrace—Ian and Audrey hugging me at the same time. The pressure feels like it might crush my bruised body, but I don’t care. I let out a deep breath and hug them right back.

“You’re alright. You’re okay,” Ian keeps repeating as he strokes my hair.

“I am. Thanks to the two of you,” I say as tears of relief and gratitude fill my eyes.

Audrey is the first to pull away, but she keeps a hand on my arm like it’s a lifeline. “Sure, I don’t know how you got yourself into this situation. But don’t you ever do it again. Do you hear me?”

I laugh, or maybe it’s a sob. It’s hard to tell at this point. “I’ll do my best.”

A wave of contentment washes over me. I haven’t known my father or my aunt very long, but I know beyond a shadow of a doubt that they love me. Enough to search for me. To fight for me. To make me feel like I’m the most important person in their world.

Then it hits me. Bridget never had this. She didn’t have a safety net. She didn’t have arms to catch her when she fell. My heart swells in sympathy for all the joy she never got to experience. Then, I remember the gun. The crossbow. The grave she dug for her own sister.

Bridget made her choices. And now I have my own to make.

“I’m done investigatin’ murders,” I tell my family. “I mean it. From now on, I’m gonna stick to writin’ stories about dogs or fishin’ or celebrity weddin’s.”

“Or the American president’s visit?” Audrey suggests. “I don’t suppose you’ve heard that your man Daniel Kilpatrick is coming to Ballygoseir in a few weeks. It's bound to be quite the to do. Surely, newspapers would pay a pretty penny for the kind of access you'll have as a local."

Focusing on what lies ahead softens the terror of the past hour. And I let myself get swept away in planning a homicide-free future in the sleepy coastal village of Ballygoseir.

We didn't—couldn't—have known then what tragedy would soon befall the place I'd begun to think of as home.

Or that as much as I may *want* to be done with murder, murder—it would seem—isn't quite done with me.

END OF WATCHING WOODS

RAVEN'S WING IRISH MURDER MYSTERY SERIES BOOK 3

I hope you've enjoyed your time in Ballygoseir!

From the coast of Ireland to the beaches of Florida, continue your cozy mystery adventure with a preview of the first book in my Egret's Loft Murder Mystery series, ***Unnatural Causes***.

THANK YOU!

If you enjoyed ***Watching Woods***, I'd be incredibly grateful if you could leave a quick review. Even just a few words can help other cozy mystery lovers find my books.

Simply head over to the product page for this book on Amazon and leave a review there—look for the WRITE A CUSTOMER REVIEW link.

Thank you so much for your support and for being a part of his journey. I can't wait to bring you along on the next adventure!

And don't forget to join me on social media for updates and info on new releases!

instagram.com/teharkinsbooks
facebook.com/teharkins.author

BLURB

Retirement can be murder....

Madeline Delarouse always thought growing old would take a lot longer. But when her adult kids move her into an upscale retirement community on the west coast of Florida, she fears her best days are behind her.

That is, until her new neighbor is found dead - a golf club stuck in her head.

Against the orders of her sarcastic son and exceptionally well-informed daughter, Madeline teams up with a wise-cracking New York retiree to figure out whodunnit. Could it be the Black Widow living across the street? The mysterious Colombian in the colored caftan? Or the ex-Super Bowl quarterback who just can't stand losing?

Against a backdrop of perpetually sunny skies, endless activities and lots and lots of over sixty-fives in golf carts, Madeline has to find out who killed her neighbor and why before her nosiness makes her the killer's next victim.

Grab your copy of *Unnatural Causes (Book 1 of the Egret's Loft Murder Mystery Series)* today!

~

EXCERPT

PROLOGUE

The day Ritchie moved me into Egret's Loft, I thought that was it, I was done for. In for life, with no possibility of parole. Extradition to a luxurious kind of prison where I, and all my new neighbors, were just waiting to die.

That might sound a touch melodramatic, but there's a pretty compelling reason people joke about Florida being God's waiting room.

Not the parts of the state furthest south, like the Florida Keys or Miami, where it's all surf, sun, and another three-letter "s" word that people of my generation don't like to use in mixed company.

No, I'm talking about the parts of the state where every restaurant has an early bird special and there are no cars on the road after eight o'clock in the evening. The kinds of places where the only children you see around town are the ones visiting their grandparents and the obituaries take up more space than the sports pages in the local newspaper.

A kind of place like Calusa, Florida—a small Gulf Coast town nestled comfortably between Fort Myers and Naples.

Population: 2,473.

Average Age: 75.

And Calusa was going to be my new home.

It was for the best.

At least, that's what Ritchie and Eliza had agreed before even bothering to broach the subject with me—their own mother. By the time I was brought into the conversation, they'd already picked out a high-end, low-crime community with guarded gates, loads of golf, and more activities than anyone over sixty-five could possibly have the energy for. But best of all, they said, I'd be around lots of people my own age.

I remember telling the kids, when they were little, that they should go play outside to be around people their own age. It didn't matter so much to me whom they socialized with, I just wanted to get them out from underfoot. This phrase has now, decades later, come back to bite me.

My outlook and attitude were grim as I packed my bags and prepared for the move to Cypress Point Avenue.

Little did I know then, the day I moved into Egret's Loft was the beginning of the most exciting chapter of my life... and the most dangerous.

Grab your copy of *Unnatural Causes (Book 1 of the Egret's Loft Murder Mystery Series)* today!